The Salt Beneath Me

NATHANAEL KOAH

For you, reader.
Thank you for taking the time to read this book.

Contents

Sometimes, something unexpected shows up or takes place, something that completely changes the course of things in remarkable ways. It takes form as a sequence of events synchronised with each other, aligned with what we are looking for, billowed into the moving scene of our life, moving swiftly into motion towards us and embodying conditions in a perfect way. Some people call them signs, some call them coincidences, some think nothing of them at all, and some treasure them as sacred gifts. And if we're paying attention, we may just notice these things, and if we follow them, somehow, they take us exactly where we wish to be.

Reminiscing on the Fifth Floor

The rain fell onto the balcony window crying out a sound that resembled needles crashing and piercing through delicate ice. Annabel noticed this and kept her ears concentrated on the sound for a little while. As she sat on her new wooden chair, leaning on the slightly tattered desk in front, the sensation of her head gently resting upon her arms made her remember the safe feeling of home and the comfort of her old room. This new room she now inhabited reminded her of something from a film or photograph she had once seen but could barely recall. The cream, rough-textured walls with inestimable tiny pieces of peeling paint evoked an inexplicable feeling of unsureness within her, but with that came a rush of pleasant anticipation. Her eyes hovered around the room as she admired the emptiness whilst silently deliberating all of the infinite possibilities of decoration and embellishment. Her mind began to wander deeper into these thoughts, and she started picturing everything distinctly; she pictured a beautifully woven tapestry, textured frames holding paintings that she admired, little ornaments, vases, gemstones, books that carried the scent of old bookstores, and candles — plenty of scented candles to fill the room with a vast range of familiar bliss. It was getting late, and her eyes began to pull down her expression and call her to her new bed, which held one of the springiest mattresses she had ever felt. With ease, she lay her head on the pillow and tucked herself into what felt like something halfway between the embrace of a hug and the fluffiness of a cloud of cotton.

Having spent the night feeling quite on edge, awaking every now and then, agitated by sudden waves of anxiety that, strangely, occasionally morphed into small flickers of excitement, the early morning buzz of the alarm clock had never sounded so grating. Annabel was not a lover of early mornings, and, whilst half-asleep, she pulled the blanket over her head to block the light and sounds of the sudden morning. The buzzing sound came from the adjacent bedroom where Dusty was most likely getting up for her morning walk. Dusty was the other tenant in the flat, and Annabel had a very brief first encounter with her upon her arrival.

The night before, Annabel arrived at the block of flats just around the corner from Highgate Station. She had been splashed by the early drops of the rainstorm and, due to an unexpected train delay, had arrived much later than she had planned. The realisation of having to carry her two heavy suitcases up the staircase to the fifth-floor penthouse came as a surprise. She wasn't quite sure why she had been convinced that there would be a lift in the building; the lift she initially had envisioned was small, but not cramped, with rustic qualities and one of those sliding gates she had seen in films as a child. Arriving at the reality of a hefty walk up a long staircase, with a heavy load to carry, evoked a huff of slight frustration, and perhaps, she thought, anticipating a certain home without the money to afford the envisioned amenities brought more sighs of disappointment than ones of joy. But all of that was something to contemplate at another time as the present moment demanded her to exercise some willpower and begin carrying her things up the steps, and for a petite being who believed that physical strength was her greatest weakness in life, this seemed somewhat of an insurmountable task.

Two very tiresome staircase trips later, she arrived at the top of the building and dragged her suitcases to the front door of the penthouse. She was greeted at the door by a tall, middle-aged woman wearing a wine-coloured nightgown, her hair in a thick bun that, Annabel thought, almost resembled a very large fur ball. There was a strong and sturdy quality to her presence, and her eyes were wide and welcoming.

"You must be Annabel," she said whilst stepping aside and gesturing for her to enter. "Welcome to your new dwelling."

Annabel gave her a friendly smile and thanked her. Then she stepped into the home and was immediately caressed by the warmth of the place. She found herself astonished by the homeliness of the flat, and the atmosphere inside was even more welcoming than she had hoped, which was a remarkable surprise. The home was warmly lit with an array of lamps, small and large, of wicker and bronze and mahogany, and on the shelves she noticed rows and rows of books and some tea light candles laying in elegant candle holders. Each room had a different quality, but every single room was graced with an artisan rug, each placed in just the perfect position to flaunt its distinctive patterns and attract admiring eyes. In the hallway, she recognised a painting, *The Old Gateway* by Thomas Edwin Mostyn, and she took a minute to look at it in the lustre of candles flickering close by.

After exploring the little details of the thoughtfully decorated living room, she wandered into the kitchen, and at first glance, it appeared to be her favourite room in the flat. She walked around slowing, admiring all the intricacies scattered around, and Dusty stood by the side, watching her and grinning, a hint of surprise in her eyes through which she perhaps happily wondered why she was so intrigued. But Annabel lived with an invariable, aesthetically oriented lens; she lived each day with an underlying keenness to be amongst surroundings with appearances that inspired her; this didn't mean she could not keep herself in an environment she deemed displeasing, but there was a noticeable difference in the tones of her thoughts and feelings depending on the presentation around her. She had always resonated with certain visual aesthetics as if something deep inside her was being drawn to particular environments, and this kitchen she wandered through swiftly drew her in. Perhaps it was the extensive collection of ceramic vases lined up along the top shelf, or the wicker baskets on display containing all the colourful fruits one could possibly need, or maybe it was the gleaming light reflecting off the shine of the cookware, emanating sweet warmth and comfort. And on top of that, the entire place yielded a delightful scent: a sugary, invisible mist spread out far and wide, touching every inch of each wall. It appeared that the risk of not viewing the flat before moving in had paid off, and in fact, it was everything Annabel had hoped for and much more.

Dusty, who told her that she had lived in the property for over a decade, spent some time going over the rules and regulations that coincided with being a tenant, proceeded to brush over some nitty-gritty details including rent and bills, then informed her that she'd be home most of the time unless out working, walking, or at the occasional dinner with her friends; although she quickly informed her that even though she was home often, she lived with a quiet presence and made efforts not to bother her cohabitants. She handed Annabel her own set of keys, then hurried off to bed. It was quite clear from the tiresome tone of Dusty's voice that she had been up waiting for her to arrive, and Annabel began to feel a little guilty for arriving so late after informing her that she'd be there by sunset. But that guilt soon vanished upon entering the kitchen a second time. She took one final look around the flat, heaved a sigh of relief as she thought about her great luck in finding such a lovely home, and then carried her things up the stairs, a minuscule hurdle after the many steps she had just climbed. On the upper floor, she found her bedroom, which was situated right beside Dusty's, and all the way at the end of the corridor there was a cutely decorated bathroom for the two of them to share. She walked into her bedroom, closing the door consciously and gently.

A few minutes after the morning buzz of the alarm clock next door, Annabel could hear Dusty clonking noisily around the room. What a heavy walker, she thought, before remembering living amongst her mother and her almost silent footsteps; she used to refer to her mother as a "grasshopper" because of her incredibly light feet, making her presence in the home often go unnoticed.

Annabel could sense thoughts of life back at her mother's home inching to her tired mind, like gentle waves caressing her consciousness, reminding her where she came from, bringing forth a slight feeling of irritation. But suddenly, the idea of it now being a place she could choose to visit from time to time without being immersed in life there gave her a sweet alleviation. She felt glad to be somewhere new, a place for which she somehow knew she'd grow to feel a strong sense of belonging. A light smile intruded her expression, and she slowly drifted back into a calm sleep.

Many hours had passed when she awakened, her eyes struck by a beam of sunlight squeezing through a tear in the blind. She peaked at the clock on the wall to see it was approaching midday. Wondering where all the time had gone, she started to regret sleeping in so late, but then came to the realisation that the long journey and late night had made her quite exhausted, and plenty of sleep probably did her a lot of good. After all, she had just begun a fresh start, she was turning the page to a new chapter of her life; and besides, she thought, no engine is ever ready to begin acceleration without fuel. So, with a lighthearted bounce, she slipped her feet into slippers and trotted downstairs and into the kitchen, which quickly, once again, sparked a gleam in her eyes, and whilst subtly dancing her way around, she began peering through the cabinets and cupboards. Dusty loved to cook, she thought, whilst browsing through the extensive collection of herbs, spices and condiments, many she had never heard of.

She soon arrived at a delicious surprise, one that ignited a temptation she could not resist. The baguette she gripped pulled her attention to a hunger she hadn't yet noticed, and then her stomach began grumbling for a quick bite. Under the packaging, she could feel the crunchiness of the outer layer of the bread, and with a light squeeze, she noticed how soft and fluffy it was inside. She wondered how Dusty would have felt knowing she'd eaten some of her food, but unable to fight the urge, she decided that a small piece wouldn't do any harm, and besides, her first trip of the day would be to the supermarket, so she'd soon have plenty of her own food. She cut herself a few slices of the bread, attempted to wrap the loaf in a similar fashion — although she quickly realised her inability to produce something even half as presentable as the previous display — and slabbed on some salted margarine she found in the fridge. She entered the living room and sat at the little dining table, positioned perfectly by the large window, with two chairs neatly tucked in and an appealingly presented vase of dried lavender. Beside her was a small, square wooden table standing under a bouquet of tulips and an antique red rotary dial phone which she thought joyfully about the prospect of using someday. Looking out the window from the high point of view, the people on the street below appeared so small; it was almost like peering on little ant-like beings, doing their daily little ant-like tasks, some talking in tiny voices among their tiny friends. There was something so satisfying about watching the world moving below her from the comfort of a tall, secluded space. There could be just about anything happening outside, and from her sheltered spot she could feel as attached or detached from it as she pleased. She could observe the constant flowing activities of city life, immersed in every scene her eyes followed, glued to the plot of each social occurrence whilst being safely tucked away. As her eyes wandered outside, she bit into the slice of bread, mesmerised by the soft and crunchy texture and the flavourful kick of the margarine. She adored the feeling of being up there, overlooking the concrete kingdom of the outside from the comfort of her own kingdom. She opened the window, allowing some cold air to flow freely around the room, refreshing her senses. The distant sound of music from a car radio and cheerfulness from playful children lifted her to a momentary air of magic. She had visited London only a few times before, the last time being on a trip with her aunt when she was thirteen years old, but this time it felt truly incomparable; she was now twenty-two, had a much greater understanding of the world, who she was, and most importantly, she was venturing out alone with no plans to return to life back home.

Back in Dean Village, Edinburgh — in the one home in which she'd lived all her life, with her mother, Edith — life had been becoming increasingly tiresome for Annabel, and the most recent couple of years had been the most strenuous, working in a local bakery and saving almost every penny towards her eventual move. She'd be lying if she said she enjoyed the work; in fact, she never truly found enjoyment in any of her previous workplaces, as much as she had tried. As a teenager, she worked part-time in a stationary shop whilst picking up extra little jobs she could find here and there, all to gift herself the camera she had so desperately wished for. At one point in her childhood, Edith, upon realising she'd save a heap of money without the temporary need for a gardener, even got her doing some weeding work on the weekends for an extra little bag of coins, usually followed by a pat on the head, an unusual form of appreciation she occasionally showed. Edith had raised Annabel with the notion that hard work is the basis of a fruitful life and that any form of fun or leisure must only come after the many accomplishments of diligence, almost like a token that must be earned from a great effort. "Things don't come easy as it seems in movies," she would often say; and Annabel did see some truth in this, although she wanted wholeheartedly to believe that somewhere, in some realm of possibility, fun and work could walk hand in hand, tasks could be accomplished without the need for stress, and hard work could ignite from inspiration rather than struggle. Deep inside, there was a part of Annabel that was a dreamer, a real fantasiser, and she treasured this part of her, this little glow of hope beaming on her path ahead like a beacon of light, a source of pure imagination on the road of sense and tangibility. And she kept her dreams to herself, shared them with no other soul, but stuck to them like a flee to a dog.

For as long as she could remember, Annabel had been a natural wanderer with a curious mind, craving a life of whimsical adventure, seeking thrills in every corner she could find them. At the age of nine, she often turned to her imagination as a source of adventure, but on one summer evening, during a sunset presenting the sweetest shade of red, her rampant curiosity pushed her a little too far. She had chased a butterfly to the tall wooden fence at the back of the garden, discovering a large crack, just about large enough for her to squeeze through. In moments such as this one, she often became stuck between the influence of her mother's voice, bouncing around her mind like a persistent echo in a cave, and that familiar internal voice of curiosity, persuading her to dive into the unknown. With some intrusive hesitation which caused the tempo of her heartbeat to speed up, she found herself edging towards the crack in the fence and peered through. The sight of a purple perennial grasped her attention, tempting her to squeeze through the crack that took her to a field of plants and flowers portraying a vast medley of colour. As she skipped along imaginary pathways and balanced along tree roots protruding out of the ground, she looked into the distance and noticed a squirrel gazing over at her, focussing its attention directly into her line of sight. With its charm and adorability, the small creature began to climb effortlessly up a tree, then glared back at her, this time from a height greater than her own. It climbed to the top of the tree, moving swiftly in a straight line, then again, turned its head towards her direction. She quickly delighted in the playfulness of the squirrel and decided to chase after it. She thought excitedly about how beautiful the little woodland would be from the view where the squirrel stood, how nice it would be to see what the squirrel saw; and moments later, she found herself climbing the tree. Each branch she grabbed onto intensified the exhilaration within her, and she climbed and climbed until she could climb no more. About halfway up the tree, she admired the great view and could see her house over the fence through which she had snuck, thinking that it didn't seem so tall after all. With wide eyes, she looked all around, hypnotised by the nature that surrounded her. Then she noticed a cluster of bird nests resting on the tops of branches not too far from the top of her head. The intricacy of them struck her; she had never seen the sight of bird nests so close before, and it triggered a sudden realisation that she had climbed far too high. Fear began to creep onto her, her palms became sweaty, and she struggled to hold the branches as her firm grip weakened, leaving her legs quivering in frantic trepidation. She shuddered at the thought of falling and attempted to step on a branch below, but the branch was weak and broke apart from the tree at the weight of her foot. She looked at the ground below in an attempt to plan a route back down, but the journey to get there seemed to be a nearly impossible challenge. If only getting back down was as uncomplicated as the climb up she would not have found herself in such a terrifying position, and she began to quietly panic with sweaty hands and shivering knees. With no plan of how to return to safe ground and no other option to turn to, she decided to call out to Edith. She hoped so desperately that the distance between where she was and her house wasn't vast enough to drown out the sound of her yells. Flocks of birds fled from the trees above as her cries yielded a sound of thunderous desperation, penetrating any space of peace around. Her blaring call for help echoed across the woodland, and in no time, she heard the sound of Edith calling back to her, and so to her again she cried, and back and forth they called to one another until Edith arrived at the bottom of the tree, looking up at her with a face of terror, an expression that marked Annabel's memory for a long time. Unable to rescue her alone, Edith urged her to hold on tight, left for a brief moment and then returned in a panic-stricken hurry with a tall, muscular neighbour who proceeded to cautiously but speedily climb the tree. With some struggle that led to a few cuts and scratches, the neighbour guided Annabel down to the safe ground and into the arms of her worried mother, who gripped her with so much mightiness that the sharpness of her fingernails engraved her distress into the back of Annabel's shoulders. For a long while afterwards, Edith scolded her for her bad behaviour, reminding her that had she not had the windows open and heard her call, she would have been gravely injured. And since that day, no matter how much Annabel tried to convince her mother that she had learned a valuable lesson and would not put herself in any danger like that again, Edith's trust in her daughter had weakened to a point of ongoing worry, causing Annabel to feel suffocated by her mother's perturbation time and time again.

Now, the drastic change in Annabel's surroundings caused her to reminisce about some more monumental memories of her childhood and adolescent years, memories submerged in her mind, begging to remain unforgotten. The newness of everything around her gave her a bright thrill that she hadn't felt in a very long time, and her senses, although overwhelmed, were being treated with a feast of refreshment. A chill came upon her as she thought about how different her life would soon become in such a vast city, which so far shared minimal similarities with her home town in Edinburgh.

With a tiny population, Dean Village was never a place she wanted to remain forever; she felt that her life there was becoming bleak and repetitious, and for some time she had been readying herself to make a move. The monotonousness of being at the same places every day, seeing the same people, and being stuck inside the house far more than she hoped had been harbouring a heavy listlessness within her, a gloomy fog dispersing hazes of melancholy, often dimming her spirit. In the past, she rarely got to experience life outside of her hometown other than a few trips abroad in her younger years, although most of the memories had drifted away a great deal. She found that there were very few people back there to whom she could truly relate; other than with a few close friends, she rarely shared her truest thoughts and interests, often keeping her flaming admiration for art and photography and the desire to be creative to herself. She occasionally spoke about these things to Joan, her close friend who was training to become an architect, but as much as Annabel appreciated that they both devoted their time to creativity, she never really experienced the exhilarative flow of two individuals discussing a similar passionate point of view. The dissatisfaction with her day-to-day surroundings, along with the mundane lifestyle that lacked anything new, gave her a persistent eagerness to leave; and she was so glad she finally did. There were, however, things she loved about Edinburgh, things she thought of fondly, and now with distance, realised she even adored: the wonderful landscape views, the stunning simplicity of daily activity, the vibrant sense of community beating through the town, the comfort of safety when walking alone on a lightless street, the sweet reverberation of songbirds chanting their chirps through tranquil neighbourhoods, the delicate smiles from strangers walking their dogs alongside beautiful architecture and a perfect sunrise. She treasured these things dearly, and although she knew she would at times yearn for these things, it was time to move on, to immerse herself in a world with unwritten potential, and she believed that in every speck of her soul.

She spent the rest of the day exploring the surrounding areas, a few hours on a bench in a green spot reading a novel she picked up from a bookstore down the street, and when sunset arrived, she strolled down the avenue with a lighthearted dreaminess floating on her gaze. It seemed the anxiety from the night before had passed, and she exerted a sigh of relief as she arrived at the entrance of the flat in which she now resided. It was starting to settle in now that this would be the place she would begin to call home, the abode where she would depart from in the morning and return for rest in the evening, and she mulled over just how beautiful it was too. She would have never anticipated how much ease came with the staircase walk that evening. And how funny that was, she thought, that something so excruciatingly tiresome one moment could be such a breeze the next.

When evening arrived, she decorated her room with a few things that she purchased in the day: a stained glass lamp with a bulb of a warm hue, a burnt gold vintage frame with a print of the painting *Unter Rosen* by Hugo Charlemont, and a finger-sized 1970s figurine of a little beauty wearing a Victorian orange dress, cape and bonnet. With careful thought, she happily placed these pieces around the room. Collecting small things like these often elevated her mood. If something ignited a glimmer of joy within her or was associated with a delightful memory, she'd hold onto that thing as a sentimental token for as long as she could, and she often stopped herself in her tracks to adore its qualities.

She spent the evening unpacking her suitcases and then crashed onto her bed with an exhale that imitated a small gust of wind. She looked over at her carrier bag hanging so proudly on the doorknob; this was where she kept her beloved film camera. She pranced over to it and took out the camera from inside a brown faux leather satchel with intricate threads, and then placed it on the desk. This camera she had very recently purchased was a rare find in the world of film photography and happened to be her most treasured belonging. She adored analogue photography more than any kind; there was no other feeling in the world quite like getting her photographs developed and being thrilled with the results. Each roll of film had thirty-six picture shots in it, and she'd often become so swept away in the unlimited dimension of possibilities that by the time the roll was full, she'd have forgotten most of the photographs taken; and that was the best part: the surprise; it was like gifting herself a moment in time that she had admired but forgotten. Annabel believed that the ability to capture a photograph was one of life's greatest gifts. In some mystifying way, she sometimes saw life as one continuously moving image, made up of a wide variety of lights producing endless images flickering by rapidly, blending to make moments that create our perceptive reality, and the ability to freeze a point in that reality and hold it in its picture forever was a beautiful thing that, she felt, was often overlooked. When she took a picture, she took it with great pleasure and relished the idea that she was taking a glimpse of the present moment into the future, and the outcome would be a moment of the past captured effortlessly, and one that would remain forever.

Whilst organising her things, she listened to some of her favourite music on the turntable — records by Maurice Ravel, Virginia Astley, and Sibylle Baier. She often turned to music when she wanted to lift her mood, feel inspired, or bask in sounds of familiar serenity. As she assigned her belongings to certain places, she wandered around the room and saw her reflection move swiftly past the cheval mirror. Then she turned to look at her reflection. Her hazel eyes shone a luminous glare. Her cocoa brown hair formed a shape that appeared like shallow waves of a dark ocean. The tiny mole resting on her pale skin just under her button nose stood out as if it were painted. She noticed, in her mind, a sudden sense of clear space, a disassociation from her surroundings, and for a moment, she was just existing, floating through an abyss of air and atmosphere. Perhaps it was the intensity of the move, the coming to terms with such a distinctly new environment, or the speed of everything happening so quickly that made her lose her bearings for a moment, but she soon stumbled back into her awareness and caught herself back into reality. She looked to her right at a few pictures she had put on the wall earlier in the day. One was a picture of her on her eleventh birthday blowing out eleven candles on a vanilla cake with heaps of icing on the top. She remembered the felicity of that day with a striking vividness because of this very picture. The one beside that was of her and Joan dancing together at a disco, travelling orbs of coloured lights scattered across their faces; she smiled as she stared into this one, reminiscing the wonderful memories she and her dear friend had shared over the years. And then, perfectly placed inside the middle of a beautifully tattered cream frame, was an old picture of her as a very young girl, standing in a forest of winter snow, holding her mother's hand. At the interlocking of their mitten gloves, the picture had been ripped, leaving half of the photograph left to remain and the figure of her mother absent from the scene. Nevertheless, this was one of those sentimental pieces she treasured, holding onto it for as long as she could remember. She recalled an old memory of her asking her mother what had happened to the other half of the photograph, wishing to have both pieces together to complete it. She remembered her mother telling her it was a gift to her as a very young girl, and one day, amidst a heated argument between the two of them, she ripped her mother out of the picture. She chuckled at that image in her head, thinking about how much of a theatrical move that must have been. She pondered about her mother, her towering posture, the dainty way she moved, the softness of her voice in the morning, the way she would firmly snap her fingers when she was cross, the screwy face she'd make at the sight of rain outside the window. Edith worked two jobs: in the reception department of a private school, and at home as a claims handler. She was often found sitting at the kitchen table, smoking and reading the newspaper with crackling news on the radio in the background. Other than on occasions that never lasted too long, Annabel and her mother rarely shared moments of strong, interchanging connection. There were joyful moments shared, of course, but these moments were overshadowed by memories of simply existing side by side, quietly being amongst one another and nothing more than that. And Edith had always been there; in fact, Annabel couldn't remember a single moment in time when she wasn't there at her call, but somehow, she often felt like sometimes her mother wasn't there at all, as if her presence was incomplete; it was an abstraction that she found difficult to wrap her head around. Perhaps it was the lack of feeling understood by her, she thought, the fact that Edith viewed her interests as nothing but small amusements, unable to take her passions seriously no matter how much she attempted to demonstrate her adoration for them. Truthfully, she loved her mother dearly but felt that it was necessary for her now to find her ground and begin writing a brand new chapter of her life. And it was relieving to be where she was, much like a tree freshly planted in new, untouched soil, where there are no obstacles in the way of growth. As she pondered all of this, she stared a little longer at the half-cut photograph with a wistful twinkle in her eye.

There are some rare moments when you find yourself accidentally lost inside a picture, surrounded by the fantasy of a recreated moment in time, a temporary escape into half-forgotten memories that blend with designs of the imagination. These moments usually only last a handful of seconds, but somehow, always feel like a whole lot more. In an instant, you become pulled in by an unfathomable force, snatched by the time that exists only there, and lost in an omnipresent world that fits inside a picture frame. Annabel had one of these moments, and as her mind wandered back to her space, she felt a tear flee suddenly from her left eye, trickle down her cheek and fall onto the wooden floor beneath her. She noticed the teardrop splattered into a tiny puddle next to her toes, beaming with all of its tiny brightness. Then, without much thought behind her glare, she lifted her foot, stepped onto the tear and pressed down firmly on it.

Epiphanies Over Tea

Turquoise, deep purple, a distinct shade of grey with a drop of blue — these were the colours that appeared in Annabel's dreams, penetrating her mind continuously, back and forth, like the oscillation of a spring. Sometimes she dreamed of colours, other times of people, occasionally of animals, and once in a long while, she dreamed of broken memories. She was fascinated by dreams, particularly their sporadic nature, the fact that the subjects of dreams change unpredictably, interweaving with one another, the fact that no matter how much we can try to influence them, or change them, and no matter how lucid they may be, we can never fully control them, or take charge over them; and when she awoke, she thought about dreams and how utterly beyond our grasp they are, how dreams are the ocean and our sleeping mind is the boat, how they pull us, push us, cover us, teach us, frighten us, relieve us, moving in and out of us as they please, reminding us that they are happening *to* us, and not *from* us.

Morning arrived swiftly with a glorious day outside the window; it appeared that the day decided to clear the skies and destroy any chance of rain. Annabel spent the morning in an effusive mood, smiling about the fact that she was now the owner of a balcony, a fine little balcony with an iron railing that danced its way to each side. And on the balcony, she sat, accompanied by a little Victorian wrought iron chair and table, sipping on a mug of peppermint tea, nibbling at some breakfast biscuits and fresh raspberries. She bobbed the tea bag up and down in the teacup as if she were bathing a puppet, and thought about how she'd eventually need to pick up a job to avoid running out of money. The idea of getting work in such a hurry didn't appeal to her in the slightest, but she revelled in the possibility of getting work in which she'd find pleasure, and luckily, she had enough money saved up to last a little while so she knew she didn't need to start worrying about all of that just yet.

The late afternoon delivered a great surprise to Annabel. She became lost in an exploration of Regents Canal, strolling down the unfolding threads of road and river, stopping often to take pictures of artful things that grabbed her wide-eyed attention. By chance, she came across something which from afar appeared to be a bookstore on a boat, floating on the waters like a luring mystery, and as she inched closer she found that it was exactly that. The water below was slowly darkening by the evening closing in and some lively jazz music was spread out far and wide from a band playing close by. The bookstore was small and quaint and required a bit of manoeuvring to get around, but it was an alluring little place, and she delighted in the wonderment of all the things around to see. There were books of just about every kind she could think of, and the entire place was decorated with hanging postcards, twinkling lights from tiny bulbs and antique typewriters. She floated around the room with a quiet concentration, absorbed by the eclectic assortment of things to see. She purchased a small handful of postcards to write in and send to her loved ones back in Edinburgh. Annabel had always found plenty of joy in writing documentations, notes and letters; during her adolescent years, she occasionally wrote a personal journal, scribbling down notes about events in her life, big and small, and she found this to be quite a cathartic activity, an enjoyable way of releasing emotions; at times it even felt as if the movement of the pen was an automatic response to her innate sensitivity, as though her psyche, in a way beyond her control, was guiding the movement of the ink as a way to express her visceral feelings. Writing, to her, was a beautiful way of portraying memories wished to be kept and stories remembered, and there was something so stimulating about finding the appropriate words to convey the emotion intending to be evoked.

And that evening, she did just that. Her hand moved tenderly along the blank page of the postcards as she wrote about her excitement, her thrill and her unpredictably wavering anxieties about moving to a big city alone. She also mentioned some noteworthy features of her new home, her new neighbourhood and some little details about her time there so far. And she signed and sealed each postcard with care and, later that day, gently pushed them inside the aperture of a bright red postbox around the corner from her flat. It was a nice feeling to be sending a little something back to Dean Village, a solicitous token letting all of them know that they were in her thoughts.

As she walked home, she looked around as she soaked into this new environment. It was the beginning of October and the trees were starting to lose their leaves; she stood for a minute and admired the soft way the leaves fell — light and playful, whimsical in movement, persuaded by the touch of the wind, each leaf dancing its own dance but altogether forming a gentle demonstration of nature and its subtle rhythms. As she watched, she began to feel the sudden vibration of her phone ringing in her pocket, and realising it had been many hours since she had checked it, she saw that her mother was calling, so she picked up the phone with a lightness in her tone.

"Ma, hello!"

"Hi dear, it's me!" said Edith on the phone, surprisingly exuberant. "I thought I'd call and see how everything's going. I haven't heard from you since you left, and I was just thinking about you. How are you?"

"I'm very well! I'm sorry I didn't contact you earlier. To be honest, I've been in such a daze that it slipped from my mind, but everything's fine, great actually!" said Annabel cheerfully. "I'm surprised how smooth everything's been. And the flat, oh Ma, I really love it! I'll tell you more about it when I get time but it's just the perfect place."

"That's great Annabel. And the other tenant? How is she?"

"Well, we haven't talked much but she seems to be quite friendly. I don't know much about her yet, other than the fact that she walks loudly."

Edith chuckled with a naturalness that Annabel hadn't heard in a while; she had even almost forgotten the sound of it. "And are you keeping warm? The wind will be getting awfully cold very soon."

"Yes, I am. I'm very wrapped up right now, in fact, a little too warm."

"And you have enough money to last a while?"

"I do."

"Are you sure? You'll need to find a job soon though, right?"

"In time I will, but please," said Annabel, "don't worry about those things, Ma. I'll be fine."

Edith exerted a little sigh. "I know. I'll try not to. It's just... It doesn't feel the same not having you around, and I know you've only just left, but it's just really different being here alone. I even left the back door open in case the neighbour's cat wanted to pay a little visit, and you know I never do that!"

Annabel laughed. "Don't worry. You'll get used to it eventually. And you know I'm only a train journey away right? I can visit any time, really."

"I know, I know. And what about London? How are you finding it?"

"Everything's great. I saw the most beautiful bookstore today. It was inside of a boat. And I've been taking some photographs too. I'll email you some of them once I get them developed!"

"I'd love to see..." said Edith, a wistful tone in her voice. "By the way, I can hear you panting over there. Is everything okay?"

"It's these stairs. I thought I was getting used to them but now I'm not so sure. I'm living on the fifth floor, and the ceilings are high, so it's quite a walk up the staircase but it's worth it for the view," replied Annabel in between heavy breaths.

"All right," said Edith. "I'll leave you to it then. Take care."

"Talk to you soon, Ma."

She hung up the phone and let out a sigh as she approached the last hurdle of steps with an unexpected spark of delight in her chest. She couldn't even remember the last time Edith showed so much interest in her affairs, and maybe, she pondered, this distance between them was just the perfect thing to ignite some enthusiasm in their relationship. Perhaps it was the lack of absence in each other's lives that was fuelling some mutual indifference between the two of them, and distance and space were all that were needed to relight their bond. It was evident to Annabel that they needed some time away from each other, having spent her entire life in her mother's tight company, the two of them witnessing first-hand every major event in each other's lives. Maybe the pursuit of maintaining their relationship from afar, keeping in touch from two ends of this somewhat vast space, was the perfect thing for Edith just as much as Annabel, who decided to hold onto this belief and take it with her into the future.

That evening, in the warmth of her new room, Annabel was greeted by a wave of nostalgia. As glad as she felt about where she was, there was a part of her that missed home, a small but unavoidable feeling of sentimental yearning, leeching onto her spirit. Having barely been away in the past, this wasn't a feeling she was used to at all, and she decided to tend to her fragile state by looking at some of her old photographs. She stored them in hardcover photo books that she decorated with small pieces cut out from books, old magazines, and other adorning things she could find. She flicked through with an attentiveness that grew with every new page, now and then revealing a tiny, bright grin which preceded an ambivalent sigh. She studied some old photographs, particularly the ones that had strong memories attached to them; people she knew, places she visited, moments of beauty, they were all here for her to see. Her favourite pictures were the ones that captured a flash of life passing by naturally, a moment that captured the heart as well as the eye. As much as she valued all kinds and styles of photography, she had never been a fan of the common photograph where one poses and smiles insincerely; she found that most of the time they sucked out the essence of the natural moment. There was nothing to her like when a picture captured the genuine feeling of a scene. A heart-filled, candid moment showcasing natural human emotion, coalescing with a beautiful collision of colour and texture — these were the components of her perfect picture. Flicking through the pages, she began diving into her mind; she thought about how many people come and go in life, the temporary connections we make that we eventually let go of, the passing moments of shared joyful interaction, places we visit that become a distant memory, chapters of our life that were once the centre of our universe and soon become cherished thoughts to recollect.

Soon after, her tender mood was met with an urge to make a hot beverage, as a means to comfort herself, perhaps a hot cocoa or a herbal tea. So she made her way downstairs into the kitchen where Dusty was sitting on the oak table, skilfully knitting a maroon blanket whilst sipping on something with steam hovering slowly from the mug. Noticing Annabel as she walked in, Dusty gave her a welcoming nod and gestured for her to take a seat.

"Annabel, I'm sorry I didn't give you a warmer introduction before. I was rather tired last night when you arrived," she said with a look of comfort, "and I realised that I never got the chance to talk to you properly. If you're not doing much right now, you're more than welcome to have some tea with me. There's plenty. It's made with fresh mint leaves I picked myself."

Annabel, who was pleasantly surprised by her affability, smiled and took a seat at the table. Dusty poured her some tea. "Is everything okay?"

Annabel took a small sip and then looked up at Dusty. "Yes, I'm fine. I started feeling a little down about things not so long ago but I'll be light as a feather again soon. It's probably because everything here is so new to me. It's exciting but just a little bit scary," she said, her hands moving to amplify her words with a slight, almost imperceptible tremble.

"I understand. A drastic move like yours is not an easy process. It's heavy on the mind, on the heart," said Dusty with a reassuring tone in her voice. "If I could offer some wisdom I would, but all I can say is that if being here is what you want, and I'm sure that it is, then in time it will start to feel like home. It may not seem like it now, but soon it will. Trust me."

Her words were nothing profound, but oddly, Annabel felt immediately reassured by them; it was nice to feel understood, for someone to commiserate with her.

"I do hope so," she said, a smile tickling the edge of her lips.

Dusty leaned forward. "When I was not so much older than yourself, I too made a big decision, quite similar to yours."

"Is that so? What happened?" asked Annabel, drinking her tea.

"Well, I was spending most of my time in an office. I had graduated with a bachelor's degree and I worked my way to the executive assistant of an established marketing agency where I was expecting a big promotion. I loathed working there but I could see no way out, and on top of that, I was engaged to someone I didn't want to be with; but one evening in the middle of spring, I was reading the daily newspaper and I came across something that changed my life."

Annabel's eyes widened and she began to listen to Dusty's words with an unshakable attentiveness.

"Throughout my whole life I was a dancer," Dusty continued. "I spent my entire childhood dancing; contemporary, ballet, ballroom, tap, I was a lover of it all. I danced every single day. As a child, I remember telling everyone that I'd grow up and become the greatest dancer the world had ever seen. A little confident I was, yes, but I had a wild dream in me."

Dusty chuckled endearingly and then had some tea, moving the fingers of her empty hand in a way that emulated the movements of a dancer.

"Anyway, inside the newspaper was a casting advertisement by a theatre production that was looking for trained and highly skilled dancers. I remember at first, I skimmed the words and the idea of me auditioning was nothing but a fantasy from a tiny voice inside, and one that I dismissed immediately. At the time I hadn't danced in years and I wasn't even sure I'd be capable of anything like that. But after some days, that voice grew louder and louder, until soon after, I listened, and I auditioned."

Taking a brief pause, she got up and walked over to the cupboard where she took out some bread and tenderly spread on some margarine. She placed it on two plates, one for her and one for Annabel.

"Here you go," she said, passing Annabel a plate. "I saw you had some yesterday, and well, I hope you love it as much as I do."

Annabel giggled lightly. "Please, carry on with the story."

"So I waited a few days for a call and heard nothing. My hope was sinking and I was beginning to accept that I didn't get the part, until one day, soon after, I received a call. It was the casting director and I was told that I got a place in the show. I remember vividly how I felt hearing those four words: 'You got the part'. My whole world elevated and I was met with this wave of euphoria. I remember trying to remain calm on the phone, to keep it professional, you know? I wanted to appear experienced. But all the while my heart was drumming inside. Anyway, I left everything and went to tour with the show. It was the best decision I ever made. It changed my life completely, and in many ways that I would have never expected. I danced for years with that show and loved every single day of it. I made beautiful connections with like-minded people, some I'm still in touch with today, thirty years later. And none of that would have happened if I didn't respond to that newspaper advertisement."

Annabel sat with her elbows on the table and her chin planted into her hands, silently mesmerised. The two of them enjoyed a shared moment of quiet, Dusty appreciating the delicious contrast of tea and bread, Annabel silently assimilating the story, occasionally taking a sip and a bite.

"And you," Dusty went on, "there's something about your story that fascinates me."

Annabel, in the midst of drinking tea, placed her teacup down and looked up curiously. "What do you mean?"

She had not spoken to Dusty about her life or plans other than a very brief phone conversation before her moving in; in the phone call, she introduced herself as a hopeful tenant of the spare room and spoke briefly of her wish to finally leave her old town and her quest to attain a new life in the big city that now surrounded her.

"I find it all rather fascinating," said Dusty, "you leaving the home that you resided in for your entire life, and now, you've arrived, you've stepped through the door to possibility, open to whatever awaits you."

"Well, it's something I've been meaning to do for years. I guess I was getting tired of the repetition back there. I found that over time things were beginning to lose their meaning for me."

"Ah, yes, and you mentioned you're an artist if I recall correctly?"

"Well, I take photographs," said Annabel, the slightest pink blush emerging from her cheeks.

"I can only imagine all of that stuff must have steered your direction too, right? The need to expand your horizons creatively?"

"Oh, yes, exactly. It was about time I found new ground."

Dusty smiled, and whilst staring into Annabel's eyes, she leaned forward.

"And what else?"

"What do you mean?" asked Annabel, her eyes scrunching a little, trying to discern exactly what her words alluded to.

"There's something there," said Dusty, almost whispering, "something deep in your eyes. A radiant determination."

Looking away, Annabel felt slightly speechless and took a final sip of her tea, emptying the cup, her attention steadily on catching the very last drip the teacup offered.

"I'm not sure what you mean," she said, catching and then losing eye contact.

Dusty leaned a little closer, her expression radiating a thirst for a satisfactory answer as if she was just about to hit a sweet spot. "Is there something you're searching for?"

For a moment, Annabel became still, staring into empty space, and then she focussed intensely on a tiny fragment of cracked paint on the wall. She turned her head to Dusty whose gaze was innocently fixated on her.

"I wish I had a magical story but unfortunately I don't. I just wanted to start something new. That's all there is to it."

Dusty leaned back into her chair and sighed tenderly. "Ah, I get it. I guess I was trying to squeeze a little extra from you. I do that sometimes, you know, try to get more out of something than there really is. But, truly, it's beautiful nonetheless, you being bold enough to go after what you want. It's inspiring. You're inspiring. A valiant one."

"That's kind of you," said Annabel, her lips forming a perky grin, whilst peering down and playing with the cluster of bread crumbs on her plate.

"All right, I'll be off to bed now," muttered Dusty as she got up with a scanty grunt. "I'll leave the lights on downstairs. Just turn them off when you go to bed if you don't mind."

"I will. Good night, Dusty," said Annabel with a pleasant charm.

"Sweet dreams, Annabel."

Dusty trodded loudly up the stairs until her footsteps faded into washed-out clumps of muffled sounds reverberating across the thick ceiling above. Annabel sat there for some time, gazing into nothingness, reflecting on the things spoken of. She was glad to have discovered that Dusty was quite lovely after all; she felt soothed because of this, as if a small weight was lifted from her, and she took delight in the thought of living with someone so pleasant after all. She brewed herself some more tea and decided to sit at the table a little longer. The silkiness of the hot liquid swept across her senses, travelling down into the depths of her inner space, melting away the possibility of unease, tranquillising any tension. And she stayed seated, rooted into the chair, accompanied by the feeling that there was something she needed to address that she couldn't ignore, and indeed there was. The talk with Dusty had driven her to ponder something she had pushed away for some time, something that was steering her without her even recognising it. Moments of quiet respiration passed by, alongside the distant clicking of a pendulum that swung ceaselessly inside a clock on the wall. As she dipped into her wandering thoughts, she couldn't keep it hidden away anymore; it was planted there in her mind and it was growing bigger, vaster and more persuasive with every second that passed, so she decided to recognise it, to acquiesce in its grip. And for the first time in a long while, she thought about it, swallowed by the thick urge of it, the urge to contemplate the true reason she came to London.

The Lady in the Blue Scarf

It was a fine evening when thirteen-year-old Annabel and her aunt Judy stepped off the train at Paddington station amidst the daily rush hour. Her distant memories of London from past visits had greatly faded, and, feeling as though she were a newly hatched butterfly in an open field, she gasped at the wideness of things around her: the size of the roads, the shop windows, the distance between the train platforms and the station entrance. As they raced in and out of hurrying pedestrians, Judy held her hand with a mighty firmness that made her feel half her age. Flocks of birds soared in their hundreds above the chimney tops; car horns honked shrill noises, intruding every ear around; buzzing humans in suits nipped cautiously around every crevice of space. Judy dashed confidently around each obstacle quickly and steadily, pulling Annabel along with her, whose feet were having a difficult time keeping up with the pace. The powerful ambience of the concrete world around forced its way into Annabel's innocent eyes and ears, producing a flickering sensation inside, almost like a buzzing concoction of fright and delight.

Judy worked as a master perfumer, often referred to as a *nose*. Her job was to create perfume compositions by blending different aromas, conveying abstract concepts and capturing the desired feelings all with the scent of smell. Annabel was intrigued by her job, drawn in by the beguiling description of it, and so it was a thrilling adventure to be accompanying her on such endeavours.

A handful of months beforehand, Judy was having dinner with Edith and Annabel, munching delightfully into the roast dinner Edith had prepared when the prospect of her bringing Annabel to London came about. Annabel briefly mentioned that she'd been reading a novel based in London and how she planned to take a trip there as soon as she was old enough to travel alone. It was clear to her that Edith wasn't going to take her, and pleading with her mother never really resulted in peaceful endings. On the topic of London, Judy mentioned that she'd be visiting there in the coming months for work-related business and, after noticing the keenness in Annabel's eyes, suggested the possibility of taking her along. Edith took some days to think about it — her protectiveness of Annabel often clouded her judgements — but with her being under the close watch of her trusted sister, she felt more at ease with the idea and eventually gave her tentative permission.

Now, pacing steadily through the busy streets of tumultuous events, Judy spotted their hotel from the other side of the road and bolted over to it like a dart to a bullseye. Inside, the two of them were greeted with a relieving warmth and together they lit up with glee at the cosiness oozing from the ravishing furniture. Annabel had never been to a hotel and the fact that she was staying in such a splendrous one was quite hard to wrap her head around. After collecting the keys from the chirpy, soft-spoken employee at the reception, an awestruck Annabel pushed the lift button, and after a smooth halt followed by a light chime, the two of them arrived at their twin room which turned out to have quite the exquisite view of the inner city.

That night, Annabel slept through a blissful tunnel of serenity, induced by the lovely cushiness of the bedding. She had never been so cradled, so supported, so embraced by a bed set, and this was the last thing she thought about before going to sleep and the first thing that came to her mind when she awoke. In the booming morning, her eyes opened gently to the soft silhouette of Judy standing in front of the window, looking meticulously into the mirror, dressed in dark velvets and a furry coat draped over herself, emblazoned with a pearl necklace and big hooped earrings that nearly reached the tip of her shoulders. She sprayed herself with a fluorescent perfume that almost formed into a mist, then turned to Annabel who was stretching her arms out, yawning ferociously.

"Morning darling," said Judy, cheerfully approaching Annabel who greeted her with a smile and another yawn. "I was just about to wake you. You looked so peaceful. Listen, I'm going downstairs to have a quick talk with one of my associates. We need to brush up on some things before all the meetings today. So get yourself fresh and dressed, and when you're ready, take the lift down to the dining room on the first floor. I'll be there waiting for you at the breakfast buffet. Oh, and the shower is wonderful but try not to be too long, okay? We've got to be out of here soon."

As Judy pranced out of the room, Annabel stood to her feet, amazed at the sudden opportunity of utter independence she'd been given. It was a treat to be left on her own in such a fine place, a place that seemed so grand, so important. Getting ready in the morning within the shelter of luxurious walls with no guardian to watch over her was like a scene from a dream. And she danced around freely, fluttering around the pretty space. She enjoyed following Judy around, and although she still often felt smothered to a certain degree in her presence, unlike being watched over by her mother, there was a noticeably lower level of apprehension, and she intended to make the most of it while she could.

She took her time getting ready, making sure to revel in the splendour and savour every second she had alone there, often taking little intervals to bounce and dance on the beds, then jumping from one to the other like an excitable toad hopping on lily pads. On her way out, she noticed there were some guest gifts on a little table by the door: a pair of cutely wrapped chocolates, tiny bottles of cologne in pouches, and little paper notebooks. She unwrapped a chocolate and stuffed it down, sniffed a cologne then put it back after a whiff of slight revulsion, then took one of the notebooks and packed it neatly in her bag.

After breakfast, during a taxi ride through the blocks of tall city structures, she took the notebook out of her bag and admired the smooth texture of the cover. She wasn't planning to write anything in it just yet, but Judy encouragingly suggested that she made notes of little cherished moments of her time on the trip, highlights she wanted to mark down to remember. Judy told her it was something she would do as a child whenever she was away from home, and how without access to taking photographs, she wanted to collect the memories of the best parts of her trips and hold onto them for as long as she could. Annabel thought that this was a fine idea and wrote down a few things:

Last night I had the best sleep of my life. I hope one day I can own a bed like the bed in the hotel.

This morning at breakfast, Judy said I could eat as much as I wanted I filled a bowl with so many different kinds of cereal and ate the entire thing. I also had a small plate of potato waffles. Delicious!

First taxi ride of my life. A monumental moment. Slight motion-sickness.

The day entailed several office meetings, the two of them bobbing from one location to the next, Annabel waiting outside the meeting rooms in close watch of Judy's alert eyes through large glass walls. At times, Annabel attempted to stroll around and give herself a tour of the buildings, but each time scurried back to her place after catching eye contact with Judy who would hypnotically gesture her to return to her seat with a simple head motion. She had tried to keep Annabel busy with a colouring book, a handful of snacks and a map of the city to study, but all of these only occupied her attention for a short while. Annabel wanted to explore, to head out into the winding pavements of a bustling city, to frolic through the variety of things to see and people to watch and activities to partake in.

The later hours of the afternoon swept by and Judy's final meeting arrived. It was located in a building just off the corner from China Town, and during the steady rush, Annabel noticed an attractive little shop that, from the window view, contained all kinds of things that tempted her eyes. She wanted nothing more than to explore it, and when they arrived at the office building she pleaded with Judy to let her go off alone to see it. Judy dismissed her request and told her it was unsafe for her to be out on her own, but after Annabel's thick, sulky silence, which shortly after led to her reminding Judy that she wasn't a little girl any more, she agreed to let her go as long as she returned within ten minutes. Then off she went, caught suddenly in the anticipation of venturing somewhere unknown completely alone; it may have only been to a shop on a road a few minutes away on foot, but to Annabel, it felt almost like a cross-country trip, as if momentarily she was an explorer with the world at the touch of her fingertips.

The interior of the shop was even more bewildering than she expected, and as she walked deeper down the aisles, she noticed there was so much to see and so little time to see it all. She briefly glanced at all the snacks in wildly animated packages, the iced teas with all kinds of blends and mixtures of flavours one could possibly imagine, the wonderfully decorated ornaments, and the collection of inventive gizmos and gadgets. She inspected some particular things that stood out to her: a facial cleansing mask that fizzed and foamed, rice cookers shaped like cartoon characters, lunchboxes that opened a dozen ways, animal-shaped tea infusers. Never had she seen a collection of so many imaginative things before, tightly presented together in such a magnificent building. On the way out, she purchased a fortune cookie — something she had always wanted to try — with a few pennies laying around in her pocket. As she walked, she deliberated if it was worth eating it right away or if she would keep it and take it home as a sentiment, locked inside its packet as a memoir of her trip, the message inside an everlasting mystery. Eventually, she gave in to the temptation and found a little corner on the road to enjoy the delicacy. There, she snapped it in half to find the message inside was written in Mandarin, completely incomprehensible to her, then she munched on both halves of the cookie, her eyes closed, taking in the sensations of each chew, absorbing all the sweetness and crunch it had to offer. Afterwards, she made her way back to the office building, holding onto the little paper message; perhaps she would find a way to translate it later, she thought, but as a breeze lifted the corner of it, the English translation was revealed on the other side of the paper. It read *Don't forget to look up.* After reading it aloud, Annabel, taking it quite literally, looked up. And maybe it was pure luck, a serendipitous instant that got a hold on her, or maybe, she wondered, the fortune cookie had led her to notice this exact spot, but right in front of her, plastered on the building wall, was a single leaflet displaying itself invitingly on an empty space.

Charity fundraising visual arts exhibition taking place in Charing Cross.

A vast collection of works from some of the finest artists in London.

Her eyes wandered to the bottom of the page.

Extra tickets at the door. Limited availability. Grab them before they sell out!

She looked at the date. It was happening later that day, that very evening, and now she wished to go more than anything.

After the meeting, it took quite a bit of persistent convincing to get Judy to agree to take her to the exhibition. Judy had planned an evening at a restaurant, to dine with the close watch of the city lights and the dazzling shine of the River Thames, and then to possibly go to see a movie, but seeing how enthusiastic Annabel was about the prospect of attending the exhibition made her eventually succumb to the persuasive teenager.

The event began at 6 pm sharp. They arrived briskly and rushed to the doors, dashing through speculating observers discussing the high demand of the show, Annabel holding her fingers crossed tightly in the hopes of getting tickets. And almost immediately, to her surprise, Judy somehow managed to get a hold of two paper tickets. Annabel often thought that Judy had a way with her words, a special gift of persuasion, and that sometimes she radiated a rather bewitching persona that often made it impossible for people to turn her down. And in this case, it worked like a charm.

The exhibition was a magical maze, showcasing an eclectic collection of hundreds of visual works of which Annabel felt so lucky to be in the presence. The two of them strolled attentively from room to room, Annabel stopping by often to closely marvel at some pieces and assimilate the meaning of them to the best of her ability, Judy showing somewhat of an interest, occasionally yawning from her doziness which eventually subsided at the sight of how lit up with energy Annabel was. She gasped in awe at some of the works, often taking time to appreciate the details of those that grabbed her interest and then jotting down the names of a few of them in her handy notebook. One of the works she was particularly fond of was a large collage of cutout photographs from the artist's travels across the mountains of the Himalayas, each photograph intermingling with one another to form a swarming display. Another one of the pieces that stopped her in her tracks was a self-portrait sculpture created by a ceramic artist with a blindfold on; the artist was interested in the outcome of sculpting their self-image without the sense of sight and relying solely on memory, intuition and the awareness of their physical touch. Another one was an oil painting on a gigantic canvas, depicting a fantastical scene of a merry-go-round in motion. Judy thought this one wasn't anything to gush over, but Annabel was entranced by it; she imagined the artist stroking the paintbrush skilfully across the scene, the vibrant colours playfully tickling the surface of the canvas, blending and collaborating.

As time passed, they came to the end of the exhibition. They had seen everything there was to be seen and were amongst only a small crowd of visitors left. Annabel, now with a plethora of new experiences in her memory bank, was filled with gladness, and as much as she wished the winding road of wanderlust wasn't over, that her adventure in London had just begun, that this newfound feeling of excitement had an extended ending, she was content as a bird in a scenic sky. But just as their journey was coming to an end, as the two of them approached the peak of the final room, she pointed out something quite peculiar: a door at the far end of the room, evidently not part of the showcase, was left slightly ajar, revealing a tiny gap where faded lively music, cheerful conversations and flickers of moving shadows seeped through. Judy noticed this too and smiled cheekily; what appeared to be behind the door seemed like something to which she was very drawn. It appeared that she was feeling frisky and ready for something exciting after hours of wandering in, what seemed to her to be through her small comments here and there, a labyrinth of eternity. And so, after a very brief pause and a mischievous giggle, she decided to take advantage of her daring mood. She squeezed Annabel's hand jerkingly a few times, and whilst no one was watching, she pulled her over to the door and, without any hesitation, pushed it open confidently and led her through, making sure to close the door shut behind her. Annabel looked up to see a vibrant party in a grand lobby, then peered over at Judy who seemed to be perfectly in her element. She had always admired this raying confidence Judy acquired, this part of her that was willing to trample on minor risks in order to get her hands on a little treat, to gain access to something special, or in this case, a lavish after-party.

There were hundreds of people around, mingling in their groups, chatting humorously amongst each other. Security guards were spread out across the area; most of them were occupied with the chuckling murmurs of gossip, so it wasn't too big a surprise that they had managed to trespass without a single raise of an eyebrow. Judy gasped at the sudden sight of little tables on wheels that held wonderfully presented collections of snacks and beverages. She dashed over to one and picked up something that looked quite like a chocolate truffle, but shinier, and perfectly round. As she bit into it, Annabel watched as her eyes rolled back in elation and she moved her hands to the rhythms of her chews in an attempt to dance with the flavours of the chocolate. Judy urged her to taste some, but Annabel was too lost in observation to consider trying some herself. She watched as Judy helped herself to a glass of something bubbly and got to talking to a group of strangers. As she conversed, she put out her open hand, and unthinkingly, Annabel took hold of it, but that familiar appetite for independence began to resurface, and so she let go, and as she wandered off, she listened to Judy's lively chatter fade into the distance, submerged in the ocean of other voices.

Her eyes moved spiritedly around the imperial room, observing the little clusters of affairs taking place around her. She watched small groups of cheerful humans huddling together, sharing slices of cake and pieces of conversation, a few giggling tumultuously, children of barons and eager investors sitting around impatiently, waiting to go home whilst their parents lurched around like giants in a playing field, a man scouting through the appetisers and nibbles, poking at them with a toothpick, a mother showing off her baby to her fellow associates, the baby in the pram giving all sorts of perplexed looks. And then the lady in the scarf, the solitary lady in the blue, willowy scarf that rested around her neck, the tassels at the ends perched delicately over her shoulders. She was sitting daintily on a bench, staring out into the open air, her expression being contentedness with a hint of craving for clearer respiration and a minute away from the noise of the eventful night, taking a sip of her drink, which was garnished with a raspberry, and then smiling and nodding welcomely at what seemed to be a friend of hers walking by. Annabel continued to inspect her with persistent curiosity, and within a twinkle of time, she became dumbfounded by the existence of this lady, entangled in her universe, forgetting her own world and merely existing in the world of her and her alone. Annabel began inching closer unintentionally with something that felt like the natural pull of a magnet until she could make out more precise features of this enigmatic being. She was older, but young, perhaps somewhere in her twenties; her gaze was precise and striking; she wore a smile that could cut through any gloom; her pitch-black hair was tied up in a beautiful bond; her hazel skin was fine and luminous like the surface of the stillest water; the way she moved her arms as she spoke was entrancing in every way. Was it familiarity? Annabel pondered. No, it couldn't possibly be. Maybe she reminded her of something she had seen before, or maybe it was utter curiosity, one of those unpredictable moments when you find yourself completely captivated by something, or somewhere, or someone, and you're hooked in within every corner, breached deeply by relentless claws. Lost in a daze, Annabel was drawn closer, and step by step the lady emerged more and more finely into her vision. Some more friends of hers were heading out, and on their way began to attempt small doses of conversation with this lady, each of them taking turns to say goodbye and greet her with good wishes. Somehow, they all passed by her breezily, but Annabel was fixated, inspecting the way she conversed with the others, the way she laughed and smiled with magical ease. She continued to step closer, unaware of her own movements, as the lady's magnetic exudation pulled her closer and closer until she was right in front of her, standing face to face with her, their feet only a foot apart.

Annabel stared into her eyes, totally transfixed, as she slowly came to her senses and realised that the lady was staring wholeheartedly back into hers. Then Annabel began to feel a sinking embarrassment as the moving world around appeared muted and everything fell silent. She watched as the lady's expression slowly turned from utter bewilderment to some kind of calm puzzlement, and her eyes began to squint slightly as she slowly leaned her head forward, seeming as though all of her attention was focused on figuring out who this young girl was that stood before. There was a concentration there, an attentiveness that stunned Annabel, pushing her off any residue of comfort she had left, until she felt the immediate need to say something, to fill the gaping space of uncertainty, to end the anticipation for the sake of them both.

"Hi... I..."

No more words could leave her mouth. Her personality had been sucked into an abyss, and there was nothing left, not even the ability to conjure a simple sentence. The lady seemed to be in a fog of confusion, and she turned her head slightly as she tried to make sense of what was happening. But still, that fixed concentration persisted and Annabel noticed the lady's eyes studying her, almost as if she were a work of art with a mystery to unravel. She felt her hands begin to tremble as she tried her very best to hold herself together. She quickly considered running away, but the need to say something struck her again; this time it felt more urgent, and suddenly, she said the first words that met her mind.

"I... love your scarf."

The seconds that followed did not feel as if they were seconds at all, but long, dragged notes that grew into crescendos of time. She watched as the lady, still looking confused, but firmly concentrated, halted, then laughed sweetly, then as she gently stroked her scarf said, "How kind of you. My mother made it for me."

Her voice, tinged with the slightest rasp, sounded melodic, like the flavour of the finest honey, and it felt like safety, a hug to ears. Annabel nodded and pretended to inspect the scarf, but as lovely as it was, at that moment she couldn't think about anything other than why she was still standing there; there was nothing to be said, not a single thought in her mind that summoned any idea of where to possibly go from there. She continued to stare at the scarf, then looked up into the eyes of the lady, which met hers with a steady attentiveness, and then swiftly diverted her attention to her own twiddling thumbs, the lady still silently concentrated before her. Annabel thought hard about what to say next, but before her mind could form her sporadic thoughts into clumps of words, she heard the sound of her name being called from afar.

And with this, she found some strength and looked into the eyes of the lady once more. "I have to go! My aunt is calling me."

Then she turned away and headed off in the direction of Judy's calls, but as she stepped away she felt the lady's hand grab her own. Her touch was soft and velvety but with an imprint of keenness, like a touch of a petal with a dynamic intention. Annabel turned to see her unravelling the scarf from her neck and watched as she placed it with a glint of affection into her hands.

"Here. Please take it," she said eagerly, closing Annabel's fingers over it to protect the delicate sliver of material.

Annabel eyes lit up with a sparkle of elatedness and she nodded sweetly at the kind gesture, smiling as she turned and ran to follow the sound of her name.

She approached Judy, who stood not too far away, next to a melted chocolate fountain, both hands on her waists, her cross eyebrows furrowed. Astonished by the beautiful scarf in Annabel's hand, she quizzed her about where she had gotten it from, and after a brief lecture about the danger of talking to strangers that Annabel wasn't focused enough to apprehend, followed by a few chocolate-dipped strawberries that Judy gobbled down hastily, they left the party.

During the taxi ride to the hotel, Annabel could think of nothing other than the lady, her striking image relentlessly ascending in her mind. As Judy stared out the window, catching the twinkling sparks of the city lights and mumbling to herself, Annabel took out her notebook and made a little note:

The lady in the blue scarf.

She underlined those words three times, then closed the notebook, wrapped the scarf around it and held it earnestly to her chest.

The feelings that stemmed from this nine-year-old memory covered her completely, moulding her movements, pervading her thoughts. She sat on the padded chair at the kitchen table, her eyes fixated on drizzles of rain tapping on the window like thousands of tiny nails of creatures begging to enter. She breathed long, sustained breaths. Never in her life had she expected to be anchored down so deeply by such an abstraction; and it was one that was attached to a fathomless set of curious feelings with no plausible direction, no way for her to make sense of them, no route for her to take them other than into an unavoidable void of longing. But what exactly was she longing for? she wondered deeply. What was it about this lady that grasped her so mightily from nothing but a simple glimpse and a brief interaction? She thought about these things now with greater detail than she ever had before. How could one tiny encounter leave such a mark on someone? Could it have just been an innocent infatuation that she fixated on for far too long? No, there was just no possibility that it could have been that. How could something like this have lingered for so many years? She knew this wasn't at all that kind of thing; she knew the difference between the fascination of infatuation and the way this felt. And she knew that it would be regarded as something negligible if she had told someone, dismissed as nothing but a little moment of fixation, and her mountain of feelings would be minimised to something so unimportant. But what else could it have been? How could it be possible to feel so strongly, to care so deeply, to be so engulfed in curiosity about someone she did not know? Perhaps it was destiny? Or perhaps they were soulmates? Or just maybe, considering all possibilities, she was someone whom she knew from a past life? But all of this was going too far beyond her analytical grasp. It was like playing a guessing game with herself but the answer did not exist.

She began remembering how huge of an impact that little interaction had on her. She recalled how for months after the day of their meeting, she did not go a single day without dwelling on the memories of that moment, often rehearsing in her mind the details of it, holding onto the image of this lady as much as she could, making sure that it would not fade. For some time, she often wore the scarf too, wrapping it loosely around her neck, forgetting it was there. The repetition of these habits led to what almost felt like an obsession; some days the picture of this lady followed her wherever she went, imprinted into the back of her mind, the continuing feeling of longing for her tattooed to the beats of her heart. She sometimes appeared in her dreams, knocking on the doors of her subconscious thoughts unexpectedly in the middle of the night. Annabel had no idea what to do with what she was feeling, no direction to steer the energy it was brewing. This compulsion lasted months, until one day she decided that it had been enough; she had spent enough time going over it, fantasising about her, and it was leading her nowhere, so she soon decided it was time to let it all go. She packed the scarf away in a place she wouldn't find it and decided to put an end to the fixation. It took a little while, but eventually, the reoccurring thoughts popped into her mind less and less, the grippy feeling of wishful yearning she thought would never leave became less intrusive, the visits to her dreams became less frequent, and eventually the image of the lady gradually dimmed into something almost indecipherable; the memory of her became a broken puzzle that could not be put back together from thought alone. But, one day, a couple of years later, that faded but familiar urge to swoop into the lingering memory of her returned and she couldn't fight the temptation to take out the scarf, wear it one more time, and flood herself in the foggy recollection of the lady. It felt different than before; plenty of time had passed, and although those deep feelings were still present, she had more hindsight, more emotional maturity, and she wasn't so preoccupied with the obsession of it, but rather wrapped in a blanket of curiosity.

More years passed by and Annabel grew through her teenage years, and all the while those feelings prevailed in a pocket somewhere beneath the surface. She seldom sat to contemplate it anymore, exhausted by the mental strain of it from the previous years, and instead, she had accepted that it just wasn't going to be understood. But something new was beginning to surface: there was a thin layer of excitement underneath the cloudy mystification, an excitement that held the tender hands of a dreamy vision of finding this lady again.

And so, as the clock struck midnight, she looked down at her empty cup and wondered where all the tea had gone. Sometimes thoughts can have such a vigorous hold on us, loaded up by all the energy we can summon at the present moment, that our awareness of ourselves and our surroundings becomes expelled from us, and we mentally travel far away, somewhere other than here and now; that's where she had been. She looked introspectively at herself in that very moment and realised that, after all these years, and after a long while keeping those thoughts locked inside a cabinet deep in her mind, the inexplainable desire to find this lady was still there, still very much alive in the depths of her nature. Undoubtedly, moving from home and breaking from the ties of her old life was something she had wanted to do for a long time, but she could see now how undeniable it was that the mere fantasy of finding this woman had greatly influenced her decision to move to London. It wasn't until this very moment that she had consciously come to terms with this. In the past, she had found the idea of this so difficult to ponder because of the heavy weight of it, the feeling of such importance it had felt to find this lady, along with the cluelessness of how to approach it; she had no plan, no idea what she would do, or say, or how she would even be towards her if she were to draw close to her again; there was nothing, not even an instinctual course of action as a way to approach this, other than the prevailing hope to find her, and it was a hope that was impossible to wipe away. And with that, in the spur of the moment, Annabel decided that she couldn't ignore it anymore. She had to find her.

She made her way up the stairs to her bedroom and searched through her belongings. Tucked into the corner of a cupboard, behind piles of folded clothes, and in a small wooden box she hadn't opened in years, was a little tin jar that was originally home to a bag of herbal tea leaves she once received as a gift. She had stored the scarf away in there some years ago, leaving it in a tight shelter to harbour in the remaining scent of tea while it withered slowly from her memory. Slowly, she popped open the lid and pulled out the scarf, which was just as ravishing as she remembered. Then she held it in her hands, admiring its beauty, moving her fingers along it to re-learn the brilliant touch of it, smitten by its softness, its texture performing the fragility of a butterfly's wings. She noticed the minor details of the design and admired it in a way she had never done before, noticing the complex white threads and blue shimmer moving along the material the way a river runs through a creak. It truly was a beautiful scarf. As her eyes embraced it, she noticed a knitted swirl in a tiny navy thread right at the edge of the material. It was words, too small to notice without close inspection, knitted in such a way that it almost appeared like squiggly patterns, but it was emulating a calligraphic handwriting style so graciously. She looked a little closer and noticed there were two words, but not just any two words, a name, someone's name. The name of the lady? she thought. It must have been. And then she realised something: the entire time, the words she had been looking for had been there, right where the scarf met the edge of its little universe. She couldn't quite believe it. During all those years her name was there, right beneath her. In disbelief, she read it: *Nina Bayu.*

She read it once more out loud, then again, and she smiled, whispered it, and then whimpered softly.

"What a beautiful name."

The Café and a Squirrel

"Nina Bayu." "Nina Bayu." "Nina Bayu."

She couldn't stop herself from saying it as she held the words in her hands. The name protruded from her lips as though it were fleeing for its freedom. She couldn't help but utter it. No words had ever been spoken by her with so much ease; it felt natural to say it, to let the words soar freely. She sat quietly for some time, alone with nothing but the name. This was *her* name, she thought. It had been sitting there on her neck during all those years, and then enclosed by the thin walls of the tin jar, hidden from her sight. She moved her fingers lovingly over the thread along the trail the letters led. She thought about how special this scarf must have been to Nina, and what a kind gesture it was to let something so precious go into the hands of someone she did not know. She imagined Nina's mother making the scarf, sewing her name dearly for her beloved daughter, and now it lay in her own hands, and she couldn't appreciate it more. How lovely it had felt to find a piece of the person she had been longing to discover; it was as if she held keys to the door to one of the many answers she was searching for. But where to go from here? she wondered. Now it was just a case of taking the next step, moving forward for more answers. She felt more confident now than ever before that she would find her, the person she now knew as Nina. She moved over to her desk and switched on her laptop, then clicked on the internet and searched for her name. Nina Bayu. Her heart raced as the results loaded. The speed of the internet connection there was slow and only intensified the suspense more. She closed her eyes for a few seconds, taking a moment to shelter in the faraway world of a long blink, and then she opened them and looked at the results.

At the top of the search page was a profile on a website that showed emerging artists in London. She clicked on it and saw a picture of Nina. It was her. Nina was an artist. She became starstruck and an outpouring of old feelings began to resurface as she stared deeply into the eyes of the familiar face on the screen. Below the picture was a small paragraph, a description:

Nina Bayu, of Indonesian and Ethiopian descent, is a painter, born and raised in London, United Kingdom. She grew up painting and studied fine art, and a few years after her studies, she and her brother opened a café. Nina spent the next ten years working alongside her brother in the café, spending half of her time there and the other half on her paintings. After years of developing her craft and showcasing her work at various galleries, she began gaining recognition and public attention. Her painting "Allamanda Dance" was recently featured in various art magazines and showcases. Nina currently works full-time as a painter.

As Annabel read the paragraph, her eyes sprung from line to line and then floated up to the ceiling into a momentary halt. She had in no way foreseen this and she couldn't quite process what she was reading. She couldn't believe the fact that within a handful of seconds, she suddenly held more information about the enigma of the lady in the blue scarf than she had in nine years of wishing to discover her. There was a photograph of Nina's painting below. It was a skilful mixture of shade and colour, coalescing with one another to depict a scene of a dancer pirouetting in a field of yellow allamanda flowers. The painting appeared before Annabel so eloquently and she withdrew to her mind to picture Nina painting it. She imagined her eyes concentrated intently on each careful stroke, her steady hand moving in slow-motion as the tip of the brush kisses the scene, the colour meeting the plain canvas and instantly forming a union with it, Nina smiling lightly as she brings the wonders of her imagination to life; everything around Nina is still, fizzled out, almost non-existent at times, and the state of being in absolute flow with insight takes over, totally transcendent; and she unapologetically surrenders to her vision. And what a fine thought it was. She browsed through some more of Nina's paintings and found herself engaged in a trance of adoration. Perhaps it was the fact that it was the work of Nina that had her spellbound so easily, but she didn't care and she allowed herself to be swept by the beauty of the work. She noticed that many of these paintings depicted a natural scene so wonderfully that it seemed almost unreal, which was exactly what Annabel strived for with her photographs, and she gazed in awe at this. The oil paint through which Nina channelled her vision actualised a serene display of light and colour onto each canvas, each shade standing alone but dancing playfully with each other, flirting, fusing and swimming splendidly across the piece like the colours of the setting sun meeting the tip of the ocean. She looked once more at the picture of Nina. That purity in her expression was just as stark and present as before. She looked older than before, but in some mystifying way even more youthful. Annabel's hand lifted and her finger floated closer to touch the picture of Nina; it felt almost mechanical, an automatic response, the way a baby reaches for a toy. She touched Nina's cheek and her curious fingertip moved down the screen slowly, the thinnest layer of oil on her skin leaving behind the faintest rainbow, garnishing Nina with a touch of her colourful joy. And joy is what she was feeling.

Consumed by all the uncovering fragments of information about Nina she could find, she scrolled, clicked and read until her eyes began to droop forcibly. She found that Nina kept details of her life away from the public; other than her art, there wasn't much of her online, no personal profiles, no public accounts on any online social platforms. Coincidentally, Annabel related to this; she herself had never been one to take part in many social media affairs. She was sure she had inspected every online site that mentioned Nina, and after being engulfed with an infinitely diverse collection of her paintings, along with some vague details of her life that only shared very little about who she actually was, she came across a contact email. It was the email address of Nina's manager. This seemed to be the only means of connecting to Nina herself, but as she saw it, she became utterly conflicted, lost in a sea of bemusement, with no idea of what she would possibly say, what words she would use to paint her mind's picture, how she would tell the story that was impossible to tell. She clicked on the contact button and stared for a moment at the blank email page; empty, with nothing to fill the bare, white void of wordlessness. And moments later, the page stayed blank, silent, and she felt unable to find the right thing to say, unable to capture any meaning she wished to convey, lost in the confusion of not knowing where to go from there. She knew that whatever she would send would potentially end up with Nina, and someone else before her, and the story would no longer be her own mystery. She peered into her mind, searching for possibilities of what to say, how she could mention their brief meeting in the past and the profound impact it had on her, but without appearing too desperate, how she could portray her overpowering desire to find her, but without appearing too needy. After all, the last thing she wanted to do was to frighten her, to come across as an overbearing admirer, or worse, a lurking fanatic. She wrote a few greeting sentences and then deleted them immediately. It seemed impossible to put it all into one email and have it make sense to someone who didn't share her feelings. Here, before her eyes was a pathway she had spent years wishing to get her hands on, and with a sprinkle of words and a click of a button she could get her message straight to the source of her longing, but she just could not do it. All she hoped for was an idea that would light her up, make her illuminate with triumph, but she was greeted with no plan, not a single idea about how to approach this, or words to type that felt satisfactory enough to send. Perhaps, she thought, she could pose as an admirer of Nina's work, or a student doing an assignment on modern artists who chose her as the subject; but this didn't seem feasible, or sustainable; it would have at worse failed to be acknowledged and at best would have only lead to an utterly unnatural interaction with her. There had to be another way. And there was. An idea sprinted to her. She would find the café, and she would go there, in hopes to learn more about Nina. Just being in the place in which she worked for ten years of her life would possibly inspire a course of action, she thought. Perhaps it would lead her down an easier path to finally understanding all of this. Perhaps natural instances would unfold that would allow her to meet Nina, entirely naturally, and Nina would feel that pull too, that pull that felt like the force of an opposing team at a game of tug of war, a feeling of desire to know her too, to make sense of the magnitude of feelings that longed to be a part of her world too, to form a deep connection with her too. But her thoughts were getting too ahead of themselves now. She would go to the café, and spend some time there, and maybe, with some luck, Nina would come in. Maybe at the mere sight of her, she would know how to approach the situation. Maybe she could follow the feelings that would emerge from being in her presence, because that's how it happened the last time, and this time, perhaps she'd be influenced to say something, or do something, or she'd understand it all, finally, assisted now by her bloomed emotional maturity, by her broader understanding of her own inner world. Maybe, just maybe, this time, at the sight of her, she would know what to do.

And so, with a little more research, she found the café. Sometimes the internet can be a powerful thing, she came to realise. She became aware of the time; the sun would rise in only a few hours. Dusty's distant snoring seeped through the wall and into her ears, and with that, it was time to sleep.

Luckily, the café was close by, only a short bus journey away, right around the corner from Hampstead Heath, a place which revealed itself to be quite a gem from her moving tower on top of the double-decker bus. During the journey there, she remained rather thoughtless, in a sheltered bubble of her mind, wilfully refusing to give into pointless anxieties. She hadn't slept much, awoken in the morning by the first touch of sunlight; she had felt too focused on her new quest to settle into a deep sleep. The café was on the edge of a small hill, much quieter than the high street through which she had just walked, and the scarceness of lively events up there made her notice that her heart was pounding like the beats of a samba; those mini anxieties she had tried to distance herself from were beginning to rise to the surface. She noticed a startling quiver inside her stomach, like frantic moths trying to escape from inside of her, bouncing onto walls, skittering around impulsively and unpredictably. But she walked on, trying her best to ignore this feeling. Outside, the café had two sets of tables with benches on either side of the front door, and cheery groups of morning lovers sat there and chatted spiritedly, chirping amongst one another like songbirds at daybreak, sipping hot teas and creamy coffees. As she walked through the entrance, the opening door gently pushed a wind chime and a soft, mystical melody danced and twirled through the room. She noticed that there were eyes on her and she presented a shy grin and nodded her head subtly. It had been a while since she had felt so fragile before and she wasn't used to feeling this way. The inside of the café was oozing with warmth and looked so charming and remarkable that she had to stop herself from taking out her camera, hoping to remain discreet and blend into the moving waves of customers. The floor was a fine shade of classic oak-brown and creaked just slightly at the weight of a step; the tables were decorated with bouquets of dried flowers; there were stained-glass lamps in different areas of the room, elevating the mood with a cosy tint of a warm hue; and best of all, paintings were hung all over the walls, some Annabel recognised as Nina's work. To her right, she noticed a striking collection of sandwiches, cakes and prettily encrusted pastries that made her mouth water instantaneously. She was greeted by a small woman in orange spectacles and curly hair, wearing an apron that had colourful stains smeared all over, and she smiled with a contagious glow.

"And what will it be for you?" she asked politely.

Annabel pinched her chin as she scanned the collection of treats. She looked up and noticed a big chalkboard displaying a drinks menu that was written in a fantastical style of lettering; each letter sprouted its lines in arbitrary directions like the roots and twigs of a tree.

"I'll take one of those," she said, pointing to a tiny mountain of glazed pastries with strawberries on top, "and a hot Darjeeling." The woman handed her the treat and the steaming tea on a vintage metal tray, and Annabel carried it over to a small table in the far corner of the café with a perfect view of the entire room. Someone else who wore another colourfully stained apron appeared from a side door holding a platter with a large violet cake. Annabel studied the room a little more from her corner-table view. On her left hung one of Nina's paintings that she instantly recognised due to the copious amount of research the previous night. It was titled *Moon replaces Sun* and portrayed a spellbinding picture of the sun setting and the moon rising, both greeting one another as the sun passes its role of radiating light to the moon. The painting was ornamented with freckles of dotted stars sporadically scattered across the sky, and whilst looking up at it, she disassembled the pastry with her fork and took a bite, absorbed by its perfectly sweet flavour and the crispy flakes of crust breaking off and melting at the embrace of a mouth. It not only tasted delicious, but it contrasted impeccably with the silky hot tea. She wondered about all the possible places Nina's brother could have been, then was suddenly met with the saddening thought that perhaps he no longer worked there and had passed the café down to someone else, but at the brief meeting of that speculation, a man walked up from the stairs that presumably lead to the kitchen on the lower floor. He too wore a stained apron, but his apron was rose-coloured, and he was dusting off his hands as if he had just finished a tiresome task. He wore a name tag on his apron that read *George*. As he passed by, he greeted Annabel with a welcoming smile and she delivered the same smile back instinctively. He had kind eyes, with a comforting warmth to them, the kind of eyes that silenced fears by caressing them, hugging away worries with gentle care. A familiarity in his features gave Annabel a striking feeling that he was indeed Nina's brother. He walked into the front room and began helping his colleagues serve the forming queue of customers. Gradually, Annabel's anxiety began to whither away as she watched him and his slow, comforting movements.

She spent some time there, watching the events of the café like a film before her eyes. George had a calm demeanour to which she felt drawn. The booming rush of the morning customers began to slow down and the mood of the room steadily became quieter. Annabel began half-reading her book in an attempt not to appear suspicious or as if she was harshly observing, which is in fact exactly what she was doing.

After a little time peering over the top of the book and then occasionally fiddling with the pages so as to appear busy and distracted, the café became very quiet, just quiet enough for her to stand out and attract attention. George was alone behind the counter now, organising and assorting some cakes and pastries. There had been no sign or sight of Nina, and Annabel decided it was time to leave and that she would come back tomorrow. She attempted to vacate the café peacefully, but as she approached the door, George noticed her.

"Before you go, would you like to try a taster?" he asked, holding out a platter of tiny chopped pieces of something sweet-looking. "It's orange cake. I made it this morning!"

Annabel smiled. "I've never tasted orange cake before!"

She politely took a piece and tasted it, gleaming at its deliciousness, its chewiness and its zesty kick. "It's lovely. Thank you."

"It has quite a magic recipe," he said, leaning forward, his eyebrows raised.

Annabel laughed. "Well, I'm not much of a baker myself but I know a delicious cake when I taste one!"

George nodded in appreciation and the two of them waved goodbye as Annabel scurried out into the daylight.

As she walked away, she thought about George. He had such an endearing aura to him, a way of being that exuded tranquillity, a way of communicating that made the other person feel so welcomed and comforted. She trod across zebra crossings and glared down at her shiny black shoes as they took turns hopping onto the white stripes. She swivelled around backstreets, decorated alleyways and neighbourhood roads as she thought to herself, unable to shake off the lingering ambivalence gripping her down to her bones. Those unshakable feelings of needing so desperately to find answers were returning, and this time she felt more determined to find Nina than ever before; and she was so close, so very close. But, in the midst of the quest emerged an utter confusion, that familiar kaleidoscope of unanswered questions about what this was all for, why the desire was so persistent, how it was possible to feel all of this, what it was about Nina that lured her so profusely, and now, most importantly, what she would do or say if she finally did find Nina. Doubts were rising, uncertainty was peaking, and as the afternoon sky began to drip splashes of cold, wet surprises, she caught the bus back home.

The journey home was a blur of daze, a conundrum of wonder and confusion. The bus halted at a red light and Annabel gazed at a tree next to her from the window. She noticed a squirrel, just like the squirrel her younger self chased up the tree, bursting to the scene. It was holding a nut, almost hugging it, soaking itself into the beauty of it and relishing in all the gratitude for the tiny thing it could find. Its quaint body held the treasured nut with a fierce love, its tiny arms wrapping around it, its fragile fingers tightly gripping the surface, its little furry body giving it a warm embrace. And it looked down at its little treasure, with a small, loving breath moving in and out of it. As Annabel stared, her mind was conquered by the sight of the squirrel; her spirit became its spirit; her existence became wrapped in the existence of this creature, succumbing to the beauties of its nature, and she smiled as all of her disquiet thoughts were momentarily wiped away by the sight of love from a little being so different to herself. She turned her mind back to the thought of Nina, and the pursuit of her, and in that instant, she decided, so willingly, so concretely, that at the sight of her, she would know what to do. And perhaps it was true, or perhaps she was convincing herself of this, but at that moment it didn't matter to her, for the squirrel felt content and so she should too, and that meant letting go of those unnecessary troubling thoughts for as long as she could. And so that is what she did.

She returned to the café the next day. George recognised her as she entered and greeted her with a merry smile. This time, it was quieter; echos of Thursday afternoon murmurs gently rippled through the room and the comforting scent of baking goods rose from downstairs like a fragrant, invisible smoke. She sat at the same table as the day before, this time with a bowl of tomato soup, a London fog — a succulent, milky, vanilla earl grey tea — and a dazzling slice of the orange cake of which George was so proud. And she read her book, occasionally taking small intervals to overhear George's conversations and peer at the entrance any time someone entered, in hopes that it would be Nina. She wished so much for some luck to be on her side, for Nina to walk in, paying a little visit to her brother, and then sit beside her, munch on something delicious and hang around for enough time for Annabel to be prompted to say something to her. She thought about all the possible avenues of their escapade into getting to know one another: their eyes would interlock and Nina would feel the hasty desire to say something, or Nina would ask her what she was reading and they would chirpily converse about their shared love of the author, or perhaps they would bond over the tastiness of the orange cake. The possibilities seemed endless. But, plenty of time passed and she did not enter. Annabel sighed as she turned a page of her book, scratching the surface of the thick pile of pages impatiently. She looked at one of Nina's artworks to her left; it was a painting of two children running in a wheat field and an aeroplane leaving a trail of thick white smoke in between two passing clouds. George was passing by, holding a tray of hot scones, and noticed Annabel admiring the work.

"You like?" he asked charmingly.

"It's beautiful," she replied.

George turned around, glanced at the painting, and then down at Annabel, who had her finger on her bottom lip and a look of dreaminess.

He grinned brightly. "It's by my sister, Nina. There's a lot of her work around the room."

Annabel quietly gasped as she looked around, unthinkingly pretending she didn't already know this. "Well, your sister is a wonderful painter."

The two of them shared a little moment staring at the painting together. It was silent; there was not a single sound to be heard, no words that made the presence of someone else known; one could have heard a feather fall to the ground at this very instant.

"There's something so remarkable about the way the colours coalesce," said Annabel. "She paints with such a heartfelt vision. I can't quite put my finger on it, but it's as if she, somehow, through her paintings, fulfils the destiny of each individual colour. It's really special."

George looked at Annabel with twinkling eyes, slightly astonished, then looked back at the painting. The silence retreated as a bird was heard warbling from outside and George let out a wistful sigh.

"I'd love to meet her. Does she ever come here?" asked Annabel, half of her still lost in the painted reality.

George chuckled. "Well, occasionally, but she's so very busy these days. We used to live and work together, but now she kind of lives all over the place. You see, her work is constantly taking her to all sorts of places."

Annabel's eyes widened as she looked at George. "So where is she now? Any special place?"

"Actually, she's here in the city, but down in the South West area," said George. "She's doing a showcase in a hotel gallery down there this evening. Richmond, that's it! Then she'll be off to Barcelona in a couple of days, and shortly after Madrid. She'll be working in Spain for some time, and then after that, who knows?"

A customer standing by the display of food waved to get George's attention.

"Be right with you!" called George, looking over, then back down to Annabel. "I'll tell her about you. I'm sure she'd appreciate what you said about her work."

He walked over to the front of the café, carrying his tray of steaming scones, and greeted the customer with his habitual kind demeanour. Annabel watched him, broodily, then came back to her senses and turned her attention back to her book and the remaining tiny pond of tea that sat peacefully in a mug of fine china.

She left the café a short moment later, and as she stepped outside into the breezy air, she noticed that familiar fluttering sensation inside again, but it was mixed with an unexpected slew of excitement, a potion churning in the depths of her. She wondered about the prospect of meeting Nina that very evening, and with every inch of her spirit she knew it had to happen, for soon she was going to Spain and so this was her moment to seize, her great opportunity to grasp. She knew where she would go next: Richmond. So she hurried home and packed a satchel of her essential items; this included her phone, her camera, a small notebook, lip balm, a scarf, and a little bag of sweetened almonds that Dusty left out for her. And then she left, embarking on the passage to find Nina, with not a single minute to spare.

At The Gallery

Whilst looking through the window at a moving world, it's easy to become swept away into thoughts and fantasies of the wandering mind, into a vortex of imagination, a rapid stream of fleeting images passing through our mind's eye.

As Annabel watched daffodils, faraway bridges and a superfluity of architecture flash by in a blurry landscape, she lost herself in this vortex, floating seamlessly between dozens of thoughts, observing them contemplatively. A building that passed by awakened a memory within her. She remembered herself, much younger, around the age of seven, standing on a balcony with her mother by her side. They must have been on a trip somewhere, she couldn't remember exactly, but some things she remembered quite vividly. She remembered the sunset beaming down courteously, gently touching the top of a building structure at the end of the horizon, and the feather-like clouds gathering in a breathtaking formation, and the cigarette smoke that her mother blew out fleeing to join the assembly of clouds, wishing to play alongside them and then melting into them peacefully. She remembered the group of shadowy people dancing on a rooftop in the distance, and the vines weaving around the balcony, zigzagging in their humorous way, and the leaves hanging down from the floor above, icing the view with a sprinkle of autumn sweetness. The moment was ethereal, and it was the first memory she possessed of feeling that genuine spark of desire to capture the moment within a photograph. But, during that time in her life, she had never owned a camera; she had never even thought of herself as someone who would own one. But at last, this moment changed that. She pictured the memory of herself and her young innocence, standing there with an aura of immense interest, admiring the view as she steadily placed her hands in front of her face, closed one eye, and formed the shape of a rectangle with her thumbs and index fingers, an action she had seen someone do on the television. She stared into the cropped landscape between her fingers and thought to herself that if it was a photograph it would be the most beautiful photograph she had ever seen. Her heart fluttered with adoration and the sides of her lips levitated into a warm smile, and with this moment, she knew that one day she would take photographs.

The train continued rolling down the trail. On her phone, she purchased a ticket to Nina's showcase, and as she did she noticed that she had been neglecting some messages from her distant mother and friends. It seemed that her intention of finding Nina had been occupying her every move and getting in the way of her other responsibilities, but she felt she was approaching the pinnacle of her search and there was no time for distractions, so she shut them out for the time being.

When the train arrived at Richmond station, she noticed the calmness first, and in a way, this calmness reminded her a little of her home in Edinburgh. And compared to where she lived now, it was quieter here, more airy and spacious than the inner parts of London she was getting used to. As she stepped out of the station and into the town, the breeze caught her off guard; she hadn't felt a breeze so lustrous and rejuvenating since the Scottish breeze, and there was a feeling in the air, a sense of slow-paced relaxation there that brought a sense of village life back to her. There were plenty of dog walkers around, trodding along with their furry companions amidst the late afternoon mellowness. As she strolled, she searched for a place to stop for a snack and to sip on something refreshing, a place to prepare for her next move in comfortable warmth. She was attracted to a little Italian coffee shop just underneath the bridge that overlooked the river that bounced around in its thousands of ripples. There, she purchased a toasted sandwich and a fresh juice and sat inside, accompanied by the rumbling rhythms of tuneful music from a crackling stereo and the clinks and clanks of kitchenware behind the counter. The gallery where Nina's showcase was being held was right along the river walk, a few minutes down the trail that emerged from the bridge. She thought about how, at that very moment, Nina was only a little walk away from her, separated by nothing but a single trail, and as the minutes passed, the possibility of meeting her was finally becoming more and more real. She was adamant to let her instincts guide her and had convinced herself that intuition would take over at the meeting with Nina, for the mere longing for her was utterly incomprehensible to her rational mind, and these feelings seemed to be produced by a force unseen to her. Thinking tirelessly about it, at this point, felt like a pointless game of mental tennis from which no conclusion or understanding was coming; so she did not think of it, she no longer thought of the way she would approach Nina or the words she would say to her. She felt she simply could not predict the chain of events that would occur, so she blocked those circling questions out, for they were only thoughts after all, and the force of nature that tied her to Nina, she felt, was much greater than her thoughts alone. And so, to let insight lead the way seemed to be the most natural thing to do.

The sun was setting pictorially as it released its glorious colours of deep red and coral-orange and glinted hints and streaks of the palest mauve through its feathery textures of light cloud; it met the twinkling river with grace and passed its colours onto the reflection generously. Geese and ducks were heard all around in their flocks, making songs and honking in joy alongside the distant sounds of rotating propellors on boats and cheery howls of children calling out to the distance. Whilst walking along the trail beside the river, she began to feel a strong sense of nervous floating, a slight detachment from her body, as if the force of her weight was only a fraction stronger than a force that could lift her off the ground. She sat on a bench and focused on the world around her as she let herself breathe for a few moments, and as she breathed she found herself again. The weightless sensation began to pass and her thoughts seemed to appear before her with more clarity. It was time to get to Nina, and she wasn't going to let anything keep her from it.

She arrived at the gallery which was a little walk along the trail on the hill and overlooked a mesmeric view of greenery and the winding river that swivelled through. The building was of classic Victorian architecture, and she took a picture of a falcon that sat triumphantly on the pointed rooftop. At the entrance door, she presented her ticket to the ticket collector and was welcomed with cordiality. The event was about to begin and so she paced inside the building, her breath beginning to move heavily in and out with great intensity as she hurried into the room where the showcase was taking place. There were plenty of rows of chairs laid out facing a small elevated stage. On top of the stage was a line of some of Nina's paintings upon metal stands that were towering over two armchairs, one occupied by a man in a suit who appeared very dapper and professional. Most of the seats were taken and the empty ones were filling up fast, so she hurried to a seat on the side in the middle of the aisle; it was as close as she could possibly get to the front. An employee walked along the aisles handing information leaflets about the showcase and handed one to Annabel. She held the leaflet in her hands and was quickly engaged by a photograph on the front page. It was a black-and-white shot of Nina sitting on a stool, her face focused as she painted on a canvas that rested on a wooden easel. She wore a glimmering coat and striking pearl earrings shaped like teardrops. Annabel thought it was an extraordinary photograph and she started to feel almost lost inside of it. She noticed the lights in the picture darkening, and she wondered how this two-dimensional Nina in the colourless scene would paint without the light, before emerging from her thoughts to see the lights in the room dimming, setting the scene for a cosy atmosphere. The murmurs of the audience began to fade and the ambience in the room became quieter as talking voices turned to gentle whispers that faded quickly into silent breaths. The man on the armchair cleared his throat and then stood up and placed a microphone to his mouth. He began talking about Nina with a charming and rather delightsome tone. He introduced her as a creative force of nature, one of his personal favourite painters as well as a friend of his, and within a small passing of time, from behind the luscious red curtains that draped down theatrically at the far back of the room, she appeared.

Between the rumbling rhythms of trees swaying in the wind in the late spring afternoon, Annabel too, swayed to the rhythm of the swing that carried her back and forth, cutting through the air like a flying dagger. She was fourteen, almost fifteen, swinging alone in an empty playground around the corner from her home. The smile that emerged on her mouth as she swung perfectly encapsulated the swift beating of elation from her heart within, intensified by the breeze that gently touched the spaces between her hair and the rush of exhilaration that came with the vast movements. The weight of her body continued back and forth, back and forth like ocean waves of the shore, and her feet lifted a little higher with every sway, blocking out the sun from her view at the peak of each swing. She closed her eyes and appreciated the sensation of being lifted off the ground and the giddy fun of teasing gravity. Gently, she stopped the swing by placing her feet lightly on the ground and sat there for a moment as the swaying came to a calm conclusion. She stared fixedly at the greenest leaves and the rosy pink damsels sprouting through the crevices of an old wooden fence at the end of the playground. A hummingbird was swivelling around the plants ahead to eat the nectar from flowers, and dandelions were blooming in their charming clusters, and the trees around continued moving and rustling and dancing to the tune of the wind. It was peaceful and comfortably quiet. She took her camera out of her little bag and took a photograph of the view before her. It was the last shot left on the roll of film, and so she rewound the camera, removed the film stock and enclosed it in a canister, then smiled as she popped on the lid and revelled in the anticipation of seeing the photographs developed.

When she returned home, she ate dinner at the table with Edith, her concentration wavering in and out of the conversations as she imagined her photographs coming to life. She wondered about the surprises that awaited her in them, the diverse mixture of marvel taking place in each shot, the sentimental feelings that would resurface again at the sight of them, the forgotten colours that would reappear before her eyes. All of these things awaited her and she couldn't wait to greet them once more. She thought about it as she rested into a serene sleep that night and remembered it as soon as she lifted herself from her bed the following morning. After breakfast, she returned to her bag to fetch the film roll to take it to be developed, but as her hand reached into the bag, she felt all of her belongings but the film canister. A feeling of despair began to rise from beneath her as she removed every item from the bag and then shook out every last crumb and fluff that was inside. It was nowhere in sight. In the living room, Edith and Judy were sitting and sipping coffee, and she ran in and cried to them. Her voice wobbled and broke as she exclaimed in disbelief that she had lost her beloved photographs. Stored inside that little canister were her most treasured memories from the many recent weeks and the outpouring of her blossoming mind. To her, it felt like losing one of her most precious belongings, and she knew that she would never be able to replicate the photographs that lived inside that canister; they would become forgotten memories and wonderful visual mementoes that could have been. Edith and Judy, upon realising the importance that finding that canister was to Annabel, reassured her that she had just misplaced it and that they would soon find it. And so they searched, tracing back her steps all the way back to the swings where she took the final shot of the film, but luck had not been on their side, leaving a devastated Annabel spending the remainder of the afternoon sitting on the stairs with her head planted into her folded arms. It took weeks for her to fully accept the loss of those photographs, and every so often she would hope that she would accidentally stumble into the canister. And she never forgot about it, and still, to this day, very occasionally dwelled on the mystery of its vanishing.

On the stage, the figure of Nina slowly appeared more fine and detailed as she entered into the light that cascaded down, adorning her with an angelic flare. There she was, in her living existence, right in front of Annabel, no longer a picture on a screen or a somewhat-remembered concept in her mind, but there, alive in her truest form. Annabel couldn't quite believe that she was once again seeing Nina before her very eyes, yet there she was, as clear as anything could possibly be. The audience kindly cheered as she was welcomed onto the stage and the interviewer shook her hand formally and gestured for her to sit next to him. She nested herself into the comfortable armchair, placed one leg over the other gracefully, interlocked her fingers and rested her hands gently on a cushion as she smiled affectionately at the audience. At this moment, Annabel felt that it was almost impossible to organise her thoughts, as she was, in all senses, utterly transfixed.

For the duration of the talk, the interviewer gently threw questions to Nina, and she, with a tender radiance, tried her best to answer each of them with her greatest insight and articulation. She spoke of her paintings and their depictions, she brushed over stories that linked to particular works and explored the conversation of her relationship to her work. She spoke about her approach to art and life, and how she looked for the rarities in life, those extraordinary moments and things that seldom come along but stand apart from the typical and the mundane. Those were the things, she said, that inspired her to start a painting. And she spoke about other painters she admired, writers and artists who inspired her, and she spoke about colour and shade, and the nighttime and how the night sky and the shadows of the night inspired her to paint. Hearing her speak was like watching water run through the rocks at the bottom of a waterfall; her words flowed with a rhythm and prose that bubbled out of her with an untouchable charm. The audience appeared to be enamoured of her words and everyone in the room was eager to hear her stories in that ephemeral moment. Annabel listened attentively to the best of her ability, but her attention was hovering, threading in and out from Nina's words to the realisation that after all this time she had finally made it to her. She found herself gravitating to the hypnotism of entrancement; she was entranced by her smile, the slight raspiness that lingered at the edge of her voice, the giddy bounce of her laugh, her eccentric habits of gesticulation, the way her eyes moved around the room, scanning to catch onto other eyes and deepen the connection with the audience. And in every way that one could, she emitted a timeless beauty. But at the same time, all of these things, as captivating as they were, felt like the beautiful outer layer of an inner core, something deeper, something inside that Annabel was unable to distinguish through her senses. A hazy dissociation from the room emerged over her, and for a while, it was only her and Nina there; for a while, when Nina smiled, she was smiling for Annabel only; for a while, her words travelled directly to her, like an arrow sent from a bow between Nina's lips to her ears and her ears only.

At the end of the talk, Nina expressed her gratitude for everyone that came along to celebrate her work and explained that she'd be around until the very end of the showcase if anyone wished to speak to her.

"This is the time," said Annabel to herself in a whisper.

The audience gave a round of applause and then dispersed from their seats, the majority of them moving into the other rooms that exhibited more of her paintings. Nina ambled off the stage and greeted a group of people that waited to speak with her, each of them standing by to congratulate her or tell her that she inspired them in some way. Annabel, standing in the middle of a moving crowd, watched as Nina embraced each and every person that approached her with an expression of presence and care, offering smiles and hugs to represent her gratitude for their kind words. She wore a navy blue chiffon blouse emblazoned with shiny jewels around the neck that glinted tiny sparkles at the touch of light, like a blessing of fairy dust. Annabel took slow and steady steps forward towards her. As she moved, the fast-paced conversations that surrounded Nina became clearer and her physical appearance emerged before her with finer detail. Struck by a burning desire to say something to her, fused with a mixture of sheer disconcertion, Annabel could feel her lips begin to quiver and her knees started subtly trembling. She watched Nina hug someone with a joyful incredulity, perhaps an old friend that came to surprise her, and as the crowd around began to subside, the two friends moved to the side of the room to continue their conversation. Annabel was now one of only a handful of people left in the room, and as the number dwindled to a few, she decided she would try again in a short moment; she knew there was no way she could interject herself into the cheery conversation Nina was now having, so she decided she would walk around and explore the other rooms for a short while, distract herself from Nina's presence, and then later when it became quieter, she would return to her.

The other rooms were spacious, and spread out evenly across the walls were many more of her paintings placed upon easels, and there was a plaque next to each one that contained the name of the painting and the year it was painted. Annabel stood right up close to one of the paintings and leaned her head forward towards it, the tip of her nose edging close, almost stroking the surface. She noticed the minuscule textures, impossible to see from a further standpoint, the minute gestures, the bumps, the tiny splats of paint, and she noticed the layers and depth of the shine, the uniqueness of each stroke. For a moment, she was not only looking at a painting, but seeing it, completely silent in mind and body, captured by the sight of a bird's eye view, peering down on tiny hills, valleys, mountains and ripples of colourful rivers that flowed along passages through vibrantly textured lands, each colour surrendering to the power of another, blanketing and elevating each other to form a brilliant spectacle, all on a single canvas.

Sometime later, as the evening was closing in, the showcase was coming to an end and the visitors began leaving the premises with satisfaction on their faces. Annabel had seen everything on display, and she composed herself and readied herself again to approach Nina. She entered the stage room and found her standing there, sharing brief moments of chatter with people as they said their goodbyes in their coats and scarves. And then Annabel noticed something about her that the others around did not seem to notice: unlike at the beginning of the showcase, she seemed tired now, and under those gleaming grins and giggles, she seemed a little drained by the large quantity of social exertion; but she continued to smile and summon all the parts of her that were happy to interact with all of those people, for they were the parts of her the people around wished to see. She had no desire to tire Nina any more, but she knew this was her only chance to speak with her, to satisfy those paramount desires, to share a piece of her world of feelings in hopes that she would share a piece of those feelings too. Once again, she attempted to prepare to throw herself into contact with her, but she just could not summon the strength to do so with all the other people around. It seemed unnatural to have her moment with her surrounded by an audience, knowing that it may only be brief as Nina appeared to be saying goodbye to everyone that made contact with her. Annabel suddenly felt a spell of dizziness pour over her, brought upon her by the nervous ripples travelling within, so she stepped outside the entrance door into the fresh air and waited at the bottom of the steps at the front of the building. She knew it would only be a matter of time before Nina walked down those steps, so she waited, and as the remainder of the people left the building into the cold autumn air, her nervousness began elevating to a level she never could have anticipated. But still, she hoped that Nina would walk towards her soon, probably alone, and it would just be the two of them, no one else, their bodies facing each other, their eyes in a private meeting.

The sun was setting, leaving darkness to expand over the town and the street lamps to wake to their marigold light. She stared at the entrance doors, seeing nothing else but those two doors, imagining the thought of them opening to Nina, until finally, they did. She was leaving, alone, waving goodbye to someone inside as she put on a long, dark jacket and buttoned it up as she walked down the stairs. Annabel remained where she was, standing restlessly by the bottom step, unable to fight off the fidgety shiver that she told herself was just from the cold. Nina approached the bottom of the stairs and Annabel saw her, up close, and stared deeply at her. But, something happened that shook her off her course completely, throwing her off any sense of direction: she became stunned; and as Nina turned to face her, Annabel looked away, as one does immediately after a brief glance at the sun, deviating the gaze. Then Nina turned away to walk down the pavement and Annabel watched her, now from behind, her tall, shimmering figure moving further and further away into the distance. She could do nothing but stand there, as still as a waxwork, and then she let out a sound, a small grunt that extruded from her mouth forcibly; it was a cry, an uncontrollable cry that broke free from its chains and released itself into the air, trying to reach Nina before disseminating into millions of particles. And she remained there, frozen, as she watched her walk further away down the hill until she seemed to be nothing but a particle herself, merging with the horizon like a single flick of colour on a vast painting. She had missed her moment and was left with nothing but the sound of her small breaths panting to and fro, flowing out into the boundless winds, until Nina was out of sight.

The Wall and The Cardigan

The moon was at its peak, perfect in its round shape, and it glowed an infinitely radiant light down for every glance. It shimmered in Annabel's vision like a floating orb of magnificent light reminding her that she was safe, that there was nothing to worry about. But how could she not be dismayed? How could she not feel upset when the one thing she had been longing for was no longer within arm's reach? How could she refrain from crying out a weep of sorrow when the person she had been relentlessly searching for was, within seconds, no longer right at her fingertips? It felt almost impossible not to sink into a strong discouragement at the sight of Nina disappearing slowly from her field of vision. She closed her eyes and thought about what to do, wondering if maybe there was still a chance to get back to her. Then she looked up at the sky that glowed behind her foggy breath. The stars were glittering like tiny bright souls and the wind blew over her, and she was overcome unexpectedly with a little spark of spirit. Perhaps, with its infinite generosity, the moon was giving her strength, because suddenly she found herself running. She ran with all her might to a point where it felt as though her legs sprinted automatically. She bolted down the hill, pushed faster by gravity until she wondered how she would stop without toppling to the ground. And then she saw her again, far away in the distance, her majestic silhouette, emblazoned with a shine by the beaming headlights of the passing cars. Annabel stopped running, caught her breath, overcome by the sudden wonder of the moment, and watched Nina as she crossed the road and walked through the entrance gates of a building — a large, detached white house. If Annabel had arrived at that spot just a few seconds later, she would have missed her, left with nothing but the final steps of the road that led down the hill. She caught her breath and then slowly walked over to get a closer look at the building. As she trailed closer, she gulped at the beauty of this house. It had a wonderful design that reminded her of a country cottage, and its walls were white as freshly fallen snow, speckless as if they had been painted that very day. The front gates had a bell on them, a bell that Nina pressed before the gates slowly opened to make way for her entrance. Perhaps she was visiting someone, or spending the night at a friend's house, Annabel wondered. She peered from afar, keeping a sensible distance so as not to appear as if she were spying on someone's property. It was hardly possible to see a glimpse of the inside as a great bush was spread out all along the front garden and the thousands of shoots and leaves filled the spaces between the black baroque wrought iron gate. She could just about see the cosiest glow of warm light from the windows, as the colours passed through the leaves and twigs in thin rays, travelling through them directly to her eyes.

Lost in a gush of sudden intrigue, she decided that she would see if she could get a better view of the house through the back of the building; perhaps the view would be clearer through the back garden gates, so she headed round the house, down the side steps of a little alleyway that led to the pathway beside the river. Boats were anchored on the bank, swaying calmly along the ripples of water, and there were endless colours that melted into the ripples, reflecting from the lights of the houses on the other side of the river. She walked round to where the back of the house was, but a large rock wall covered the view of it completely. The wall was tall, but not much taller than she was, and without much thought, she jumped up to it. Her arms held onto the top of the wall and her feet struggled as they scraped on the rock, kicking off repeatedly in an attempt to climb and heave herself up. As she stumbled and very slowly struggled her way up, the weight of her legs pulled her back down to the ground, and just before she could try again, she noticed a hand reaching down to her. Somebody else was sitting up on the wall, their dark attire blending into the darkness of the evening, almost completely unnoticeable. For reasons unknown to her, she felt no hesitance and decided to take hold of the hand, and with a little push and pull, she stumbled onto the wall, balancing herself into a centred position, one leg on each side of the wall. She looked straight into the eyes of the person sitting before her and smiled as a slightly reserved way to thank them. The person's figure blended in obscurely with the shadowy tree that lay behind. Without much light to see, Annabel concentrated her vision and noticed his wavy brown hair, the tiny freckles on his cheeks, and the set of striking brown eyes greeting her. He wore a dark brown jacket that went all the way down past his knees and he was sitting in a way that made him appear to be in total comfort: one leg up on the wall, the other leaning off the side, his elbow rested on his knee and his chin planted tenderly into his hand. He reached into his pocket and pulled out a small crinkling packet.

"Here, take one?" he said as he tilted it towards Annabel, shaking it a little. "They're dried red currants."

His voice was soft and husky, and, smitten with the sound of his question, she reached into the packet and pulled out a handful of the little red currants. She realised how hungry she was as she stuffed her mouth with them, and then, almost embarrassed, giggled endearingly.

"Thank you," she replied as she chewed. "They're so sweet."

"Ah yes! Just how I like them. I'm Emile by the way," he said, smiling with his eyes.

Annabel stuck out her hand, raised her chin slightly and said, "And I'm Annabel."

She wasn't quite sure why she chose to introduce herself with a handshake. She had never been the kind of person to initiate a handshake; she usually would settle for a head nod or, on some occasions, a very subtle bow.

"What brings you up here, Annabel?" asked Emile playfully, shaking her hand. "To be honest, I didn't expect to have the pleasure of company up here."

"I was just... I felt like climbing, getting above ground for a bit," she replied.

"So you like to climb?"

"Yes, well, kind of."

"Interesting! Your technique suggested otherwise," he said with a chuckle.

"Well, I just haven't done it in a while." She looked down at her floating feet.

She could see him looking at her with a noticeably puzzled countenance, but also a look of amusement. He took a few nibbles of some berries and then leaned his head a little closer. "Really though, you don't climb much, do you?"

Annabel sighed. "Never. I never climb anything. I climbed high up a tree once when I was a child and it almost ended very badly, and since that day, I can't remember ever climbing again. Maybe you can't tell but I'm actually quite frightened."

"I couldn't tell," said Emile with a glint of affection, "but don't worry, okay? You're perfectly stable in that position. You're not going to fall, trust me."

And she did, in fact, trust him, and whether it was because of his reposeful demeanour, or his soothing words, she wasn't quite sure, but all at once, she felt safe and her discomfort began melting away. As she settled into her balanced position, she turned to face the house. There was another black gate a couple of metres ahead which guarded the edge of the garden. The grass was freshly cut and lanterns were hanging from the trees that gave light to wooden swing chairs, and all along the garden were trimmed bushes on the edges of a pathway that ran all the way to the back door of the house. The upstairs windows were small and had their curtains draped over, but downstairs, the windows were large and the curtains were drawn so she could just about see a peek of the inside. Through one window, she could see a small group of people sitting on a large sofa, chatting and laughing. Through the other window, there were a few people in the kitchen, conversing and drinking from tall glasses. But, through both windows, there was no sight of Nina. Noticing her own trancelike state, Annabel turned her head back to face Emile, who seemed to be studying her with an inquisitive enthusiasm.

"So why did you climb up here?" he asked.

She looked into his quizzical eyes, and for some strange reason, she felt no timidity, no detectable feelings of disconcertion that she would have expected from herself at the interaction with a stranger in such a bizarre setting. The question echoed inside her and she felt a sudden need to answer it truthfully, and for reasons she was unsure of, she had a feeling that she was about to tell someone about Nina and the pursuit of her, for the first time. And then she did. She began telling him that she was looking for someone in that house, and after his lively response that unveiled his keenness to know more, everything began to pour out of her like an endless fountain. She told him everything, from the beginning, and the more she told him the more questions he would ask and the more details she would share. She told him the story of when she encountered Nina at the exhibition after-party, and her overwhelming feelings about wanting to know her, how for a long while after that day she obsessed over the fantasy of meeting her, of knowing her and them being in each other's lives. She told him, how after meeting her, it oftentimes felt impossible for her to shake away the thoughts of her from her mind, how she wondered what she was doing from time to time, whom she was spending her time with, what activities she was doing, what she decided to wear, what she was eating, the things that made her laugh, cry, the music that made her dance. She told him about how for years she pushed down those feelings of longing, and then how they resurfaced after the recent conversation with Dusty, how she came to acknowledge the fact that after all this time she was still searching for her. She told him about the scarf, how she treasured it and how the recent discovery of Nina's woven name in tiny threads led her there, to that very moment. She told him about George, about the café, about how Nina was soon going to Spain, and about how just moments before, she had stood right by her, and how she had missed her chance to say something to her, and then followed her to the house that now lay beside them. And after explaining everything, she exerted a sigh that she had never sighed before; it was a sigh of alleviation, an unstoppable expression of release that flew from her body, the final utterance to mark the end of her story.

Swept away by what he had just heard, Emile sat there, speechless and fascinated. He appeared to have fallen so deep into the rift of her words that his face suggested he had briefly forgotten how to speak his own. The two of them shared a moment of peace, somehow comfortable in silence as if they had known each other all their lives; the only sounds that remained were the chords of their intertwining breaths.

Eventually, Emile shuffled a little in his seating position, pinched his chin with his finger and thumb and opened his mouth to speak. "So, you're telling me that Nina is somewhere in that house over there, right this moment?"

"That's right," said Annabel, nodding.

"And before meeting her nine years ago, you hadn't ever seen her before? Not even once?"

"Nope. It's disturbing, I know."

"I don't think it's disturbing, but I can't say I've heard anything quite like that."

Annabel looked at the house, then back to him. "That's why I've never told anyone. I could never rationalise it myself no matter how much I tried. And if I can't understand my own feelings, how could I expect someone else to understand them?"

"And what is it about me that made you want to tell me?" he asked.

"I'm not sure exactly, but believe it or not, this is the first time I've felt the impulse to tell someone."

They shared another moment of quiet, meeting one another on a plane of connectivity with their amicable eye contact.

"Did it ever cross your mind that maybe you and her are soulmates?" he asked.

Annabel smiled and shrugged. "I've thought about it, but I don't know much about those things. And I guess there's no way for me to know that unless I got to know her personally."

"Well, I do know one thing," said Emile. "Sometimes we come across things or people that awaken a desire within us, a burning momentum. I can't say I've experienced anything to the level that you have, but I've certainly had strong feelings of longing, so I think I understand you to a certain extent."

"What was it that you were longing for?" asked Annabel, consumed by interest.

"Well, it was a long time ago, about ten years ago. I was in town with my parents and I saw the most beautiful acoustic guitar through the window display at a music shop. I was thirteen, almost fourteen years old and I hadn't ever played guitar before, let alone music. As a kid, my parents would fill the home with music from their old records, but until that day, I hadn't even the tiniest slither of interest in music. It had always just been something I'd listen to passively, until the day I saw the guitar. I remember that feeling I had when I saw it, the feeling that told me I was supposed to play it. I couldn't understand why I wanted that guitar so much, but I remember at that moment it was the most important thing in the world to me. We had very little money and my parents told me that if I still wanted it after some time they'd save up to buy it for me as a birthday gift. But my birthday was a few months away and I felt inside that I couldn't wait that long. I didn't want to."

Emile took a moment to stare into his thoughts. He had a look of thoughtful reflection as if he was reliving the memories. He smirked and released a small fragment of laughter.

Then he continued, "Anyway, those feelings I mentioned, that desire I had to play the guitar kept on burning within me. I started listening to music much more intently, hearing it in a way that I had never done before. And then it hit me. I wanted to be a musician. I wanted to be a composer. I wanted to play songs just like the artists on the record players my parents used to play. And I thought about that guitar a lot. Some nights I could barely fall asleep because of it. I would imagine holding it in my arms, strumming the strings, and seeing the expression on peoples' faces when I played. I don't know, the fact I could make people feel certain emotions by playing music to them, that was a concept that excited me so much. So I decided I'd save up for it myself. I got a little cash-in-hand job helping out at a car wash. It was pretty hard work, but the vision was so immense that I gave myself no choice, and in no time, I had enough money to buy myself my very own guitar. It turned out to be the best decision I ever made. I never stopped playing."

The night was leaning into total darkness and the wind was turning colder, and it blew past them daintily, stroking their skin with the touch of a frosty kiss. Annabel took her scarf out from her bag, wrapped it around her neck and then hugged herself in an attempt to find more warmth as she listened to Emile's words with a natural focus.

"I know there's a big difference between my teenage longing to play the guitar and what you're experiencing," he continued, "but I think what I'm trying to say is that if those feelings are as important to you as you say they are, then I guess you must follow them. Maybe something remarkable will come out of it. You never know, right?"

"I've never wanted anything more," she replied, "but the thing is, I don't even know what it is from her that I want."

"Do you think, perhaps, in any kind of form, you love her?"

"I don't know. All I know is that when I think of her, when I hear her name, when I see her, something takes over me. It feels like an overwhelming desire to fill a purpose, and in some strange way, the purpose is *her*, but how she is the purpose, I don't know. Even trying to put it all into words confuses me. It's totally incomprehensible."

"So, what are you going to do now?" he asked curiously.

Annabel turned to look at the house. There was still no sign of Nina.

"She's in there, I'm out here. I'm pretty much out of ideas. Not that I had any truly great ones anyway."

"Hey, I'm certain she's going to do more of these showcases when she gets back from Spain, then you'll have plenty more opportunities to meet her," he reassured her.

"Yeah, you're right," she said, receiving his words with a narrow smile.

But waiting was the last thing she wished to do at that stage. She knew it would be a long while before Nina returned, and deep inside she did not feel that she could wait any longer. The thought of waiting months with no definitive idea of when she would return from her interminable travels felt like a kick to the stomach.

The heaviness of the night was closing in and Emile looked at his watch. As he proceeded to shuffle his legs in a way that indicated that he was preparing to leave, Annabel felt an abrupt feeling of unease. She didn't want him to leave. Never in her life had she felt so comforted by the presence of someone she only just met.

"I was so entranced by your story that I didn't realise the time," he said as he looked down at the ground, then back up at her. "I've got to go, but maybe we can continue talking some other time?"

"I'd really like that," she replied.

"I enjoyed meeting you up here and I'm fascinated by your story, Annabel, really I am," he said as he tightened his shoelaces.

The murmuring sounds of the night enveloped the town and small howls of owls hooting bounced around the edges of the wind. Groups of strolling people passed by along the trail in their herds of big and small, as they headed home with their glowing eyes and tender yawns, some linking arms, some huddled closely, others connected by the chilly air.

Annabel and Emile exchanged phone numbers. It seemed like the most natural thing to do after the synergy of their engagement.

"Would you like me to accompany you to the train station? I'm walking by that way," he asked.

Annabel looked back at the house and then turned to face him. "No, it's okay. I think I'll stay up here for a little while longer before I leave."

"Okay. You'll be fine getting down though, right?"

"I'll be fine, thank you." She nodded and smiled sincerely.

Emile carefully jumped off the wall and the two of them waved goodbye to one another. She watched him walk away, stepping chirpily in his long buttoned-up coat, the size of his hazy figure steadily decreasing.

She was met with a sudden, tenuous shiver that travelled through her chest and down her legs. It was the time of autumn when the temperature of the air began to drop and the nights laid down a frosty breeze in preparation for the coming wintertime. She gazed at the house again, closely inspecting everything she could see through the windows, with every drop of focus she could evoke. Someone in the kitchen went to smoke a cigarette by the window, and as they opened it, out went the soothing sounds of jazz music launching into the open air. Annabel noticed some of the lights in a few surrounding houses switching off, reminding her that it was getting late and she really should have been returning home, but her adamance to stay prevailed and she continued waiting for the chance to see Nina. She hadn't the faintest idea of what she would do if she did see her through those windows, but the chance of catching a glimpse of her had all the reason she needed to wait. So she waited, her gaze fixated sharply on the windows, and then out of the blue, she saw the figure of someone draw open the curtains from one of the upstairs windows. It was her. Annabel became perfectly still; the only part of her that moved was her chest breathing vehement breaths. The opened curtains revealed what appeared to be a bedroom, and she could just about see the inside. She watched Nina open a suitcase on the bed and take out a robe. It was a ravishing robe; perhaps it was velvet, or a material of similar tone, Annabel wondered; the way it shimmered in her hands was startling, astounding. She watched her slip her arms through the sleeves, wrap herself into the robe, swallowed up by its warmth, and then leave the room, switching off the light behind her. She was powerfully irresistible, and Annabel, once again, became taken over by the spell of her. She waited, counting the seconds before Nina appeared downstairs, joining the people in the kitchen with their shiny, bubbly drinks and pleasant smiles. She seemed happy to be around these people; they seemed close to her, and her to them, and her contented expression shimmered and shone as she conversed with them. Annabel leaned forward a little, attempting to hear anything she could, even the tiniest crumb of broken words, but every word spoken was slurred, incomprehensible, drowned out by the bustling jazz. Unaware of how much time was passing, she continued to watch from afar, her attention stolen completely by all of the wonderment of Nina. Everyone in the kitchen made their way to join the others in the living room, and together they toasted their drinks and continued talking and laughing together, lost in their joyous world. As she watched, she felt those familiar sensations of longing drooping over her, melting into her, but this time it felt different — it was mixed with a powerful feeling of eagerness, as if a part of her was being pestered by an unbridled desire to do something, anything that would get her into the realm into which she peered from afar, to have her presence and the presence of Nina entwine and become one. But it was a problem without a solution, an ache with no relief, an itch that could not be scratched.

As the moments passed, she watched large conversations break into smaller conversations and then build up again into larger ones. She observed as people dipped in and out of moments of sweet chatter and playful chuckles with one another, and she witnessed the transformation of ambience, as the evening drifted from a buoyant tempo to a mellow, restful atmosphere. She observed as one person said their goodbyes and left, and then a pair did the same, and then another, and another, until there were only three people left in the house: Nina, and what appeared to be a couple — a man in a vivid yellow shirt and a woman in a glittery gown. From her observation, Annabel gathered that the house must have belonged to the couple, and Nina must have been a friend of theirs and was now staying the night there.

The aftermath of the gathering was much quieter, but the pleasantness that exuded from the windows remained, as the three of them sat down together, talking and resting in their mutual delight.

After what felt like a series of timeless minutes, Annabel noticed that her continual leaning towards the direction of the house caused her bag to lean over the side of the wall, prompting her camera to fall out of the side pocket and tip right off the edge. In the second that she noticed this, everything suddenly stopped; the world moved astronomically slower and the camera fell as if it fought to resist the pull of gravity. She reached her hand out to grab it, and as she did, the weight of her travelling arm tipped her over the edge of the wall and she fell down along with her belongings, her body slamming into the grass and soil, her chin and hands planting themselves vigorously down into the ground and the dirt of a moonlit garden. Total darkness was all she saw before she lifted her head from the ground and looked around her as she wiped the mud from the side of her face. She was in a patch of grass, a couple of metres in width, right between the stone wall and the black gates that guarded the back of the white house garden. It was dark and she struggled to see clearly, but it was the darkness that kept her unseen by those in the house. As she got up slowly, she felt a twinge of pain on her chin and her chest, but to her luck, by virtue of the padded grass that embraced her impact, at most, she would have suffered a few bruises. She looked towards the end of the little space of garden in which she stood. The end of the iron gates were anchored to the stone wall which continued round to shield the edges of the garden. She was stuck, sealed away like a caged animal. She packed her camera back into her bag and then walked down to the tip of her freedom and noticed that there was an old wooden door in the wall from which she had fallen. It was wide and arched and had a large keyhole right on the side. With some force, she pushed against the door, and something about the way it felt as she pushed made her feel as though it hadn't been opened in many years. The door did not budge, so she pushed again, much harder, with all the force she could muster, but all that followed were specks of stone dust that fell onto her and a creaking sound that revealed the door's antiquity. She took a step back and jumped up to climb the wall, failing again and again and then trying again each time. Her arms and legs trembled with each attempt, but without a hand to assist her, it was no use. As she stepped away from the wall, she breathed with focus, all of her intention towards remaining calm, to steer away any approaching panic. She turned around to face the black gates. They were tall, around the same height as the wall, and at the top of them were tiny spears that pointed to the sky, but the possibility of getting past them instead of the wall seemed more promising to her now. She studied them, placing her hand along them to feel the gaps between the metal railings. The spaces seemed larger than those of most gates, maybe just large enough for her to push herself through, she weighed. Then she thought for a moment about the possibility of calling for help; it was likely that her calls would be heard, either from someone on the other side of the wall or someone in the white house, but the chance of Nina discovering her like this made it just about impossible for her to even consider calling out. She stayed still for a moment, thinking, holding her effort to inhale and exhale with composure, until she had a plan: she would get past those gates somehow. She noticed there was a pathway on the side of the house that connected the back garden to the front gates. She would sneak through the garden, follow through the side pathway and exit through the front gates of the house. As she placed her hand between the railings again, she was met with a sudden instinct, an inkling that somehow, with a squeeze and a push, she would make it through. She took off her boots and placed them, along with her bag, through the gap onto the other side of the gate. Then she put her hand right up to the gate and slowly pushed her arm straight through, inching her shoulder through very carefully, and then her head, squeezing through the solid pressure of two railings, until she was through up to her ears, and then she turned her body sideways and began to squeeze her chest through. Her space to breathe was so restricted that for a split-second it seemed as if she was on the verge of fainting. She pushed herself through with tremendous effort, forbidding even the tiniest hint of expansion from her body. As she pushed forward, her voice uttered all sorts of grunts and shrieks. The feeling of compression on her struggling body was almost unbearable, but she kept going, inch by inch, until her head had squeezed all the way through, and then her chest, and waist, until she was pulling through her leg, and then at last, her foot. After the final inch of her passed through the gap, she plummeted straight onto the ground. Her body was aching, but as she lay there, the feeling of now being on the grass of an open garden outshone any pain she was feeling. She rolled onto her back, allowing every limb to surrender to relaxation. For a second, the brightness of the moon and the stars, along with the refreshing air that caressed her, caused her to forget where she was; but it was just a fleeting instant, and when she was reminded, she knew it was time for her to get home. Now it was just a matter of sneaking through the garden and then out through the entrance gates without anyone noticing. She put her boots back on and her bag over her shoulder and then rolled onto her stomach and looked ahead towards the windows. Nina and the couple were still lounging in the living room. The lanterns in the garden continued glowing and she knew that once she started moving forward she'd enter into the light, and in that light, she would be seen easily. So she waited some time, keeping herself low and hidden in the darkness at the edge of the garden, fretting often about the likelihood of being caught, hoping that soon they would all go to bed so she could make her escape. But it wasn't long until she watched the man in the yellow shirt walk to the back door and open it to catch a breath of the fresh air, and then make his way to the middle of the garden to adore the night sky. He was just about close enough now to discover her if he looked in her direction, she was sure of it, and her heart began thumping as she searched for something, anything to hide behind. She started crawling surreptitiously along the grass towards a tree at the far corner of the garden, hoping the darkness would not fail her, keeping her belly and legs down on the ground and pulling her weight along with her arms. When she got to the tree, she stood up and flung herself behind it, making sure not a hair of her was seen. She wished so eagerly that the man would leave the garden, but to her dismay, he not only remained there in his continual excitement but called out for the others to admire the sky with him. Annabel sighed and winced in worry and frustration. Never in her life would she have expected herself to feel contempt for the beauty of the night sky, to curse the stars for their resplendence and charm. She heard Nina and the other woman join the man and behold the sky with him. She was unable to see Nina, but she pictured her smiling with gladness and delightedly pointing to her favourite star, praising the bigness of everything above and the rarity of the view. Annabel waited, repeatedly stating in her mind that they would soon become sleepy and make their way to bed, and then she would leave quietly and return home to her own bed that awaited her, finally enveloped in a cradle of safety. Then she heard the couple exclaim how wonderful the nighttime view was from the top of the hill, and Nina, seemingly lost in the euphoric energy of the stars, insisted that they take her there to see it. Annabel could hear the sound of their fluttering voices getting smaller and smaller as they entered back into the house, presumably to wrap themselves up in warm coats and then exit through the front gate. And then they were gone, and the second she heard the sound of the front gate closing, she began pacing her way through the garden and then along the pathway on the side of the house, but she came to a sudden halt when she arrived at another gate that connected the back garden and the front garden. From afar, it must have hidden in the shadows of the night, but up close its presence was alarming. The gate was of a similar height to those that surrounded the house, and it had a keyhole right on the side, and as she attempted to open it she was slammed by the crushing realisation that it was locked, utterly and hopelessly unmovable without a key. The gate stood tall, looming over her, daunting her and mocking her, and the spaces between the railings were even smaller than the gate she had only just managed to squeeze herself through, forcing onto her the certainty that there was no alternative plan to get past it. Her only means of escaping now was to get to the front garden through the inside of the house. There was no time to stop and think of another route or plan, so she headed round to the door at the back of the house. Luckily, it was left unlocked and so she pulled it open and stepped into the living room and continued through until she got to the corridor. She hurried along the corridor, disassociated from her surroundings. As she got to the front door, she turned to look behind to make sure that she hadn't left any dirt marks on the pristine carpet, and was suddenly distracted by something that rested on the bannister finial on top of the staircase. It was a cardigan, a deep forest-green cardigan, watching over the crimson carpet that cascaded down the staircase. She was drawn to it, and not in a simple way of adoration; there was something else, something deeper about it that called forth every grain of her attention. She could feel what almost felt like the sensations of déjà vu radiating from the cardigan, and somehow she was filled with a solid knowing that it belonged to Nina. And perhaps that was why it drew her in so much — the fact that one of Nina's personal belongings had chosen to present itself right before her, flaunting itself for her eyes to behold. For a slither of time, she questioned why she had not yet fled, for she knew that they would soon come back home and to be discovered there would be not only dreadful to her but frightening to them. But a feeling had overcome her; it was a feeling that convinced her to take a closer look at the cardigan, for inspecting it by the touch of the hands may give her some form of gratification, a temporary fulfilment of the desire to be closer to Nina while she had the chance; maybe it would lead her closer to understanding these feelings that knocked on the door of her mind so vigorously. She found herself in the absence of conscious volition, seized by a force outside of her worrisome thoughts. She walked up the stairs, her hand sliding up the bannister, convinced by the idea that getting a closer look at one of Nina's personal belongings was worth the loss of a few wasted minutes in the house. She was getting closer to a piece of Nina's world, and in that instant, unlike her anxious mind, the feeling that came over her, the feeling that was so enticed by the opportunity to get closer to Nina, knew no risk; it was simply just trying to satisfy its curiosity, to quench its incredible thirst. All at once, she was endowed with a tenacity that moved her directly towards the direction of her fascination, overpowering her concern for time. At the top of the stairs, she touched the cardigan, gliding her hands over the soft fabric. It was a very particular piece of clothing, a one-of-a-kind. She picked it up, holding it in her two hands. From close inspection, it revealed itself to be an old cardigan, used and worn out over many years, but blessed with a timeless character. The colour appeared to be faded from its oldness, but the richness and vibrancy of its tones were still alive. Then, out of the blue, she was struck with the smell that arose from it. The remnants of perfume met her with a soft touch that had an unexpected power, a rich potency that enlivened her. It was a scent that was rare to come across, but there was a forceful familiarity about it that she found startling, and it brushed through her with a comfortable intimacy. She placed the cardigan up to her face, burying her nose into its warmth, her eyes closing naturally, and she breathed in the scent like the ocean enveloping itself. It was a smell she knew, but she could not reach far enough into the depths of her mind to realise how she knew it. For a small moment, she was lost in that smell, soaring in its vast skies, swimming and flowing in the currents of its rivers, and she was engulfed by it so much so that she almost failed to register the sound of the front gate opening. She froze in horror. They had returned already.

Light Breaking Through a Cracking Shell

With the suddenness of waking from the pinnacle of a nightmare, Annabel pulled away from her daydream. She figured it would be seconds before they walked through the front door, so she quickly placed the cardigan back onto the finial and scurried upstairs and around the bend of the bannisters, her feet moving like nimble feathers. She peered over the end of the bannister, nervously anticipating the opening of the door. A severe flooding of regret washed over her; if she had just fled when she had the chance she would have avoided such a horrifying predicament. And then, after the rattling sound of keys, the door opened. She ducked down. It was too frightening to look, so she stayed low and listened from above. She tried her best to conceive an escape plan, but she was too lost in a panic to be able to think sharply. If they all went back into the living room, she thought, she would likely be able to sneak out quietly through the front door without being seen or heard. But, the night had other plans for her. She faintly heard the woman in the glittery gown express her need to use the bathroom, followed by her footsteps dashing up the stairs. There was no time to remain still, and Annabel, in silent distress, got up and turned to face the corridor. To her right, there was a door ajar, exposing the view of a bedroom in misty darkness. It wasn't the bathroom and that was all she needed for the time being, so she speedily tip-toed into the room, closing the door as silently as she could. She stood for a few seconds by the door, holding her breath until she saw a shadow of footsteps flicker by the gap at the bottom of the door. Her stomach began to convulse into a whirlpool of terror. She placed her shaking hands in front of her, drawing out the motion of steady breaths. She knew there was still a chance for her to escape as long as she could find composure, so she focused every bit of her control on calming herself down until the rampant attack of panic had subsided. Then she turned to look at the room in which she stood. The first thing she noticed was the white light of the moon sweeping in through the large windows, and, along with a few distant street lamps, it superseded the darkness that lingered. The room was spacious and the bed was large, and long dark curtains were hanging by the window, and to her side was an open door exposing the view of an ensuite bathroom. As she looked around, she quickly realised that she was in the room in which Nina was staying. On the bed was Nina's open suitcase, revealing an assortment of her folded clothes, and to her right a desk, where Nina had placed some of her personal belongings; there was a perfume bottle with a red ribbon wrapped around it, a scarf with a prominent delicacy, and some pieces of paper laid out with a swivelling layer of black ink written across. Then she heard the woman leave the toilet next door and, once again, held her breath until the running shadow swept under the door like a scouring crow seeking her presence. She put her hands on the door, and then placed her ear onto it, following the sound of the footsteps that scurried back down the stairs, then counted up to ten inside her jittery mind and opened the door with as little sound as possible. There were murmuring echoes of speech rising upward from downstairs. Their voices did not sound distant enough to provide her with a sense that it was safe enough to attempt an escape, so she waited a short while, but still, the closeness of their voices remained. She turned around and approached the window, trying to find another route out of there, but as she opened it and peeked down at the distant garden, not a single strategy of escape came to mind that wouldn't result in an imminent injury. And then, once again, she heard the sound of footsteps treading up the stairs, causing her heart to pound with a heavy impact as if it were tangled in thick strings of distress and was punching and kicking to break free. She hoped with great vigour that it wasn't Nina walking up those steps, but then she heard something that crushed her hopes with such a force that she almost forgot how to breathe. Nina was calling out goodnight, and the distance between Annabel and her merry voice was decreasing with every second that passed. She was moving closer and closer, and Annabel, suddenly sucked into a void of horror, threw herself behind the curtains that draped down the sides of the windows. She stood there, still, as if frozen by a spell, tucked away behind the thick, long curtains, merging her body heat with the sweltering space where the air was dense and hot and sticky. Before she could muster a single thought, she heard the sound of the door open and then close behind tender footsteps. With all of her spirit, she forced herself to stay as quiet as she possibly could. The footsteps continued, and they were soft and gentle, as if Nina planted her weight onto the carpet with a purposeful fragility, each step carrying a piece of her thoughtful mind. Then Annabel heard the switch of a lamp, and she noticed some light breaking through the spaces between the curtain and the wall. She felt as if the barrier of her safety was weakening, as if the shell she covered herself in was cracking at the edges and the light was breaking through to expel her guard. And then she heard Nina coming closer, and it sent a chill up her spine that caused her shoulders to tremble and her jaw to quiver. Then she heard nothing, but curiously, she could sense the space between them, and she knew that Nina was close, close enough that she could touch her through the curtain if she just lifted her hand. The sound of the window opening belted out a whining creak and within inches of her ear, she heard the abrupt sound of the flick of a lighter. With a rapid force, she squeezed her lips together as tightly as she could, refraining from uttering even the tiniest sound. She discreetly turned her head slightly and moved her eyes to the side, and through a small space that fluctuated in size as the breeze moved the curtain, she could see Nina's hand holding a lit cigarette between two fingers. A small gush of cold air touched her face, and it was so fresh across her sweating face that she felt a glint of gratitude for it. The trickles of smoke that rose from the tip of the cigarette danced into the moonlight, and an occasional gust of smoke that blew out from Nina's mouth poured over the starry sky. Annabel held her lips together tightly shut. Her heart was pounding so powerfully that for a moment she worried that Nina would feel it. There was a sense of disbelief that came over her, a feeling that tried to convince her that she was dreaming, that if she pinched herself hard enough she would wake herself up.

After the final exhale of smoke, she heard Nina shut the window and then amble further away again, and then she heard the light switch on in the ensuite bathroom, followed by the sound of water running from the tap. She briefly considered running, bolting out the door, down the stairs and then out of the house, but there were too many hurdles between where she was and the road to freedom outside the front gates that she just couldn't conjure the strength to take the leap. Her mind began to race with worrisome thoughts, flashing through her like harsh lightning. Would she make it out of the room before Nina saw her? If Nina were to scream, would those screams reach the others in the house before she could even make it to the staircase? Would she be able to unlock the front door in time before she was caught? And then there was the gate, the wretched front gate; even if she were able to succeed in all of that, would she then be able to figure out how to open the gate fast enough to make it out in time? She wrestled in her mind these turbulent questions until she concluded that running and making a scene was not a feasible option; she would wait there until everyone had fallen asleep, and then she would make a smooth and tactful exit. The sound of Nina cleansing herself in the bathroom continued. Annabel noticed that as the minutes went by she was finding it more difficult to breathe with ease. She couldn't quite believe what she had gotten herself into, how she had managed to get herself into such a state that she was hiding behind the curtains of a house that she had trespassed, all to escape out of a mess she had gotten herself into after chasing the person she was now hiding from. If it wasn't for her desperate need to remain silent, she would have laughed and cried and wailed at the absurdity of it all.

Clouds of thoughts of the outside world began floating in her mind. She thought about her mother, and what she would have been doing right at that moment. She imagined that she was most likely on the telephone with a friend or a relative, sitting in the kitchen, occasionally wondering when she would receive a message from her daughter. And she wondered what she would say if she knew about this terrifying situation she was in. She remembered her friends back home and wondered what they would have been doing, and the words they would say to her if they could have seen her, standing behind that curtain, hiding for her life, holding onto any sliver of hope she could find. Then she pictured Dusty and imagined her sitting comfortably in the living room, next to a cosy flame blazing in the fireplace, eating a slice of pie and sipping on hot tea, enclosed in the comfort of home. How much she would have loved to be there with her, safe and sound and sheltered in warm company. Then the thought of Emile came to her, and what he would say about all of this, and how she wished so deeply that she had just gone with him to the train station when she had the chance.

All of a sudden, she heard Nina leave the bathroom, and then the shuffling sounds of movement and the sound of a suitcase zipping, followed by the ruffling of materials. Along with the muffled sounds, she pictured the image of Nina going through her things, organising her belongings and tending to them with a sweet and gentle hand. And then, she heard something that welcomed her with the softest touch; it was a sound that trickled out and across the room in silky textures. It was the sound of Nina humming, and it was so beautiful that she almost felt she had lost the strength to keep hiding, to hold up the guard that refused to surrender; and though she was drowning under tides of fear that pulled her below a murky surface, something about Nina's voice shone a glowing light above those waters, sending her hints of its benevolent rays. Her voice was warm and gentle and it wavered between the notes like a feather swaying in the wind, lingering in frequencies that for the briefest moment put all troubles in a calm place. It sounded golden, as though if the colour gold were to be a sound it would be the sound of her voice, and it flowed like melodious honey that transuded out of her in tiny drops of her love.

What came next was the sound of footsteps walking by across the corridor, and then the closing of a bedroom door. It gave Annabel a speck of hope to know that everyone was now in their bedrooms, retreating to their beds. It seemed there was a foreseeable chance now to get out without anyone noticing, and if everyone just went to sleep she could perhaps soundlessly make her way out without her presence being discovered.

Then, in a sudden instant, she heard Nina walk right up close again, causing her, once again, to freeze, still as a marble statue. She felt Nina's hand brush across the tip of her shoulder, just layers of fabric between the contact of their skin, and then the whooshing motion of the curtains closing over the window which caused her heart to jump in a flashing fright. But luckily, she remained hidden still. Then she heard Nina make her way into bed, settling herself into the cosy fabrics with an exhale of sheer pleasure, followed by the sound of the turning pages of a book. Annabel remained sedated in silence, impatiently wishing that Nina would find tiredness somewhere in a little gap of time between the pages. She hung on tightly to every minute that passed, minute after minute until she heard the sound of the light switch off, and immediately, everything was dark. There was no longer any traces of light seeping through the sides of the curtains. She was submerged in total darkness, unable to tell the difference between open or closed eyes. The dreary thickness of the sultry air behind the curtain persisted, and, along with her distress, began causing her to feel hot and faint. She hoped and prayed with unwavering severity that Nina would fall into a deep sleep. As the silence continued, she thought about attempting to leave, but her fear planted her feet to the ground and forced her to wait, to be on the safe side. Those drawled minutes in pitch-black felt like an eternity, and every minute or so, she prepared herself to leave, but each time she was overcome with doubt that convinced her that the risk was too high and to wait a little longer. She counted down from ten in silent whispers, telling herself that she would leave when she reached number one, but each time she did, the fear of Nina still being awake vanquished her hope and inhibited her ability to move. So she waited longer and longer until it had been so long she was sure that Nina must have fallen asleep. Silence remained, but now, it was accompanied by the faintest, almost imperceptible sound of Nina's sleeping breaths. Finally, she prepared herself to get moving, and this time she forced herself to lean slowly out of the curtains. Other than shades of darkness that melted into one another, she was still unable to see anything, so she began moving gingerly and as quietly as she could, taking tiny steps forward, her hands in front of her to feel any potential obstacles. It took a solid minute of furtive movement to get from the curtains to the door, and when she finally reached it, her heart began punching through her chest again so rigorously that she almost believed it to be the loudest sound in the room. Her hand moved through the darkness like a hazy ghost until she grabbed onto the doorknob and turned it, but as it turned, it let out a creak. It was only a small sound, but within the silence that conquered the room, it erupted like a flaming howl. Before the door even became unlocked, with the suddenness and flash of a lightning bolt, she could see her trembling hand clenching onto the doorknob. For a split second, she thought her eyes were playing tricks on her, but then she realised what was happening and saw that there was now light in the room. She froze, in complete denial and disbelief. At that second, she could have opened the door, ran out, sprinted down the stairs and out of the house, but she heard a gasp behind her, and in response to the sharp utterance of surprise, she turned around to see Nina staring directly at her, moving into a guarded position, with a face of shock. There were a few seconds of silence as they appeared before one another in the probing light of the lamp beside the bed, both of them glaring into one another's startling appearance, their eyes meeting for the first time in nine long years. Annabel fell victim to overpowering immobility, unable to move her lips to form the shape of a single word. She wanted so desperately to say something, to assure Nina that everything was fine and she was harmless and was just trying to get out without frightening anyone, but the shock of all that was happening made her powerless in the fight to deliver these words. But, in that inability to speak, some part of her wondered if Nina would recognise her innocence without the need for words. And Nina, with a look that suggested she had adjusted to Annabel's apparition, did not scream, nor did she make a single sound to indicate that she was frightened, and Annabel watched her as her gaze began to sharpen as if she was now staring deeper into her. Nina's face began morphing from a look of surprise into something else, something completely elusive. It was a look of perplexity and bewilderedness, but it had traces of a deep zeal to fathom something, an indescribable eagerness for an understanding; it was as if, beneath the surface, there was a thirst for some kind of answer, and it was an expression that Annabel had never been on the receiving end of. Whilst the utter incapability of speaking lingered, Annabel blinked herself back to life, turned around and opened the door. Then, for reasons she did not know, she turned back to face Nina who was still there, pushed up against the upholstered headboard and gazing at her with a persistent, mysterious air. Annabel turned back around to see the corridor that was now right before her, offering her a direct route to freedom. And then, an impulse that urged her to leave right that second kicked in with a burning momentum. Without looking back again, she took the leap and ran through as nimbly as she could. She paced right across the corridor and then down the stairs and out the front door, and then through the front garden and finally out through the side of the black gates which, to her luck, opened with a hard push of a lock. Now she was on the pavement, with nothing in her way, and she ran, galloping down the street without a second to pause, moving faster than she had ever moved before. She ran until her heart couldn't take it anymore and her lungs compelled her to stop. She was at the bottom of the hill, away from the house, with her hands on her knees and her back hunched over, trying to catch her breath with heavy pants and gasps. Tears were falling from her eyes onto the ground, moving swiftly one after the other, and she noticed them and realised that she was sobbing uncontrollably. But, for reasons unclear to her, she felt numb, removed from the feeling behind the tears, but despite this, they continued to pour out of her like an overflowing fountain. She tried to understand why she was crying, but she was unable to discern her feelings, unable to determine whether she felt scared, relieved, angry or ecstatic; perhaps, she thought, she was somewhere caught in the middle between suffocating panic and the euphoric release that came as a result of her escape. When she caught her breath, she hurried on and turned down a small alleyway, moving through the tight roads that offered minimal light, turning left, then right, then up a stone staircase, then through a pathway and down another stone staircase, until she ended up in a patch of grass. She threw herself onto the grass, rolled over onto her back and then looked up to the sky. And she stayed there for a while, accompanied by the moon and the stars until the rhythm of her breath had returned to a calm sway and the final tear had fallen.

Emile's Disposition

Without the consciousness of being completely awake, it is often easy to mistake reality for dreams — that's what happened to Annabel early the following morning. She awoke, wrapped in a blanket draped over her that she had somehow tangled between her legs, her mind halfway between sleeping and waking, and fleetingly, she was convinced that the events of the night before were nightmarish memories of a dream that had visited her in the night. But then she awoke fully, and whilst rubbing the sleepiness out of her eyes, she was stunned with the realisation that the events of those memories did, in fact, really happen. She looked around the room. The sun had just begun rising and it shone a shimmer of light through the windows. She was in a living room, nestled into a sofa, surrounded by cotton cushions.

The night before, after she had exhausted herself from running and tumbled to the ground, and every tear she could cry had trickled deep into the soil beneath the grass, she was left exhausted, emptied of energy, and frightened of the possibility that her whereabouts were being searched for. She was so eager to tell someone what had happened, anyone who was willing to listen, and she thought of Emile; she had only just met him, but now he was the only other person that knew about the story of Nina. And in her despair and desperation, she called him, and he listened to her as she spewed a stammered story about what had happened. As she cried through the phone, it was clear from Emile's silence that he could sense the fright through the shakes of her feeble voice, so he comforted her and told her that she was welcome to come and stay the night at his home, and did not have to leave until she felt better. His kindness was alleviating. His reassuring words spoken through his warm voice, although dampened through the phone speaker, eased her and endowed her with a touch of strength to lift from the ground and up onto her weary feet. She did not question her decision to go to him; somehow she felt an astonishing sense of trust towards him and the last thing she wanted in that moment was to be alone.

His flat was directly above a flower market in Islington, a train journey away, and she arrived there a little after midnight. At the door, he greeted her with empathetic eyes and welcomed her inside with careful attention to her needs. His home was small but cosy and full of quirks and colour and antique decorative features that Annabel took an immediate liking to. There were lit candles around the room, random piles of old music magazines, several large plants that bloomed with stark beauty, and there were framed vinyl records hanging around on the olive-coloured walls. The two of them sat by the heater and sipped creamy hot cocoa in the iridescent light of the moon. At first, Annabel did not have the mental clarity to muster anything other than broken words, but after a moment of settling into the safety and the feeling of calmness, she was able to see her thoughts clearly again and she told him everything that had happened, from the very moment he left her sitting on the wall to the moment she called him. He listened with open ears as if his mind was an empty bucket. And he was a brilliant listener. His fascination with her words and his curiosity to understand the thoughts behind her actions along with his lack of judgement made it easy for her to confide in him. And when she had finished talking, he comforted her with his words and accompanied her until her eyes began to fall, and then he made the couch a comfy haven with a plethora of blankets and cushions, and encouraged her to get some sleep. They spent a little more of the night together in comfortable silence until she fell asleep, her tired body sunken into the gentle layers.

Now the morning was rising and the lively sounds of nature were beginning to unite, and Annabel was waking to the vivid memories of the night before. In hindsight, it was an inconceivable and somewhat terrifying night of first experiences. Finding Nina, and then following her footsteps, like chasing a rabbit to a hole in the ground, then pouring her heart out to a stranger on top of a wall, then wounding up in a trap, and then trespassing and hiding in someone's home — these were the components of the absurd night before, a night she knew would never wither from her memory. But above everything that happened, she just could not shake from her mind the desire to know what Nina must have been thinking when she saw her in those ephemeral seconds of eye contact before running away. That was the moment that kept replaying in her mind: right before she had run out the door, she turned and looked into Nina's eyes, and Nina into hers, and it was just that and that only for a timeless instant, two wondering gazes meeting and nothing else. She remembered that feeling of so eagerly wanting her to understand that she meant no harm, to see her for what she truly was and not some frightening stranger lurking in the dark. She recalled wondering, as their eyes made contact, why Nina did not scream, speak, or even make a sound; she simply just sat there in elusive silence, backed up against the headboard with the most mystifying radiance in her eyes. And she remembered the look on Nina's face, that specific expression she gave; it was an expression that suggested more than just surprise; something else was there, bubbling below the surface like a question tugging to reveal an answer.

Annabel lay in bed, her body resting upon the sofa as if she were glued down to it by the safety of the bounce of its fabrics. She gazed mindlessly at the tiny bumpy textures on the ceiling but saw only the memories from the night before; they came in fuzzy, flashing pictures that tickled her bleary vision. The search for Nina and all of her decisions that came as a result of it had carried her to a point of hopeless surrender. She believed now, with a lens of clear reflection, that it had to end, all of it, at least for the time being until she could figure out how to regain power over her actions. Those moments of mesmerism she had been experiencing, those which had each time caused a cloud of hypnotism to come upon her, had gotten the better of her every single time and led her down paths that had only made everything worse. And now, those dreams of meeting her for the first time and all of the visions of the wondrous possibilities of connection with her had been washed away, flushed into a void where nothing but lost possibilities remained. All she had hoped for was to find Nina, and for Nina to see her, to truly see her, and not as an alarming figure exposed by the lamp light, smeared with mud and frozen and incapable of making a sound, but as a human soul with a spark that poured into her direction with innocence and admiration and a joyful hope for connection. And now, Nina *had* seen her, but in all the ways she would have wished to never be seen. And on top of that misfortune, she had frightened Nina, and to have frightened her, she thought, was a big enough reason to let her be. She thought about, how after everything, she had hurt the person in her field of hope, the person whose existence somehow livened her, and although this was never her intention, the thought of hurting her any more was too much to bear.

She yawned. It was early and she still felt overwhelmingly tired, so she allowed herself to drift off back to sleep, and when her eyes opened again, she saw the freckled face of a young girl, her hair in two ponytails, dressed in a tweed dress that had patches of strawberries scattered all over, peering over her with large amber eyes that resembled those of a night owl.

"You're awake!" said the girl delightedly.

Annabel slowly lifted herself and sat against the cushions, yawned and then smiled at her.

"I am."

"When my brother told me someone was sleeping on the couch I didn't believe him so I came to see for myself. You sleep just like a kitten!"

Annabel laughed sweetly. "I didn't know Emile had a sister."

"I'm Sylvie," she said with a large grin on her face.

"I'm Annabel."

With a melodious hum and a playful skip in her step, Sylvie pranced out of the room. The curtains were closed but a bright beam of sunshine was slipping through a tiny seam. Annabel stretched out her arms and yawned away any drowsiness that lingered inside, then planted her feet onto the ground and wrapped a blanket around herself. She walked out of the living room and into the kitchen where Emile was standing by the counter, skilfully cutting into fruit. As he reached his hand into a box of fresh kiwis, he turned around and saw her standing in the doorway, wrapped up like an otter in kelp in the wintertime. He smiled and chuckled breezily then grabbed a mug from the cupboard and a teabag from a tin and poured in some hot water from the steaming kettle.

"Morning!" he said cheerfully, handing her the mug. "Have some tea."

Annabel gleamed. She always drank a cup of tea right after she awoke, and she wondered if she had told him this and forgotten or if it were just by chance. Nevertheless, it was a kind gesture.

"You may have seen my sister. She stays here with me now and then," said Emile as he continued cutting fruit. "My parents occasionally have some business in London so they come here from France, and Sylvie, she comes along with them and stays with me."

"How lovely," replied Annabel.

As she stood by the doorway and sipped the tea, she couldn't help but think how kind Emile had been with his generous hospitality and his incessant sweetness.

"Emile, I just want to thank you for everything you've done. I'll just drink the tea and then I'll be out of here."

"You're leaving already?" he asked as he cut into the juicy strawberries. "I was just preparing a fruit salad. I thought I'd take Sylvie to the park for a little while. It's such a beautiful day. If you're not doing anything, join us?"

Annabel shrugged with glee. "Well, I'd be happy to tag along. Fruit salad sounds delightful."

"Great! I'm sure Sylvie will be happy. I've left a spare toothbrush and a fresh towel for you in the bathroom cabinet. You can help yourself to any of my clothes if you like. Not sure any of it will appeal to you but I'm certain you can find something."

Annabel thanked him once more and then drank the rest of the tea. She headed upstairs and into the bathroom and then walked up to the sink. Her reflection gazed at her from the rose-gilded mirror above. She noticed that her eyes seemed different, smaller and less round, as if cursed by a stiff heaviness and emptied from their tears. She splashed her face with cold water and let the nipping shock on her skin wake her to the day. The sun had risen with a warm surprise to the cold autumn and it was making itself known through the circular window in the top corner of the room, the scintillating rays shining through to wake the world.

After freshening up and a little bit of rummaging through Emile's wardrobe, she returned downstairs, dressed in an oversized polo shirt and loose-fitting linen trousers. The other two were sitting down by the garden window. Emile was playing on his acoustic guitar, humming along to the melody of *Freight Train* by Elizabeth Cotton, and singing little fragments of mellifluous lyrics from time to time. Sylvie had her hands and forehead pressed into the window, appearing as if she was lost in deep observation.

"Come see this, Annabel!" she called. "There's a moth over here!'

Annabel sat next to her by the window and the two of them observed the moth that alighted itself on the other side of the glass. They noticed the brisk but slight movements of its body on the glass and examined the intricate layers of beauty on the wings. Emile proceeded to play, going on to play some songs by

Simon and Garfunkel, and Carpenters, his gentle voice skipping along the ripples of rhythm and melodious tune of the guitar that resounded through the room, bouncing off the walls. Annabel looked around and, unexpectedly, she felt a feeling of pure safety, almost as if she was home.

At the park, the birds sang a beautiful hymn and the specks of sunlight came in transient moments through the spaces between the clouds. The three of them walked side by side along the assemblage of nature, Sylvie striding slightly ahead. When they reached the top of a small hill, Annabel and Emile sat together and watched Sylvie dance a cheerful dance before them. She flung her arms around as she swayed from side to side and occasionally span in playful circles. Her feet jumped and landed on the grass and her hands stroked the sky and painted the clouds. A large bird swooned over them and, with an incredulous gasp, Sylvie stopped dancing to admire it. And Annabel and Emile — both of them lost in utter amusement — chuckled at her whimsical mannerisms.

After eating, the three of them sat under an elm tree, each of them resting on spots of padded grass between the large roots. There, they felt safe and cradled, as if to be beneath the thousands of leaves that sprouted from the twigs was to be guarded against the dangers of the world. It was a place of comfort, a place to be wrapped in the blanket of shade that blocked out any trouble, acting as a dome that protected bright moods and joyful thoughts. The wind was playful and capricious and it soared with a fluent musicality and charm that gave rise to the soaring birds that sang erratically. In the distance, someone flew a kite in the vast winds and it sparkled against the sun, uniting with the feathery white clouds that gave way to the vivid blue in the pallet of the sky. The kite soared brazenly and without a care in the world, swift in its rhythm, quick in its dashing movements, catching the eyes of those who looked up to notice; and then it pirouetted in a fanciful, vivacious way towards another kite that floated aloft alongside it. Then the two kites danced together, catching the sun and jumping through the air around them, tickling the gusts of winds above them and beneath them, and then falling as if swooning and then rising even higher as if to chuckle at the humorous deception. As the three of them watched, they all giggled at the animalistic movements of the kites as if it were a performance, then they lay on the grass and gazed up at the top of the tree and the beautiful presentation of autumn leaves above them; some were copper, some a dark mahogany, others bronze and crimson; some fell to the ground, forming heaps of leaves on the grass, whilst others remained on the trees, waiting for their time to fall and join the departed ones.

Sylvie noticed a flock of pigeons not too far away and dashed over to them, tiny seeds spilling out of a little pouch in her back pocket as she ran. Annabel and Emile sat up and watched her take out small handfuls of seeds and throw them towards the avid birds. Eventually, more birds came flying in to get a taste of the seeds and she welcomed them with an ovation, looking back often to share the joyful moment with the other two. Emile and Annabel cheered for Sylvie, and then after a moment of quiet, Emile spoke.

"So, what do you think you'll do now?"

Annabel could tell that he was alluding to the situation with Nina and the happenings of the night before, and when she turned to him, he was looking at her with thoughtfulness on his face and slightly furrowed eyebrows that revealed his heartfelt concern. The question gently probed her as if it knocked on a thin layer of glass with which she had been guarding herself. She stared out to the horizon and then sighed a small breath.

"It's hard for me to explain this, but each time I saw her or got close to her I kept on losing the ability to speak sense into myself," she said slowly, with a broken emotion in her voice. "It felt as though I had lost myself to some kind of powerful daze, and each time it pulled me in deeper and deeper, and every single time that feeling came over me I surrendered to it, like falling victim to a snake charmer."

Emile took a moment to not only hear her words but absorb them, as if through his empathy he was inserting his imagination into the experience of her, to try to see it through her eyes as best as he could rather than through his own disconnected reality.

"So, after you found yourself trapped in the garden, did it ever cross your mind to call for help?" he asked.

"No, I was too scared. Honestly, I didn't want to risk being seen by Nina like that. I thought I could get out, and I almost did."

"And it was the cardigan that held you back?"

"Yes. I don't know, there's a part of me that is so utterly drawn to her, and with that, there's this tremendous curiosity to discover why, and that curiosity came over me with so much force that I guess I just lost myself to it."

"And when you saw her in the bedroom, was she frightened?"

"At first, I think she was, but then, something in her face changed. It was almost as if she was overcome with curiosity too, and somehow she wasn't scared anymore. But maybe inside she was scared, and the curiosity I saw on her face is only my wishful thinking. But she did become calm. And her eyes, they were so striking, so inquisitive. Part of me wanted to say something but my mind went blank and then fright took over and all of a sudden I wanted to be as far away from there as possible. That's why I ran."

Her words pushed aside the surrounding sounds of the park and everything other than her words became muted in the distant background.

"Anyway," she continued with a shake in her speech, "what could I have possibly said to her at that moment? I don't think there is anything I could have said that would have made her understand why I did what I did. I can't even begin to understand it myself."

Emile sat in quiet contemplation, and Annabel — lost somewhere in her thoughts — stared up at the drifting clouds. She so fervently wished to know what Nina had been feeling and what thoughts were going through her mind in those moments after she turned on the light and saw her. And then there was the aftermath, the moments after she had fled: she wondered what Nina could have possibly done, whether she stayed under the sheets and up against the headboard, in shock, or whether she chased after her, or if she woke the others up and told them that someone had been lurking in their home, and if that was the case, whether or not they called the police or went out to find her. But then, as she pondered, another thought occurred to her: maybe it was true that Nina hadn't been frightened after all; maybe the intrigue she felt in that moment was big enough to overshadow any fragments of fear; maybe, as someone who drew creative inspiration from the extraordinary, the uncommon and the rarities of life, the experience fascinated her; perhaps she could even sense that she wasn't a threat, and instead of feeling threatened, she felt the need to know why that peculiar-looking girl with remnants of soil smeared all over her was standing in the room whilst she slept. At least, Annabel hoped that was what had been occurring in Nina's mind.

And then, unexpectedly, Emile turned to her and hugged her without an ounce of hesitation, drawing all of her troubles towards his chest, gently. At first, she was surprised by this kind gesture, but then she held him too and as she did her hands squeezed onto him tightly. She could feel his good-natured care fall onto her until it felt like the fluctuant waves of worry were tormenting her less and less, and then suddenly, everything seemed covered in a cloak of tranquillity. She could faintly feel the soft touch of his heartbeat thumping tenderly through the current of her own, and for a brief moment, she could see things with an alighted spark of hope. A soothing little smile came over her; it was a smile of relief, of solace, a smile that flew out of the depths of assuagement. Finally, everything was calm.

A New Season

The city was moving into colder days and the collective moods of those around had entered into seasonal excitement. Darkness lingered over the skies for longer, leaving the days to feel shorter and the air colder, but with that darkness came millions of twinkling lights that beamed from trees, rooftops and windows. When the rain fell, there were hopes that in time it would thicken to streaks of glorious white snow, and at night, when the skies turned to navy blue and the cold air whispered through the spaces between homes, children went to bed waiting for the day they would eventually wake to a white wonderland.

Many weeks had passed since the night of Annabel's encounter with Nina, and despite all of the overpowering eagerness that previously had gotten a hold of her, she had not attempted to make any further contact with her or George at the café since then. The events of that night had somehow punctured a hole into her hopes like a dagger into a daydream, shattering its abstract components into near-impossible pieces that had once formed a steady stream of desire. What started as a decision to let the whole endeavour rest for some time had turned into a prolonged wilful detachment from it all. Initially, her conclusion had been to step away and focus on other things until everything became clearer and the waters that carried her towards Nina had settled, but even after time away from it all, whenever she thought of her, those waters only began to rock and tremble again, as if stirred by an unseen force way beyond her control. And she was persistent in her restraint, although sometimes at night, in the passageway towards sleep, when her mind drifted and roamed in the depths of curiosity, she thought about Nina, picturing a near-perfect image of her, wondering what she was doing, what adventures surrounded her, and if she had returned from Spain. In those moments, the longing for her rushed from beneath her like a sudden gust of wind. As she would lay there, she would also speculate about whether Nina ever thought about her too, how often the unsolved mystery of the girl in the bedroom visited her mind. But those moments seldom lasted very long; whenever she noticed herself getting caught up in it, she would shut those thoughts off and tell herself that to be drawn in by all of that was not worth any more of her time, nor would it be good for anyone. She had given up seeking an explanation for the immense feelings that often grasped her so tightly, for the mere pursuit of gaining any sort of knowledge about them had only ever driven her to a sticky confusion through which it was impossible to navigate; so she began to learn to let go of the need to know why. And whenever she considered even for a speck of a moment to act upon her desire to find Nina again, she was only met with probing anxious thoughts that told her if she decided to act on those feelings she would only fall into the same trap all over again. And so, to entertain the tickling urges that prompted her to find Nina would be to fall into an endless cycle that looped and looped and came to not a single conclusion.

Luckily, there had been other things occupying her attention, such as her blossoming friendship with Emile. Emile had quite recently moved to London from his family home in Avignon, in Southern France. He had come with a wish to step into new experiences and with the hopes of getting more musical opportunities in the city. He worked in the art department for an independent record label on the south bank of the river, as well as a session guitarist in different spots around the city.

As the days turned to weeks and the weeks rolled on, the two of them spent plenty of time in each other's company, often visiting one another and sometimes venturing on outings together. It felt natural for both of them to be in the presence of each other, and this naturalness lead to a remarkable companionship that seemed to grow a little stronger each day, a connection that Annabel hadn't anticipated in the slightest. Their relationship contained all of the zest and enthusiasm of a spirited song, and it was without an ounce of conflict or unspoken tension. Emile often expressed genuine curiosity and encouragement towards her love for taking photographs, and she did the same towards his musical endeavours. They both had a wild curiosity for the world, and a knack to discover, to learn, to understand the meaning of things, and when they were together there was a wonderful intermingling of their minds. One particular trait they had in common was their affinity with *things*, things in all their particularity and specificity, and their inclination to explore these things, whether it was the particular colours of the sunset, or the fine details of design on an artefact, or the way a song made them feel and the memories it ignited. Annabel had found someone who noticed the nuances of life just as much as she did, someone who could bask in the littlest to the largest details of something they admired, someone who could see something and not only it but everything it contained and adore those little things just as much. They understood each other; they captured one another's words with an appreciation for them; they thought about things similarly, and when their thoughts differed, their words linked and connected in a beautifully organic way until those thoughts came together, like two puzzle pieces forming into a whole. And they were both explorative thinkers; when together, their musings and reflections bounced off one another with passion and ardour, and when not in discussion they could sit silently beside each other, together in a bubble of utter comfortability; and that was something Annabel had never had before. It had only been a few months before meeting Annabel that Emile had moved to London, and he often expressed to her how great it was that they found each other, and how he hadn't anticipated making such a wonderful friend in such a short time. And she, too, treasured their friendship. Sometimes, when thinking of her life, just the knowledge that she had a friend with whom she felt so close was a cheerful enough thought to ignite her day with joy.

One afternoon, whilst the two of them were sitting on the balcony enjoying the view at the break of dusk, Emile gently strumming the chords and singing along to *I Believe In Dreams* by Doris Day, Annabel had a spontaneous idea to wander around the streets to somewhere they had never been before. Emile liked the sound of it, so off they ventured, down the back of side streets and narrow roads, through the passageways ignited by golden street lamps.

After getting rather lost, they came across a warmly lit pottery shop and looked in through the windows to admire the vast assortment of pieces on display. On the shelves were sculptures, vases, mugs, bowls and other kinds of ceramic works. A sweet-looking woman was turning off the lights and making her way out, and as she locked the front door, Emile asked her if she was the owner to which she replied with a smile that she indeed was. They told her just how beautiful the display was, and the woman, who introduced herself as Muna, was so pleased to hear of their adoration and told them that everything was made by hand by her and her girlfriend, Adia, and that they would work in the early hours of the morning before the opening of the store. There was an amiable charm in the way she spoke and moved, and when she smiled, dimples formed in her cheeks like two miniature craters. Dazzling blue rhinestone earrings dangled from her ears and her hair was cut in the slickest black bob. The three of them talked a little more, and Muna expressed that she and Adia had been having a bit of a hard time in recent months running the business and doing everything themselves. She told them that they had been thinking about seeking some help, and then, impulsively, but with genuine excitement in her voice, Annabel told her that she would love the opportunity to help out there, and after a little more discussion about the work and all that it entailed, Muna offered her a part-time position with an enchanting smile across her face. It was a fortuitous moment and it came just at the perfect time; Annabel had been preparing to look for work as the city expenses were beginning to cause her savings to dwindle, and this seemed like just the perfect thing.

So she began working there a few days a week. The job was relatively simple; she would arrive in the morning and leave in the afternoon, and the work mainly consisted of selling the ceramic pieces to customers. There was also a section of the shop where customers would mould and paint ceramics and she would sit by and supervise them, accompanied by a book or a magazine to keep her company when she was left alone.

One day, she came to work extra early. She wanted to see the process of ceramic art after some weeks of growing intrigue. It had never been something she expected herself to be greatly interested in, but after being there for some time, she noticed that her attentiveness to it had been steadily blossoming. Muna and Adia were in the creative room in the back of the shop, sitting down and focusing as their hands worked magic, and Annabel watched as they made beautiful ceramic pieces. She sat there, enamoured of the way the pottery spun on the spin wheel, transforming and moulding the way a ballerina moves through the notes of a piano, passing through transient structures and shifting constantly. The way the ceramic responded to the touch of a hand seemed almost unreal, a pleasant sorcery, as if the crafter cast a spell of metamorphosis; the skill that they possessed was so brilliant and so refined that the workings of it seemed effortless, and that was something that struck a light of wonder inside her. She found it entrancing to see such exquisite pieces coming to life before her eyes and she was fascinated by it so much so that she came early again the next morning. Muna soon noticed her steady interest and taught her some basic forming methods: slab, wheel, coil, pinch and mould. There was a whole lot to the process and in the beginning it was extremely challenging, but after the first few stages of trial and error and some hard effort, it became quite thrilling, and when she came early on the third morning, she practised by making a small vase for Dusty. With warm affection, Muna and Adia told her that the vase was truly impressive for someone at such an early stage, but with just a little glimpse, it was clear to see that the vase was rough and crooked. Nevertheless, Annabel quite liked its peculiarities and gave it to Dusty who received it with an excitable squeal of delight and then placed it on the mantelpiece over the fireplace and filled it with a bouquet of dried palm leaves.

Annabel's relationship with Dusty had been pleasantly developing as time living together passed on. They had settled into a pleasant dynamic in the home where they gave each other a healthy amount of space, and then sometimes they shared sweet moments in each other's company. Dusty spent plenty of time by herself, satisfied with her solitary avocations, and Annabel often found her in quiet solitude sitting and reading or knitting or baking in the kitchen. Occasionally, they would drink a warm beverage together and munch on sweet treats that Dusty would bake and prepare, and they would share stories over the candle-lit table. Dusty was a focused listener and always took time to receive spoken messages, however, she had a special way with her words; it seemed that she possessed an impressive ability to say the right thing at the right moment to ignite the joy and the heart of a conversation; it was as though a great gift of the ability to lift spirits and alleviate any apprehension was bestowed upon her. Her presence was soothing and — unlike her hefty footsteps that bounced around the place often — gentle as a pillow. It was lovely to share a living space with someone so kind and with such an illuminating presence, and after living tightly enclosed with her mother for so long, it was just the thing Annabel needed.

She and Edith spoke on the phone now and then. Their conversations were usually comprised of Annabel's little anecdotes and updates on her wellbeing, followed by Edith's newsy chatter about the current events in Dean Village and her little daily activities, and they usually ended in her forlorn, dreary expressions about her solitude in the home. This was something that had steadily increased as Annabel's time away had gone on, and it wasn't easy to hear that her mother at times had been feeling lonely, but Annabel knew that she mustn't let that get in the way of her vision. She would be there for her mother whenever she could, and she would check up on her every so often; she had even been planning to visit her soon and it was clear through Edith's habit of reminding her of the upcoming date that she was very much anticipating it. And that kept Annabel at peace, to know that her mother was looking forward to something. She also occasionally sent her mother letters written on postcards in which she shared little notes of things that occurred in her busy days. She also sent a few letters to Judy and some of her friends, and one day, on a fresh morning, she awoke to find that she had received a letter from her friend Joan.

Back in Dean Village, Joan had been one of her closest friends since childhood. They had lived on the same road for most of their lives and grew up alongside each other at school, and throughout the many years, they had always remained good friends. In the letter, Joan wrote that she had been inspired by Annabel's move and had recently moved to Liverpool where she began working as an architect. She shared stories of her adventures in the exciting new city and wrote that she often thought about her and cherished the moments they shared over the years. Annabel treasured the letter. She wrapped it in a fine thread and kept it neatly tucked away in her bedroom. It was always such an astonishing surprise to her when someone wrote back to her, matching the energy and the enthusiasm of her own epistolary endeavours. After she read Joan's letter, a memory sprung to her mind and she remembered it with the precise detail of a picture. It was during the week before she left for London. She and Joan were strolling along a trail in their neighbourhood, under the shade of lofty trees. They were discussing Annabel's big move, and as Joan spoke, hints of melancholy began spilling out from her voice. She told Annabel how important their friendship was to her and how she hoped dearly that their connection would remain after the distance and time away. Annabel reassured her and told her that nothing would change; she was sure of this. Their group of friends was small and it was a rare occurrence to see someone so close travel so far, but Annabel's time over there had come to an end, and Joan knew this too.

And now, the city that surrounded her had gradually become her new home, and although it took some time for her to feel settled and truly rested, she had now adjusted to the ambience of it. And she was beginning to understand it too, to fully grasp the inner workings of the metropolis and the pace at which everything moved. Most of the time, it felt as if the city lay somewhere right in the middle between calm and turbulent, as if at any moment the rush of commotion could roar over the town and then swiftly pass by and leave a soft serenity to remain. She enjoyed being amongst so many people but felt out of place in hectic crowds, so she would typically leave home in the quieter hours and then retreat home in the busier hours. Once in a while, there would be a vigorous air to the city and it felt as if it were a frenetic jungle, so every so often she would escape for the day to the quieter parts on the outskirts of the city. This was a perfect balance for her and she found plenty of joy and restfulness in these days. She also adored the art scene in the city; never before had she been amongst such an enormous variety of art, immersed in the opportunity to see and experience so much. Here, she felt she had everything she needed, and when she became tired of one aspect of the city she could run to one of the many others. And she felt balanced when she looked around her, as if for the first time in a long while she truly resonated with her surroundings, with her home. And then there were the opportunities for her creative endeavours; the things and people and instances there were to take photographs of were endless. She could spend a day out and about and walk into unending wonders. Here, she could express her creative mind to an extent that it had not yet reached, and after being amongst the same places and people and things for so long, this was the missing substance her photographs needed. And she loved the photographs she was taking; slowly but steadily she was forming a wonderful assemblage of them, and to her, they were better than anything she had taken before and evidence that she was growing in the right place at the right time. And though she hadn't any idea about what she would do with this collection of works or the avenue she would eventually take them down, she felt gladness within her whenever she looked through them.

It seemed, at last, that things in her life were taking shape, and there was much to appreciate, and as the weeks came by, the appreciation lingered.

The November morning rose. Annabel freshened up and slipped into a grey turtleneck that she tucked into denim jeans. She opened a large jewellery box and pulled out a floral pendant necklace and placed it around her neck.

Downstairs, there was a smell that waltzed across the hall with a pungent richness. As she breathed in the smell, it beckoned her with a sweet touch, melting through her layers of hunger with a flair of irresistible persuasion. Upon approaching the kitchen, the smell grew even more delightful. It appeared to be the lingering scent of freshly baked goods. There was a little note stuck to the oven window. She walked up to it and read it. *Blueberry crumble. Enjoy!*

She opened the oven door and was faced with the most ravishing oat and blueberry crumble. It winked at her with a face of utter beauty that to deny a taste would have been a crime against her senses. She prepared herself a slice and ate it in the comfort of the living room, cradled into the embrace of the fluffy cushions that lay on the sofa. It was a special moment to have such a delicious treat for breakfast, so she relished every second of it, chewing out every little drip of sweetness that erupted from the treat.

Whilst flicking through television channels, something swiftly greeted her: she was overcome with a desire to sit in nature, to feel the flow of the breeze of the outside and hear the flapping of the wings of birds and the rustling of leaves. So after finishing her platter and getting informed about the upcoming weather on the television, she packed another small slice of crumble and headed out.

For a November's day, the cold was surprisingly tame, so she decided that it was a good idea to take a walk in a nearby park and eat the rest of the crumble amongst booming verdure.

At the park, she sat next to an oak tree. There, she ate and felt rested as she observed the people and creatures and nature passing through. The wind blew elegantly all around and she looked up to see the leafless branches of the tree shimmying. A small tingling sensation emerged on her hand and she looked down to find a ladybird crawling up the edges to the very tip of her finger. She lifted her arm and pointed her finger up to the sky to get a closer inspection of the little red beauty with tiny black dots speckled all over. Its movements were mesmerising and emitted a tiny perkiness. Its minuscule footsteps tapped in tiny droplets up and up as high as it could get. Then it reached the tip of her finger and rested on top as if it successfully ascended a hill, and, refusing to fly away, it rested up there, allowing the breeze to brush over its small body. A twinkling glow from a sun ray that cut through a gap in the clouds surfaced on the tip of her finger, knighting the ladybird with a cloak of light, and it bounced off in golden flares to travel the distance of its destination. Something about the creature and its perky mannerisms alighted a spirit of zeal within Annabel. The ladybird seemed so fragile yet so important in its stride, so conscious and sentient yet so indifferent to the world and the puzzles and adversities that can tangle the human mind. It had no problem to solve, no item to gain; its only mission was to exist and to play its role in the circle of nature; the ladybird had no plans and knew no time or schedule; it had no concept of structures or systems — the fact that it was a Wednesday morning meant nothing to the creature — or class or race or religion; the fact of its beauty was even unknown to it. Yet despite all of this, it somehow contained all of the phenomenal complexities of life and the wonder and mysteries of creation. Annabel giggled brightly. What a wonderful little thing, she thought.

The Flautist

The air was graced with a rich coldness that came from within the vibrant breezes; it was the kind of air that would never go unnoticed, and it swept by with terrific electricity, like a dramatic refreshment for every person that stepped out to feel it.

As Annabel exited through the door of the pottery shop in the pleasant early afternoon, the breeze not only blew past her, but through her, stealing any hints of somnolence that abided within her and granting her a newfound energy. To her, the cold air was a gift, such as the rain is a gift to the plants and vegetation; the cold air gave her sustenance and vitality. And she knew the cold air almost as if it were a friend that came and went every year, and each time it revisited it arrived with the same vibrancy and freshness as it always did, never once falling short in its delivery. And now for the winter to be present and for the breadth of the city to be bathed in the coldness of the air was a sheer pleasure to her.

Through the large windows, she waved goodbye to Muna and then turned to face the street. On the other side of the road, Emile was waiting for her. He was leaning against a lamppost, his hands tucked into the pockets of his corduroy jacket, and he bopped his head up and down to the rhythm of a song that played from a store behind him. Annabel crossed the road and they greeted each other delightedly. They had planned to wander the market of Portobello Road for the afternoon, so they took a bus ride and got off at the tip of the market.

At the market, the atmosphere was spirited and filled with vibrancy, and a cheerful energy seeped through every corner. To the left of them, some people behind stalls called out to the passersby to come and take a look at some handmade watches, and to the right, a small elderly man behind a lemonade stand drew attention with his unwavering smile. Beside him was a large heap of piled lemons, so tall it was impossible to miss. There wasn't a single customer at the stall; perhaps the cold weather was keeping people from wanting a taste of fresh lemonade, but it didn't stop Annabel, and she headed over to it with a festive prance in her walk. The old man had an earnest glow about him, accentuated through the lines in his face when he smiled and the iridescent sparkle in his eyes. He got to making her a cup of lemonade, pushing the sliced halves of lemon into the juicer, and as he did his expression contained an unfaltering ray of glee. His movements were skilful and precise and it was clear that he had squeezed the juice from lemons countless times, that each lemon he held was only one of the thousands upon thousands that he had held before, but still, underneath the fact of monotony, there was an essence of enjoyment, of fulfilment; there was something in his presence that seemed to know only the purity of the very moment and nothing else but it. Annabel observed him with curiosity. She pondered about how someone could be so blissfully content in the repetition of such a simple task, how someone could be so removed from the innumerable memories of recurrence so much so that they experience each moment as it comes and goes with so much delight.

As the stream of lemon juice poured into the paper cup and mixed with the sweetness of the syrupy water, she couldn't help but become enticed by the satisfaction pouring out from the juicer. When the cup was full, he passed it over with care and with the sweetest look of thankfulness.

Annabel and Emile walked nonchalantly along the pathway, through the spaces between excitable visitors and shoppers, taking turns to sip on the lemonade, and sighing with pleasure after each taste. The roads were wide but the spaces to walk were narrow, filled with the swarms of people around. All along the road, the market followed, and wherever the market reached there were plenty of people around. After inhaling the scent of baked bread and sweet cinnamon, Emile noticed a bakery stall and stopped to purchase some soft, sugared buns to eat along the journey. And they ate as they carried on, in and out and around the attractions of the market. There was one particular stall that stopped them in their tracks. A woman with a small, hunched figure and large beady eyes stood over a gargantuan selection of handmade necklaces. Some were small, others were large, but every single one had a timeless beauty to it, and they were each laced with detailed features and fascinating blends of colours and remarkable textures. The woman, who was pleased that they had stopped to take a look, moved her hands in a mystifying way over the necklaces as if they were seeds and she was watering them with an invisible liquid to help them blossom forth. Then Annabel noticed her own hands waving over them, her fingers moving back and forth whimsically as if the air held the keys of a grand piano. Then her hand gravitated to a single necklace amongst the many others, and, noticing her interest, the woman lifted it for her to see it closely. It was a forest-green Alhambra pendant on a gold chain and it shone with so much magnificence that she felt compelled to try it on, and when she did, the woman cheered as though it were a sight to behold. And Emile also found a necklace he was enamoured of. The necklace in his hand was an ocean-blue glass pendant with silver inlays on a long brown cord, and as he held it up it sparkled as a reflection of white light ricocheted off it. They purchased the necklaces after what almost felt like an inspired inclination, and they wore them around their necks as they continued down the market.

A little later on, as they turned round a bend, they encountered a flautist who played his long wooden flute in the corner of the street. He was dressed in brilliant greens and black shiny boots that gleamed in the light of the day. He played like a musical wizard, drifting through the sweet notes, his torso swaying gently and his feet bobbing up and down. His eyes were closed and his eyebrows were furrowed, and throughout the song, his head moved as if it were tracing the lines of a mandala. The music oozed out like velvet, smoothly filling the air with a heavenly melody that made it practically impossible not to stop and witness the virtuoso in his element. They stayed and watched in awe, and Emile, in some kind of a reverie of admiration, wanted to signify his admiration, so he dropped a few coins into his basket. After the flautist finished the song, he bowed before the groups of people who had stopped by to listen, took a small moment to breathe and take a sip of water, and then delicately slipped into the next song. Again, he appeared to enter that blissful state. It was a place beyond himself, a place of magic, where momentarily nothing other than the music existed, where the melody held the entire world within it. And then, Annabel, whilst transfixed on the musician, mused about the wonderful peculiarities of the scene before her — how deeply and perfectly intertwined with the music he was, how gracefully fused his heart was into the melody he played; it was as though he produced every note as if it were the first time, as though every time he breathed through the instrument he was hearing the sound for the very first time, discovering the beauty of it again and again, perpetually. Perhaps it was the fluid way he moved, or it may have been the distinct jubilance in his tapping feet, or his face that painted the scene of his mind, revealing its absence from the world around as if it were drifting in spaces beyond himself; he and his mind were utterly submerged in the call of the flute, and, for those sweet moments that he played, no other thing could reach him.

When the song ended, Annabel turned and saw Emile wipe a tear from his cheek. He was greatly touched too. And afterwards, they continued moving down the road beside each other with contented faces.

After a few minutes, Annabel turned to Emile. "Did you notice that?"

"Notice what?" he replied.

"The flautist. I mean, clearly he's a master of it, and I can only imagine he's played those songs time and time again," she said, "but he played in a way I don't think I've ever seen before. It seemed like nothing in the entire world meant more to him at that moment than those songs. And somehow the way his face responded to each note was as if it were the first time he himself was hearing them."

With a calm reflectiveness, Emile placed his hand on his chin and his eyes suggested that he was thinking deeply, almost as if he was looking inward to discover more answers.

"Yes, you're absolutely right," he said with eyes that lit up. "I haven't seen anything more magical than someone lost in music, in their element." Then he placed his hands in his pockets and looked up. "I'd love to write a song as beautiful as those someday."

As they carried on, Emile shared small stories of other times he had witnessed that magic. He told her of a bird feeder he used to see in the park when he was a child, and how she would feed the birds every day for hours as if it were the most wonderful thing in the world, and how sometimes he would sit by and watch her and try to see the wonder of it through her eyes. He told her of a baker he had known, a sculptor he met abroad, and a harpist he had seen on the television, and how he witnessed in each of them, whilst seeing them work their craft, a magic that is not often come across; it was a yielding to a current of bliss, a sort of rapture, just like that of the flautist.

The afternoon was slowly melting into the early moments of the evening. They turned down a cobbled road, and they wandered along with no idea of where they would end up. Annabel was in a mood of quiet cheerfulness, and Emile was animated and full of bubbly words, so she listened with pleasure to the stream of consciousness that he spoke aloud. As they walked on, they stopped by some more places that caught their attention, and then, just moments after they cheered over the prospect of finding a place to drink a warm beverage, they were bowed at by someone in a ravishing waistcoat and a bowtie in the colour of fine red wine. The person was walking perkily out of a building, and they had a moustache that smiled along with their grin. Annabel and Emile noticed, with curious gasps, that the building was a tea lounge, a hidden gem of a place, and so they climbed the wooden stairs up to the lounge to see what lay above. Up there, they were seated by a window that overlooked the bustling road. Annabel looked around the room in quiet veneration of the interior design. The table they sat on was carved from the warmest red oak, and on top, a candle inside of a lantern flickered in silent prances. Along the corners of the room and the edges of the walls, green leaves on long vines climbed and sprouted and travelled throughout. Behind Emile, there was a crimson wall, and piles of antique hardcover books were neatly piled on top of wooden shelves. On the side, a framed picture of a painting that Annabel recognised as *Coffee* by Pierre Bonnard hung on the wall, and all around the edges of the frame were dried fennel flowers sitting prettily. On the windowsill were small, circular rocks with intricately painted scenery on them. She looked towards them and noticed the lovely medley of colours and the delicate touch of the brush strokes. Then she turned to Emile and noticed that the rich brown of his jacket blended just wonderfully into the harmony of colour happening behind him, and the lush waves of his hair added a nuance of detail to the spectrum of patterns and forms, like a flick of texture, a glaze of grandeur. She took out her camera and captured what she saw, and as she caught the shot, she felt a subtle sensation of exhilaration move through her body. The feeling was obscure and in some way indefinable, but it came with a spring of joy and she was sure that it was the feeling of some kind of creative satisfaction, and she captured it just as she captured the memory inside the photograph, and it came in a flowing gush and sent an effortless grin to her face. They drank tea from iron teapots, and throughout their stay, a sublime selection of acoustic music played through the room. Those sweet sounds filled the place with a vast magic, a magic that swirled in lustrous rhythms through the air, like a wind of sound. Then, as the night continued, the room became merged with a wonderful scent of sweet-cinnamon incense. Emile did not stop tapping his feet to the rhythm of the music, and his shoulders swayed and glided along with each song. It could have been one or two or three hours that went by, and yet they were unaware of the passing time, sunken in the gladness of tea and tunes.

When the nighttime came over the city, the two of them said their goodbyes at Notting Hill. Emile strolled into the train station, waving goodbye to Annabel as he turned the corner to catch his train. Annabel headed to the bus stop to catch a bus home, her scarf wrapped around her neck and her belly full of tea. As she waited for the bus to arrive, she reflected upon the events of the day. It had been a day of such sweet memories, she thought, a day with moments to cherish.

At the top of the bus, she smiled all along the journey home, and when she reached her stop she pranced all the way to her flat with a playful little dance with each step of her feet. It had been a while since she had felt so chirpy and full of zest, and she hoped that Dusty was still awake so she could share the moments of her day with her, but when she arrived home the lights were off and a calm silence filled the rooms, so she quietly crept up to her bedroom, and after closing the door gently, threw herself onto her bed and let out a great, satisfied exhale.

When it was time to sleep, she melted into the warmth of the bedding and listened to the distant sounds of cars passing by every so often, along with the wind that came flowing in whispered breaths. The air in the room was cold, but underneath the covers, it was just the perfect temperature of warmth to be swept into a fine slumber. She felt herself drifting away until the padded pillow on which her head rested became a cotton cloud; and then she was floating, hovering over the swaying waters of her mind. Then the memory of the music of the flautist came pouring through the ears of her drifting awareness, and she could hear it all once more — that soft melody, the tones of hope and tranquillity, the soaring notes with ends and beginnings that gently touched as they moved through one another with the fluidity of a running river. It was serene, touching her as if tickling her mind with a bird's feather, soothing her to rest, into an unconscious bliss, until those sounds carried her into a deep sleep the way a lullaby carries a baby.

Throughout the night, dreams were floating through her mind, vivid and ethereal, and when she awoke abruptly in the middle of the night, she remembered the dream she had just been in the midst of as if watching it through a window. She was dreaming of someone, someone within a memory, a memory she hadn't revisited in a while. And that someone was Nina. She had seen her face, so vivid and real, and she had on a red dress, as red as the reddest lipstick, or fresh blood from a beating heart. In the dream, they were inside a dimly lit room, Annabel sitting down with her back against an armchair, her head resting on the soft padding. She felt safe, and comforted, like a bird cradled into a nest under the sheltering leaves of an elm tree. Nina was in front of her, sitting in a chair by the window under the midnight moon, looking out to the misty town within the dark horizon with deep concentration. She was singing something softly to her in that soothing voice of hers, lulling her to a dreamy state where the air became wavy and her vision hazy. The words she sang let out a spell of calmness, almost like a sedative. Annabel tried her best to listen with attentive ears, and the more Nina sang the more comforted she felt. Gently, Nina turned to look at her and then their eyes met as she smiled with a warm sincerity. Immediately after that, she woke, and that was all she remembered. But then slowly, the picture of the dream in her mind began to fade, vanishing with no wish to remain, the way the sun fades into the night, the moon into the morning, or footprints fade in the sand as the ripples of waves wash over them. And then she couldn't remember anymore. The words Nina sang were evaporating into the air and the memory of the room was vanishing into dust until she remembered nothing of the dream, nothing other than Nina's dwindling silhouette. For a moment, she tried to remember again, but she knew she must forget about it and fall back asleep or she would spiral trying to remember something that was no longer there. And as she looked outside to the night sky and then at the tiny splatters of rain residue on the window, her eyelids began to seal until she drifted away to sleep once more.

Her, By The Door

The last days of November had arrived, making way for December. Scarves wrapped necks and vapour flew from breaths, and the coldness of the air was growing richer and more potent with every day that arrived. Most days, Annabel rose to black, frosty mornings, and she stayed warm with woollen socks and knitted jumpers and a mug of hot herbal tea between her hands. Some mornings, when she would get up early for work, she sat on the balcony to hear the dawn chorus by the wrens and the warblers chirping their lively melodies across town. As she sat there and listened, she often fell into daydreams and tunnels of contemplations that came without notice or reason. It was during those early hours that she would descend into these inner spaces, somewhere that bordered both a zone of conscious rumination and one of a space of endless possibility, and she would drift somewhere in the middle where she would be guided through a journey of spontaneous reveries. It was at this time of the day that she found she could observe her thoughts without living in them so much; somehow they appeared before her in a way that made her feel as if she were a spectator of her own life. But these moments occurred transiently and they seemed to come and go as they pleased. She regarded this feeling as the zone her mind entered when in a state not yet fully alert, a place where her awareness of herself had not yet arrived at the forefront of her mind, and whatever was happening behind the scenes made itself known in thousands of little particles of thought.

One particularly dark morning, she sat on the balcony and listened to the melodic layers of birdsong, and as she listened she began to think about herself and her place in the world.

The city around her was yet to wake and the acceleration of her day was yet to begin, and it was during this time, this fragile space at the edge of the beginning of the moving day that she was able to see herself almost as if she was unattached to her own life, as an entity that was separate from her own human condition. And with this view of observation, she somehow felt contented, endowed with genuine satisfaction that she could sense within her. She thought about where she had been this time the previous year, and how, at that time all she wanted for herself was to be a part of something greater, to be extricated from the banalities and the monotony of her days. A small, bubbly feeling of gratification came upon her. When she observed her life in this way, she narrowed the feeling down to the fact that — underneath the occasional thoughts of worry and self-doubt — she was proud of herself, proud of how she had grown, proud of the way she had leapt into a new pond, how she had created a new trajectory and settled into a new life for herself. And that was where her attention was, not where she had been or where she was possibly heading, but where she was at that very moment. This had been the longest time she had gone without stopping to worry about her life in the future, and that was something to be pleased with.

She breathed in the sultry morning air and rubbed her hands together to bring forth some comfort. Then she noticed the early stages of the light coming to meet the sky, and with that, she stepped inside to get ready for the day.

A little later, when she went downstairs to fetch herself something to eat, she encountered Dusty peeling some oranges on the kitchen table.

"It's a sweet morning," called Dusty.

"It is! Ah, those oranges look so tasty!"

Dusty handed her an orange with a twinkling countenance and with the same radiance that beamed from her eyes every morning.

"I picked them up from the market yesterday! You wouldn't believe the weight of my basket by the time I was finished there."

"The flavour, it's so rich!" said Annabel, biting into a piece.

The two of them exchanged grins and then Annabel grabbed a loaf of olive bread and began cutting into it on the countertop.

"It's funny," she spoke, "when I was a child I only ever got to eat oranges when I was sick. But then one day, an orange tree blossomed in the garden next door and my neighbour would sometimes throw oranges over to me and my mother. We would keep them in the fridge overnight and then eat them cold in the morning."

"Ah, there's nothing like fresh oranges in the morning!" said Dusty with zeal in her voice. "Feel free to eat as many of them as you can while they're ripe and juicy! Oh, and there's also raspberries, melons, grapes, and the crunchiest pink lady apples in the wicker basket!"

She continued peeling and Annabel spread butter on her bread and then joined her at the table.

"Before I forget," began Dusty, "I spoke to someone at the market yesterday. He was a photographer just like you. He told me there's some kind of visual arts exhibition down by Greenwich that's happening throughout this week. I know you're interested in these sorts of things so I took a booklet in case you'd be keen on going."

"Oh, I'd love that!" said Annabel, biting into her bread.

Dusty reached into her bag that was sitting beside her, pulled out a small information booklet and slid it across the table. Annabel opened it and turned the pages, her eyes moving left to right as she read the short summaries and skimmed across a list of names. And then, after turning a page, she read something she would never have anticipated. Perhaps her eyes were misleading her, so she blinked and read it once more, but it was clear and it was right there in front of her, driving itself into the spotlight. There were many names on the page, but they didn't matter, they may as well have been erased, for there was only one name that settled: Nina Bayu. The image of those two words carved themselves into the frame of her entire sight, piercing right through with its pointed edges of ink. It had been a while since she had seen the name written before her eyes.

"Everything all right?" asked Dusty with a hint of concern.

For a few seconds, Annabel gave no response, let alone any sign that she had heard her words. But then she found herself again and swiftly closed the booklet with a firm hand and slid it into her jacket pocket.

"Yes, just fine!"

But as those words came out, they were so far from the truth. She was stunned, completely stupefied, by both the shocking coincidence of it all and the fact that she had far less control over her reaction than she would have hoped. And amidst that fortuitous instant, beyond her placid demeanour, her mind soared countless times through the image of Nina, and the words of her name probed at her from each and every direction, filling her with a desire to drop everything and leave right away to see her paintings at the event, along with a cold, sharp urge to drop it and refrain from entertaining those thoughts again. She did not wish to fall into the unending whirlpool in which she had found herself countless times before, but to ignore it and go about her day whilst pretending she had never seen it was just plainly unachievable. So she would go to work, she decided, and become distracted in the happenings of the day, and then perhaps it would begin to fade and then she would let herself forget about it.

So, she said goodbye to Dusty and set off to the pottery shop. But even over there, forgetting about it all was not a natural response; the booklet not only lingered in her thoughts but it overshadowed her capability to focus on her work responsibilities. At one point, she took it from her pocket and opened it again to triple-check that her imagination had not been deceiving her, but that didn't help the situation one tiny bit, so she attempted to throw it away, but she couldn't make herself do that, so she held onto it, with no clue of what to do with it but with the hope of figuring it out eventually.

The afternoon came, and when given the chance to take a break, she stepped outside to catch a breath of the outside air, and there, she called Emile. Discussing it with him was the first and only thing she wished to do at that moment. She told him exactly how she felt about the situation, that she was lost in a medley of confusion and unease and that she could also see this was now mixed with a strange excitement — although she had some difficulty articulating the depth of what she felt — and she told him how there was an eagerness within her to go and see whatever it was she had the opportunity of seeing, to dive into the pursuit of whatever it was from Nina that she longed for once more; but, moulded into that, was a reaction of distress that was brewing within her, a fear that if she did follow these feelings, she would be opening a gateway to an obsessive fixation, one that resulted in an insufferable itch of dissatisfaction, that familiar road with no end that she knew all too well. And along with all of that, she was meddling with the actuality that, after some time she had spent purposefully detaching herself from Nina, the mystery of her was somehow making its way back into her life. She told him how a part of her wished she could let it go, forget about it or pretend she never saw it, but somehow the opportunity had found her without her looking for it, and perhaps that was the reason she couldn't let go of it. Emile listened to her without interjecting, and after she said everything she wished to express, with keenness, she asked him for his perspective, and he gave her a thoughtful response. He told her that maybe the worst thing that might happen wasn't actually as bad as she would expect, to which she responded by telling him that she wished to no longer be haunted by the compulsions that got a hold of her so much in the past; that, and the small chance that if Nina were there and caught sight of her and recognised her as the girl in the bedroom, she wouldn't be able to give an explanation for her past actions. It frightened her that a possible scenario could take place where she would have to give an account of her reasons for that dreadful night and explain her inscrutable feelings to the one person to whom all of it was directed. But she *did* want to go, so much so that it felt almost as if she was compelled to; she wanted to see the latest paintings, to witness Nina's imagination and her expression all over again, to see artwork she hadn't yet witnessed, paintings that maybe had been formed in the recent months, painted on days after the moment their gazes met. Then Emile, after taking a few seconds to gather his thoughts, asked her if his fellowship, the thought of him perhaps being there beside her to offer her a helping hand, gave her enough support to feel as if she could follow through with it, without the possibility of it consuming her the way it had in the past. He told her that if she wished to go then he would accompany her and see her through it, and as he spoke these words she began to feel calmer at once. His words highlighted the fact that she now had someone with whom she could share her feelings about this entire bewildering journey, someone she could rely on to help guide her back to herself in times when she reached for guidance. She absorbed this and thought about it deeply. She pondered now, with a clearer mind; it was different now, she thought, of course, it was; she had something now she hadn't had before; she had support, a friend with whom she could share things she didn't wish to face alone, a friend who she knew would try to make her see the light when she couldn't see it alone; and perhaps, that was all she needed in the past, and now that she had this, things would be different. So she told him this and he told her that it would be a pleasure to go with her, that he would stay beside her, and that whatever would happen afterwards, he'd be there. Annabel smiled. These words had somehow gently assuaged her. She realised that it was time she allowed herself to lean on a shoulder, something she had never fully been able to do in the past; she had been so incapable of letting someone else into her inner world, partly because she tended to feel as if she had to go through everything alone, and also because she never felt that anyone really understood her, until now.

The following day came, and Annabel, with Emile closely beside her, walked through the entrance doors of the large, three-floor building right by the pier. The building's walls were made of spotless glass that stood high, and inside, the appearance was simple, but grand and imposing with an immensely high ceiling and thick pillars aligned in symmetrical positioning. They took a lift up to the third floor to the event, and when the doors parted, they stepped into an enormous room full of hundreds of people, all walking around slowly, taking in the large selection of artworks placed neatly throughout the spaces of the room. There were large partition walls that separated the room into smaller sections, and on each wall were a myriad of paintings and photographs and poetry. Placed in an orderly fashion throughout the room were glass display tables with ceramics and sculptures among a plethora of other hand-made creations. There was so much to see, so much to soak into the brilliance of, and as they wandered through slowly, Annabel couldn't help but anticipate seeing Nina's paintings creep from behind the corner of a wall. They walked slowly around the other visitors and through the room to take a look at some of the works. Then they stopped by some photographs which were so wonderful that Annabel momentarily forgot what she was looking for. Emile stopped to inspect some ceramic works and Annabel took a moment to read some poetry, and afterwards, they came back together and continued. They came to a halt when they passed by a film of some sort being projected on a cloth. Emile sat on the long wooden bench to take a look and Annabel stood behind him, and then she noticed a flutter of nerves within her chest. Her hands were tucked into her jacket pockets, her legs were crossed, and she bit her lip and swayed her head side to side gently as she watched the flickering images of the film flash across the cloth. Emile seemed to be quite enticed by this and he leaned forward, but Annabel could feel anticipation thickening inside of her more and more, building up with every second. She turned her head to the side to catch a glimpse of what lay beyond, and she could faintly see from afar, through the small spaces between spectators, an assemblage of paintings hung up on one of the partition walls. Something about the paintings captivated her, but from where she stood, she couldn't quite tell if they were paintings by Nina or those of another artist, so she began walking in their direction. The paintings were becoming more real and the depictions clearer with every step she took, and she approached them slowly, gazing through spaces between bodies until she was close enough to see Nina's name on a wooden plaque on the wall. There and then, something happened: she became almost mesmerised, and she moved closer until she was standing in front of a large painting, her head floating past the velvet barrier. Under the painting was a plaque that read *Two Hands*, and showed two hands reaching out to one another, submerged below the surface of a misty water-like substance, distorted by the currents and waves and overpowering movements. She thought the portrayal was enchanting, and her eyes moved along the scene, noticing every stroke, every layer, every movement in which the brush swayed, and capturing every detail, every touch and nuance of the oil paint. In a reverie of adoration, she became immersed in a world beyond her surroundings, motionless, soundless, captured in a place of infinite colour beyond the partition wall. No painting had moved her quite like this, and she breathed deeply as though her soul was gasping at such a profound work of beauty. Then she moved along the wall to study the other paintings, all the while submerged in a dreamlike state. The buzz of the room washed away into a faded hum, and now she was somewhere above it all, afloat in a bubble above everything, where only herself and the artwork could exist. She studied every painting with a striking infatuation and unfaltering preciseness in her gaze that scarcely came upon her, and she leaned in gradually, and each painting stood before her majestically. Her eyes were transfixed, aware of everything from the fine strands of detail to the blends of colours to the waves of meaning that crashed down all over her. What could have been a minute could also have been five, or ten; time was now shattered into fragments, and all that could be and all that was now dwelled on the canvases. Each painting was unique and carefully executed, portraying moments of human emotion through scenes of a limitless imagination; some spoke words of grief and sorrow, others of joy and hope. Then she stepped towards the final painting at the end of the wall. This painting was titled *Her, By The Door*. It was of darker shades, and it appeared gloomier than the rest, with much greater obscurity. Throughout the sides of the painting, dusky shades of dark browns and shadowy greys and black swirled in an unending motion. From the bottom right corner, a gold ray of warm colours blended into the darkness and lit up the scene, moving right into the middle where it met other colours of illumination. And in the middle, submerged in that marigold light, there was a silhouette. The figure was dark, blended into the shadows, and the features were nebulous, but the silhouette stood there with a soft, tender presence, drowned in the compound of lights and darks that fought against each other with such potency. It was unclear which direction the figure was facing, what they were wearing and what the expression upon their face had been, and yet somehow, there was transparency there, an air that made it clear that the person was stuck between both directions of light, halted right in the middle between two worlds. Annabel noticed a tingling jitter of disquiet palpitate inside of her stomach, and the tiny hairs on her arms stood, and she felt the ground rumble beneath her feet and send a thundering shiver up through her legs, past her chest and up through her neck to the top of her head. And the world stood still, and the walls of the room seemed boundless, and then her eyes blinked forcefully and she breathed a tiny, crackling gasp. An expression of surprise came from a voice beside her and she turned to see

Emile standing next to her, his eyes squinting incredulously as he pinched his chin. Then he removed his glasses and rubbed the lenses on his cotton shirt before putting them back on and leaning in forward to get a better focus on the painting. In silence, and with her mind in a wordless blank, Annabel stared into the painting once more, her point of focus fixated upon the shadowy silhouette. It was as if a denseness filled the air around for her breathing no longer felt effortless, but heavy and onerous. In an almost synchronised manner, the two of them turned to look at each other, and immediately, without the need for discussion, they knew exactly what the other was thinking. And then, as if pushed by the hands of a benevolent wind, they stepped out of the room to flee from the noise and congestion. In the quiet air of the lift, they didn't speak, but instead, they stood closely beside one another whilst they both endeavoured to comprehend what they had just seen. Outside, the refreshing air gave them some clarity of mind, and they walked down to the river and sat on a bench that overlooked a view of the boats on the rippling surface of the water and a bridge that led to a mass of historical buildings. They sat there for a little while, thinking about what they had seen until Emile let out a little chuckle of befuddlement. Annabel turned to face him and noticed his astounded demeanour, catching glimpses of her own feelings in him, and then she too chuckled, and soon after, Emile began giggling which caused her to giggle humorously, until they were both laughing almost hysterically, rocking forwards and backwards with their hands on their stomachs. Annabel knew of no reason for their laughter — it was clear that Emile hadn't the faintest idea either — yet it came so naturally, and perhaps it was the perfect remedy for such an absurdly perplexing situation. So they continued to laugh, their infectious sounds mixing into the ambience of the pier and their amusement rubbing off on each other. And shortly after, their jubilance faded into the air, and they both sighed in unison, leaned back into the bench and fell into a mellow state of repose.

Salt

An infectious excitement was brewing as Annabel and Emile leaned on the railing of the second-floor balcony of the train station, watching the shifting crowds below them. They were taking a trip to St Ives, Cornwall — something they had spontaneously planned one evening after agreeing to escape the wildness of London for a little while. And they had even invited along some friends to join them on the adventure; Annabel had invited Joan, whom she had not seen in months, and Emile invited two friends, Nolan and Giselle, who waved up to them with swinging arms and big grins from down below. The two of them were in a band — Nolan played the keys and Giselle the bass guitar; and they were close friends of Emile; he had met them many years ago at a music event during an old trip to London and had stayed close with them ever since. They stood on the ground floor, waving up to Annabel and Emile to get their attention. Nolan was tall, with distinctly green eyes and dark ginger hair and he stood with his shoulders back and a spirited demeanour, bobbing up and down to say hello from afar as if his feet were on springs. Giselle had long and curly cinnamon hair, with the curliest fringe that dangled down above her large glasses, so large they covered her cheeks, and she stood with a calm countenance and a liveliness shining through her smiling eyes. Upstairs, the four of them greeted with amicable hugs and then together they watched the display board, eagerly awaiting the announcement of their train. It was the early hours of the morning, and they all delighted in the excitement of getting on a train in the midst of dark, when most people were at home and tucked into bed.

A melodious chime sounded and the announcer called out the number of the platform for the departing train to St Ives, and so they made their way to the train with ardent strides. Upon boarding, Annabel noticed the lovely soft colours and tones throughout the interior of the train. They each sat on comfortable mulberry purple chairs, surrounding a spacious table and beside a large window to catch the passing views. Overjoyed with stirring anticipation, they discussed amongst one another things they wished to do and places they wished to see in the little town of Cornwall. They talked with enthusiasm, their mutual excitement bouncing off one another, back and forth, until eventually, the train began to move and the sounds of their voices melted into the constant hum of the train engine and the clanking of the wheels on the tracks. Emile handed out some snacks and Annabel took out her flask and poured everyone some steamy tea in small paper cups. Then the train began to roll on down the tracks. Flickering city lights whizzed by, appearing like fine crystals tightly organised together in their thousands. Annabel noticed the small, inconspicuous rock of the train, the movement of the carriage swaying her to a sweet state of calm, and from the window view, city architecture slowly turned to trees and fields, and country homes and cottages that overlooked large spaces of tranquil land. The husky trees were flowing past in an evanescent manner through the darkness, like hazy, shimmering beasts flying through the frosty air. She leaned her head on the window and stared through the blur of the rushing waves of the night. It was wonderfully warm and homely inside the train, and the chairs were cushiony and comforting, and she listened to the resonant sound of the tracks and the faint hum of Giselle and Emile's music fusing, the melodies blending into each other. Nolan was reading a book, seemingly engrossed as he turned the pages with an evident keenness. As Annabel stared through the window, she couldn't help but observe how the shapes of the branches merged into one another as they passed by swiftly, moving into a distorted fusion of shadowy colours against the dark sky; and as she stared deeper, she noticed how the shades of those trees were much like the shades of Nina's painting. It had been a week now since she had seen that painting, and although the sight of it was brief, somehow the vision of it within her mind was still fresh as if it had only just come into her sight. It was the details and the textures of it that she recalled so distinctly, the way every colour and shade amalgamated into something so poignant and so expressive, and now it was appearing before her again, revived by a nebulous blur. In recent days, she hadn't thought much about that painting for the fear of falling into unending contemplation, even though at times it felt as though all she wanted to do was imagine it and wonder why Nina had chosen to paint her. And although she was without confirmation of that, there was not a single doubt in her mind that the painting was of her, for who else could that startling silhouette have been? She was sure that it was her in the painting, it had to have been. And when she imagined Nina painting it, and pictured her retreating into her memory to conjure the hazy remnants of the image of her silhouette standing before her in the dim shadows in that mysterious and somewhat harrowing scene, it sent tingling chills that travelled through her. But all the while, there was no doubt in her mind that the experience inspired Nina, for after all, the memory of it gave her something she wished to paint, and in some peculiar way, that was a comforting thing to know. As the trees rolled on, she thought of it all now, and she couldn't help but wish to discover the inner workings of Nina's mind as she painted it, to catch a glimpse of her thoughts, like peering through a little window at the edge of her psyche into a world that only she knew.

The crescent moon made an appearance through the flickering treetops that whizzed by, and as she stared into it, her eyelids blinked once, then twice, and then they closed gently and she drifted to sleep, the last thing in her sight being those evocative dark shades travelling at high speeds. And then, like tumbling down through a tunnel where darkness washed over spangling light, where hands reached out to meet nothing but air and no feet touched the ground, she descended involuntarily into a dream.

She was standing on the pavement, looking through the windows of a building on the other side of the road, flashes of cars and buses passing by in between. With a moment of inspection, she realised that it was George's café she was looking at, and through the glass, it was Nina she was searching for. Colours and lights blurred recklessly into each other, and shapes and forms and movements happening all around seemed vivid and real, but all the while, heavily distorted as if looking through a shard of glass that warped the image and gave the scene a fluctuating speed of motion making it difficult to recognise how much time had passed. She could feel her heart thumping in her chest, relentlessly turbulent, and though she was aware that she was in a dream, she questioned if it were the heart of her dream body or her real, physical heart in a rush of alarm; and in that focus of something other than what she was looking for, Nina appeared through the windows, completely out of the blue, as though she were summoned from the air. It was unclear exactly what she was doing inside the café, but she was talking and interacting with other people around her, smiling so genuinely that happy tears could have fallen from her eyes. Then she turned her head and, in an instant that came so suddenly it took Annabel chillingly by surprise, made eye contact with her, strong and unwavering like a summer's sun. It was only a dream, and her conscious mind knew this, but even with this partial lucidity, a shadow of fear slithered into her bones, and in that hollow feeling she turned away and began to flee. But when she looked back, Nina had left the café and was crossing the road, making her way to her eagerly, and this eagerness was in the urgency of her footsteps, and it was written on her face too, in the widening of her eyes and furrowing of her eyebrows. And so Annabel increased the pace of her footsteps, and as the volume of her breathing grew, so did the sounds of the environment around her. Rain began to pour and thunder struck the skies with a tenacious power, stirring the entire dream into a swirl of hysteria. She looked back, expecting Nina to be far away from her, but instead, she was even closer and getting closer to her with every passing second. Now Annabel felt panic consume her, and to whatever direction she turned, the roads grew into expanding trajectories that formed endless routes. And then, with an abrupt stop, she stood still, suddenly overpowered by a part of her that had had enough of her constant running away, a part of her that grew so tired of it all that it gave her no choice but to surrender. She stood there, in stillness, her wildly frantic lungs calming down, and she began counting every second until she would hear Nina's voice from right behind her ears, or feel her soft hands meet the back of her shoulders; but as those seconds passed, nothing happened, and when she looked back, Nina was no longer there. Now only the teeming sounds on the road and a flock of birds that rose in the sky breathed life into the dream. There was no sight of Nina. She walked slowly down the road, her vulnerability melting like hot candle wax, the rain calming down until not a single drop fell. She looked down to the ground and a puddle beside her shoes reflected her image, and in that reflection, behind the incandescent glimmer of lights on the surface of the fallen rain, she saw Nina. A sharp shock seized her body and she froze, and after an instant of telling herself that none of it was real and that it was just a dream from which she would very soon wake, she decided to look once more into the puddle. So she bent her knees, arched her back and leaned forward slowly until the striking features of Nina's face were glaring right back at her. She placed her hands on her face, touching her skin that felt so unfamiliar, moving her fingers over her eyelids, down her nose and across her lips, and then placed her hands over her cheeks. Then she woke. And when she opened her eyes to the passing scenes through the window, she remembered that dream so clearly that it felt almost surreal. Perhaps hours had passed, she thought as she noticed the other three curled into their deep slumbers, so she checked the time to see that hours had indeed passed. But the dream was *without* hours, or any time at all; it was, in a way that seemed only comprehendible in that moment of waking up, sealed within a sphere where no time existed. And as she found herself in the alertness of her waking mind, the dream began changing, but it wasn't changing its contents, only its form. It was being unhooked from numerous trails of feelings, ripped apart from all of its abstract complexities that were incomprehensible to a mind that was awake. It was now becoming something seeable, a single scene, a moving image that could be processed by memory and remembered with ease. Now she just simply remembered it.

With a slow and steady stop, the train approached the final destination, arriving at St Ives in the middle of the morning winter sunlight. A sweet-sounding bell chimed and the arrival announcement was made, and so the four of them opened their eyes, curved their backs and stretched their limbs before looking out the window to see the vast coastal landscape. Bushy trees stood clumped together on hills that surrounded the outline of the lightest blue ocean. The ripples in the water were tame and the ocean foam touched the faded-yellow sand and moved across it, stretching out so far it almost appeared like a rapid glacier of ice at the tip of the ocean. Through a gentle fog, sweeping lands on further hills appeared, and on top of them were distant clusters of cottages and little towns connected through unseen roads. In the sky, the white clouds made way for the vibrant sun to touch the hills and kiss the sand and send rays to the ocean.

They walked out onto the concrete ground and let the crisp air wash over them as they breathed in its enlivening touch. The colour of the sky was an arctic blue that fused with a foggy white, and effulgent streaks of feathery clouds, broken and brilliant, hovered slowly together, scattered across in disarray like paint thrown arbitrarily onto a work of art.

They walked along the platform, their bags on their backs, inhaling the salt air and absorbing the light of a beautiful day. And when they got to the exit of the train station, Joan was there, waving her hands beside her gleaming smile. Her almond-coloured hair swayed in the wind above her shoulders, and she stood there, arms open, with an artless grin painted over her face and a dimple on each cheek. She wore a bright yellow raincoat that was impossible to miss and her eyes held a magical, glistening glow that even from afar was noticeable. Annabel ran to her and the two of them hugged, holding each other dearly, their cheeks pressing into each other.

"I'm so glad you came!" said Annabel, leaning back to meet her eyes.

"*I'm* so glad I came!" replied Joan.

Then Emile, Giselle and Nolan approached and Annabel introduced them to Joan and Joan to them, and after an instant of genial embraces, the five of them set off to their accommodation.

Along the pebbles of the stone pathway that traced through a little hill, they strolled merrily until they arrived at their destination. Before them was a large stone cottage with a pointed rooftop and wide windows, and below each window, clumps of the most vivid pink and red geraniums blossomed from baskets. A swing sign that read *Blue Water Guest House* hung from above the entrance door. Emile walked up the steps and pressed the doorbell, and in the silence of their anticipatory waiting, the distant sound of the herring gulls on the shore below the hill echoed through the air. Then a whispering creak emitted from the door as it slowly opened, and standing in the doorway, someone in denim dungarees, small and hunched over, welcomed them in and showed them to their room on the uppermost floor of the cottage.

The room was somewhat cramped, but cosy and airy, and there were paintings of the town in gilded frames over a dainty floral wallpaper. The carpeted floor was thick with a soft touch and there was a patterned rug in the middle of the room underneath a wooden table holding a bouquet in a pretty stained-glass vase. The fragrant smell of the flowers dispersed across the room and a touch of a breeze came through the slightest gap in the window and filled the air with a wintry touch. On the side, pushed against the wall were a couple of beds and bunk beds placed next to each other in an orderly fashion. Nolan jumped enthusiastically onto one of the beds, breaking out a small cry from the springs.

"I'll take this one," he said as he laid back, crossed his arms and smiled.

Emile and Joan went to look out the window to see the coastal view, and then Joan unlocked the latch, lifted the window and threw her head out to feel the crisp breeze wash over her and hear the chirping of the birds above her head and the faint humming of the pushing and pulling of the ocean. Giselle stood by the table and leaned over to smell the flowers, letting out a peaceful sigh. Annabel stood by the door with the whole view of the room before her. She lifted her camera to her eyes and captured a photograph.

"You gotta take a look out here!" called Emile from the window, looking back at her with a fervent glow.

So she went over there and stuck her head outside, emerging her breath into the breath of the breeze that touched the roof of the cottage. As a strong gush of wind came by, her hair whooshed frantically in the impact of it, like leaves in a whirlwind, and the coldness tickled her skin and enriched her spirit. Then as the wind passed and the loudness of its power calmed she could hear the coastal sounds fading in, and her eyes widened to see the beautiful homes tightly clumped together along the hills and bumps of land; and she saw the clouds kissing the summit of the hills and the birds soaring around them, and at the bottom of the hills, she saw the ocean and the millions of ripples amongst the stillness that constantly remained beneath its movements and its noise. And she saw the tiny moving dots of people on the sand, there to admire the ocean and witness its grandness and be a part of such a riveting landscape. When she pulled her head back into the warmth, Emile had turned on the kettle on the small kitchen countertop at the side of the room and was opening packets of coffee and matcha powder for everyone. Joan, Giselle and Nolan were sitting on a bed, conversing and mingling. Annabel went and sat beside them and leaned her head gently on Joan's shoulder, listening to the lighthearted conversation.

They spent some time talking in the comfort of the room on top of the beds, and after a little while, they decided it would be a great idea to grab some local food in the town, so they went down the hill to a little restaurant. During the walk, Annabel and Joan walked arm in arm and Joan caught her up on things she had missed since the day she left Edinburgh. Annabel told her about her days and affairs in London, and small details about her life that she hadn't mentioned in the letters she had sent. She told her about the unexpectant instance of how she met Emile, what it was like living with Dusty, and her job at the pottery shop with Muna and Adia. After they had strolled down the hill, past the beautiful array of cottages and leafless winter trees, they stopped by a coastal café that Emile spotted from afar. There they sat and snacked on toasted sandwiches and chatted and laughed and relished the sweet escape of the moment and how delightful it was to be where they were, temporarily outside of their bustling lives.

As the day turned over a page and swept effortlessly into the afternoon, Annabel realised just how lovely it was to have some time away, and to be surrounded by such wonderful company was just the perfect addition to such a wondrous trip.

After dessert — a succulent sticky toffee pudding — Nolan and Giselle shared some anecdotes about their recent adventures touring in a band across different cities, and Emile told everyone about his recent endeavours in London and moments he and Annabel had shared, and then out of the blue, Joan asked Annabel an unexpected question, as though she had pulled it out of thin air; it was an innocent question, a question that came as naturally as a breath, but it sent a tiny quiver to Annabel's lips and caused her chest to sink into itself. She asked her why, at the moment she and Emile first met, she had been trying to get on top of a wall in the first place, knowing her prolonged fear of heights. It was only a question, a simple question, and it posed no threat whatsoever, nor did it come with a single hint of malice; it was an easy, innocent enquiry, but it approached Annabel with a heavy thump. She froze, and in her peripheral vision she saw Emile calmly sip his drink, and knowing that he was calm made her a little calmer too, but still her mind lurched to every wall in the room as it tried to find an answer. Shattered silence surrounded the table and curious eyes probed her like those of owls staring through the shadows of a forest. She breathed in as if to speak but then even her breath froze as there were no conclusive thoughts behind the incoming words. Now Emile was watching her too, and it was clear he was wondering what she would say, but all the while there was a comfort to his eyes, almost as if he was silently reassuring her that it was okay if she didn't feel comfortable sharing that part of herself, but also that telling them would not be even a fraction as bad as it seemed. And she had no response in her mind other than the truth; and perhaps it was evidence of her growth, a testament to her overcoming the bulk of her internal struggles, but she told them exactly why she was trying to climb the wall that night. As she spoke, she was unsure why the words came so suddenly; it was as though she was persuaded by a swift push that overcame the anxieties. Naturally, their curiosity inquired more, and with every question she dived a little deeper and deeper until she told them the entire story of Nina, how she had been looking for her, and of the night she went to meet her and hid behind the curtains, and of the painting of her silhouette; and when she reached the end of her story she sighed and shrugged and then smiled with watery eyes. Emile was smiling too, looking at her as if to tell her he was proud of her, and Joan reached across the table and held her hand in her own. And Annabel, upon realising the careful attention to her feelings and the scarcity of judgement from her friends around the table, could now feel nothing but sweet relief. And with that, the moment moved to the next and the afternoon rolled on into a calm and serene evening.

As the sun turned to the moon, the sky revealed hints of violet and pink, and the clouds were fading to invisibility as the nighttime came lurching in over the faint shimmering of stars. They walked along the pathway on the edge of the coast. Calmly swaying boats were scattered across the waters like sleeping animals floating and catching rest in the night. All along the road that ran along the coast, golden lights from street lamps glowed, and the clean surface of the water reflected back those golden colours like a dusky mirror, but alive and with a unique charm. All of the colours reflected on the waters appeared to be like something from a painting, a vivid and ethereal display of stark beauty. The cottages and homes on the hills revealed dots of glittering lights, alight in their brilliant colour. Annabel took a photograph of Joan reaching down to grab a stone on the sand in front of the grandeur of a wonderful view.

Then the nighttime had arrived and shone its full, ardent presence over the town. At some point, they walked by a tavern where streaks of the most soothing music came seeping through the windows and the walls, so melodious and delicate it sounded just heavenly. They peered through the windows to see a violinist playing in front of a crowd. Quietly, they entered the tavern and sat on empty seats in the back of the room. The violinist played with such precision and concentration that it felt only natural to sit and witness the prowess before them. Annabel listened meticulously, and in an instant, something compelled her to close her eyes, and as she did it felt like the music was there just for her and her friends, as if it were dedicated to them, laid out across the air that they breathed to endow them with a magic touch, a life-giving song. Then she opened her eyes and saw the violinist rocking her head back and forth the way a ship rocks on moving waters. She played the melody to Annabel as if with a needle she were sewing it through the ears of her soul, sailing along the vast waves of her heart like the captain of a ship, and moving her, deeply, traversing through her inner walls and gilding her with unfathomable droplets of pure light. Annabel heard nothing else other than the sounds of the instrument, for no other sound reached her; everything else fell silent, as if all other existing sounds, upon realising their unworthiness, yielded to the brilliance of the song of the strings. She looked beside her to her friends who were also lost in a similar daze. Then she looked up to the ceiling at the intricate carvings of patterns and the geometric forms with interlocking parts, and the brass lantern that hung from above like a tiny, iridescent planet, and the windows above where gentle splatters of rain began to fall. And as the swiftly moving notes of the violin swirled around the room, everything felt just right. She realised that it had been a long time since she had felt so comforted, so at peace. And she felt hopeful, too, more hopeful than she could remember feeling, hopeful about where she was heading, about the choices she was making and those she would go on to make; and wherever she looked, that hope lingered. She found it at the edge of smiles around her, in the flicker of the candle in the corner of the room; she found it in the tone of the violin that cascaded out of the instrument, and in the rocking and the swaying of the violinist. For a passing moment in time, she was in a place where only harmony existed, where problems ceased to be and where comfort caressed her, and it didn't matter to her how long this feeling would stay, for it was with her here, and for now, that was all that she needed.

Later in the night, in the cottage, the five of them relaxed and laughed together, a mutual jubilance bouncing off their smiles. They lit some candles around the room from which the light blended with the light of the moon that shone through the window. With some grooving jazz playing from a radio in the background, Annabel and Joan giggled amusingly as they reminisced about memories of their younger years. At some point, Giselle pulled out a deck of cards and she and Nolan taught the others a game, which shortly after prompted howls and cries of laughter. Then later on, Emile taught Joan some French phrases after noticing her intrigue in the language, whilst Annabel, Giselle and Nolan watched the stars glisten in the sky, lost in conversation. There was a sense of vitality in the air, a stream of enthusiasm enveloping the entire space, and they could all feel it. And as the day was coming to a close, and when the ambience had moved into quieter moments, Nolan and Giselle fell asleep on their beds, breathing deeply into their dreams. Joan was sat up on the kitchen counter and Annabel and Emile stood close by. They were conversing in whispers and decided — from their collective energy that made them reluctant to sleep — to go for a little night walk around the neighbourhood. So they put on their shoes, sank their arms into their heavy jackets and noiselessly stepped out into the freshly ripe night. They walked along where the lights of the street lamps followed, the wind breezing through them. After a few minutes, they arrived at wider roads where lanterns and seasonal lights hung across the road from the chimneys of the buildings, swooping across strings, painting an atmosphere from a wonderland. Curtains were drawn by windows, unveiling the beauty and homeliness of the buildings behind them. There they sat on the steps at the entrance of a small, quaint hotel, where dazzling sounds of a piano whispered through an open window above. Annabel told them of the dream she had on the train earlier that day, recollecting the details and the imagery of it, and although, with this hindsight, she wasn't able to sink fully into the depths of the oddity of feelings within the dream, she tried her best to paint it in words that made the picture of it crystal clear.

"Honestly, after everything you've told us," said Joan, "it sounds to me like you're letting go of fear you've been holding onto for a long time. The whole thing is just so fascinating." She sat with her elbows on her knees and her head rested on her hands.

Annabel smiled tentatively. "You don't think it's peculiar?"

"Not to me it isn't," replied Joan. "I guess it can be whatever you think of it. I think, to me, it's pretty magical."

Emile leaned in and looked at Annabel. "And do you remember the way you felt in the dream, knowing that she was going to catch up with you?"

Annabel thought in silence for a moment. "I remember I was frightened at first, but then that was washed away by something else, something bigger. And I found control of myself, and when I stopped running away, I guess I felt some kind of release."

Joan leaned back a little and looked up at the sky. "I think dreams tell us a lot about what's going on inside of us. The very fact that you stopped to finally let her catch up with you, that says something. Maybe you're letting go of the fears of her seeing you, *really* seeing you, in all of your curiosity and confusion."

"Yeah, maybe you're right. If I picture myself meeting her, I don't feel as scared as I used to, and now, it's more of an intrigue I feel above anything else."

She recognised this dream now with so much solidity. Somehow even talking about Nina now felt different than before; somehow she was accompanied by a newfound poise right beside her, and when she thought of Nina and the pursuit of unveiling the feelings of longing, she felt that she had released herself from the claws of it that had been so utterly inextricable before; but somewhere beneath her heart, right on the edge of her mind, there was still that feeling of longing that desired to be fulfilled; but it was subtler now, and it had less control over her temperament than in the past. And for the first time, as she watched its existence pulsating within her, she noticed something about it that had changed: unlike in the past, the feeling was no longer one of sadness, but one of hope, and this hope, although she had caught small glimpses of it in the past, had somehow blossomed. Now it was a sense of purpose to seek and discover the answer to a great mystery, a hopeful longing.

"And to see her once more," said Emile, "is that something you'd want?"

"Well, I'm done chasing after her now. I know that for sure. But if she did ever wish to find me, I know that would mean a whole lot to me. After all, I still do want to know her."

"She must be curious about you now," said Joan. "She painted you after all."

Annabel pressed her lips together firmly and thought as she looked up at the trees standing before the night sky. "In the dream, I became her. That's the part that doesn't make any sense to me."

"Do you ever imagine being her?" asked Joan.

"Not really. I've tried to imagine the thoughts in her mind, and I've tried to picture what it would be like to see things through her eyes, but I've never fantasised about being her in the flesh, no."

"Maybe you're relating to her now in a way you haven't before, no longer putting her on some pedestal, but now at a human level where you can empathise with her point of view," Emile chimed in.

Then Annabel sighed, but it wasn't a pitiful sigh, it was a sigh that signified her relief in getting to talk about these things with her friends. She could feel the warmth of them both, to her right Joan and her left Emile, and they were hearing her and guiding her with thoughtful detail to her feelings. Tuneful melodies of the piano came pouring down from above, and they sat there in quiet contemplation, allowing the sounds to wash over them and the lustrous air to breathe through, until a mellow sleepiness came over them and it was time to get back inside.

A shimmer of white light came breaking in through a tiny gap in the blind, falling onto Annabel's face, waking her to a new day. She had been sleeping lightly ever since the first ray of sun hit the sky, rolling in and out of dreams and waking up to see the lightening room, and when her eyes opened to the light, she knew she would sleep no more. The day was calling her, first from the light and then from the faint whistling of birds and the sound of a wind chime that made itself known with its gentle melodious notes. The others in the room were fast asleep, and the whistle of Nolan's snoring trickled along the room. She looked at the ticking clock in the upper corner of the room as the hand approached 7:37 am. The morning ambience was peaceful, and outside, sounds of roaming life came out through chirps of birds and horns of cars and bells of bikes. She quietly made her way out of bed and slipped into her morning robe. Then she stretched out her arms and yawned silently, and then drank a few handfuls of fresh water by the kitchen sink, before splashing the cold water onto her face. There was a tingling sensation in her chest, like a remnant of a feeling attached to a dream she could no longer remember, but it was fading with the cold water that met her skin and woke her entire being. With a mug of peppermint tea in her hand, she went over to the window and stared outside. The winter sun was rising just perfectly over the hills, its light touching the tip of the ocean that abided on the side, and the clouds were clearing out for a blue sky. Then a feeling came over her that made her want to be outside, so she slipped her feet into shoes, put her satchel over her shoulder and headed out. When the front door opened and she stepped out, the air that breezed across her face endowed her with a flair of life, a refreshment that gave her a gift of vitality. She walked along the pathway, making her way down the hill slowly.

About halfway down, she purchased a fresh orange juice from a little fruit shop that tempted her with its display of fresh fruits, and she continued down and sipped the juice along the way, lost in awe at the growing morning around her. The sun kept on rising until it was at its highest point, aligning in impeccable formation, enveloping the sky in its power and filling the town with light to begin the day.

With footsteps that moved as naturally as the air, she reached the coast. The wind was stronger here, and it brushed past her with a beautiful, magic sway. Moving closer to the ocean, she approached the sand. She realised that, before this trip, it had been a while since she had seen sand, and now that she was by endless heaps of it, she wanted to step into it; she wanted to feel the feeling of the countless grains underneath her feet, pushing into her under her weight, so she kicked off her shoes and left them on the side. With firm steps, she walked along the sand towards the calmly swaying waters, until the tip of the edge of a little ripple kissed the tip of her toes, slid over them and then enveloped her feet. Then she took a few steps forward, allowing the waters to weave through her, coming up to her ankles. Her eyes closed automatically, and without sight, the commanding touch of the wind and the sand and the cold waters pierced her like a needle through a cloth, and the enriching feeling of these wonders had intertwined with her, endowing her with a physical sensation she hadn't a slight recollection of feeling ever before — it was like a spring of rain giving life to wilted plants, and then it morphed into something that felt like the flutter of a bird's wings dancing around her heart. The moment was breathtaking, and for reasons unbeknownst to her, she wanted to remain there, where the ocean washed over her feet, deep in that sense of natural comfortability. Somehow she could see things clearer; just being at the tip of the great ocean, far away from where any of her troubles resided, gave her the ability to see past the restriction of walls she had not yet been able to see beyond, walls that kept her enclosed in the bounds of them. She noticed her emotions and how the intensity of them was rising just like the level of the water below, and as a tear trickled down her cheek she realised that she was thinking of Nina. She could remember the melodic, melancholy sound of Nina humming, and it sang across her mind, appearing to her along with the wind that reminded her that she was safe and sound. With a blink, she witnessed a tear fall, her own drop of salt merging into the salt of the ocean, becoming a tiny fraction of its greatness. She looked down at the swaying waters, the endless wobbles and ripples, the deep blue and the reflection of sunlight, the salt beneath her. She thought about how beautiful the ripples of light looked on the surface of the waters, dancing ribbons of white, sparkling and shimmering in sprightly sways. And she thought about salt, how on a wound it feels unpleasant, but then heals; how it stings, but then purifies. Then she thought about how, in some strange way, the impulse to find Nina was just like the impulse to dip her feet in these waters and feel the cold touch of it caress her skin. And maybe she'd never know the reason for her desire to find her, maybe she'd never understand those driving thoughts that led her to her so many times, but now, finally, she was fine with that. It was the fact of not knowing that pained her most in the past, the fact that she was without any understanding of her own feelings. But now she was letting all that turmoil sway along. Now she was learning not to force, but to flow, just how the water flowed, and to let things be, just like the water. She let out a great exhale, a breath that flew out into the air. And it was a big release, a freeing of energy that she no longer wished to hold, a goodbye to old feelings. And that misty cloud of breath led her eyes to the rising sun that rose from the other end of the ocean.

An Unforgettable Landscape

At the guest house, breakfast was served by Emile. He had laid out platters of finely sliced fruit, buns of soft bread and steaming tea and coffee on the table. There, the five of them sat around and ate together, munching into the succulent food, sipping the tea and coffee and passing the platters around to make sure everyone had enough on their plate. As Annabel fed herself spoonfuls of the reddest pomegranate, munching into the crunchy layers and tasting the delicately sweet juice, she was enriched with a burst of life, a certain freshness that had come ever since her early morning coastal stroll. They had planned to set out on an excursion, to wander down the endless trails of Cornwall and end up wherever the roads led them. So, after breakfast they set out, making their way down and around the hill until they reached a trail that cut through rows of frosty trees of great height that spread their hundreds of branches, appearing like wooden hands with numerous spindly fingers pointing in endless directions, and the tiny twigs at the tips of each branch scattered out like nerve endings connecting to the sky. They wandered happily, scarves wrapped around their necks and mitten gloves on their hands. The sky was a wintry blue with scratches of thin clouds frantically scattered around. Crinkles of frost on the dormant grass and thin layers of ice cracked below them, breaking under the weight of their bodies. When they had walked a while, Joan pointed to a river that glinted from afar, and they headed over to it. The river was quiet and still as if it were a picture on a wall, so still it appeared as a stainless mirror to the trees and the sky and all of the life around it, a mirror from which the image was reflected in a crystal-like glass, so clear that perhaps a bird would dive downwards into the reflected sky. Nolan attempted to skim a stone on the surface of the water, but instead, it fell right through at the sudden touch, quickly enclosed under the reflection, creating a perfect ripple that expanded out until it touched every edge. Then, again, the river found itself in stillness, returning to its everlasting place of calm; nothing could prevent it from returning to that place; it was uncompromisingly always finding its way back to its quiet place. They remained there for a little while, warmly huddled together on a bench, and when they felt the urge to keep on moving, they continued down the trail until they unexpectedly arrived at a stone castle. The castle stood mighty and tall, flaunting a great height and pointy roofs, and it overlooked a town from where sounds of human life seamlessly echoed. From the height where they stood, the view of the town seemed dreamy and inviting, so with keenness, they walked around the castle and onto a road that came across from the other side of the hill until they arrived at a bus stop; it was a wooden bench surrounded by brick walls and sheltered by a roof. There, they fiddled their fingers inside their pockets and bags for spare coins so everyone could afford a ticket, and soon a blue and white bus approached and stopped before them, and they climbed the steps and seated themselves at the back. The bus rocked as it moved along the turnings in the road that lead the way down the hill, stopping every so often at the bus stops. Annabel was staring out the window when she saw the castle come back into view. It was far away now, at the top of the hill, standing brilliantly over the town. The cottages below, with their slight wonkiness and thatched roofs, appeared in a pretty formation below the castle, and then a windmill and a scarecrow came into view. Overcome by an impulse that came like a sudden gush of wind, she went to pull out her camera, but just as her hand reached inside her bag, the bus turned down a bend in the road and the view vanished from her sight. The bus sped up its velocity as the hill became steeper, racing past the cottage homes and the fields and thickets until it went over a bridge built over a little streaming river, carrying them into the town. Then it slowed down to a halt and off and out everyone went.

They stepped off the bus and strolled along down the pavement of a road where there were plenty of other people passing by, some strolling through town, getting out into the pristine air, others walking alongside chirpy dogs. The glowing shine of the sun came cascading down in whips and waves through the thin, vaporous clouds. Someone on a bike with a basket of fresh bread zoomed by, and then a church bell resounded, sending out a melody to praise a new hour. After a gentle stroll down the lane, a glow of lamps attracted them from a window and, upon noticing it was a rather inviting antique market, they stepped inside. The entrance took them into a long corridor with colourfully patterned rugs leading the trail. There were rooms on either side of the corridor, each with its piles and collections of numberless items imploring to become possessions through vibrant and classic features. Everything was laid out so wonderfully that they couldn't resist stopping to admire the detail in each assemblage. They wandered through the rooms, getting lost in their worlds. Joan was drawn almost immediately to a patched coat on top of a shelf, so she stepped up on a mini wooden ladder to grab it, and in the instant she held it up to inspect it closely, she was bedazzled and threw it over her shoulder to hold onto. Giselle, Nolan and Emile browsed the many music items, skimming their fingers along the vinyl and tape records and all the goods in the music room. Annabel was in another room, alone, carefully going through a collection of postcards, photographs and books. In the middle of a pile, she found old letters that enticed her with their elegant flow of writing. She picked out a letter and held it up to read it. The ink had faded through the years but the words were still intelligible, and so her eyes skimmed the lines, scanning the many words briefly. It was written to a friend of someone who wrote about how they missed them and longed to see them once more. The words moved along the paper like a swift dolphin under the surface of water, smoothly, gracefully bringing back to life a world from the past. She looked through some more letters, and then from another pile picked out some postcards with paintings that captivated her. Then she found an old photograph of a dancer, the figure a blur in the midst of a pirouette; she thought she'd give this to Dusty. With a little more browsing, she found an old stained book with pictures by Vivian Maier, a photographer she admired; she held onto this one, thinking it would look nice with her other collections. Then, through echoes that floated in from a distance, she could hear faint sounds of music, and she walked into the other room to see Emile plucking gently on an old acoustic guitar, Joan standing by watching him, and Nolan and Giselle still lost in the thrills and surprises inside of boxes of tape records. The guitar in Emile's hand was worn out, but beautiful, with ornate patterns on the body, and as he played each note, small clouds of dust met the ray of sunlight that came in from a stained-glass window above them, creating a moving mist that rose to the rows of books sitting daintily on the bookshelf behind him. He was in a sort of flow, playing the strings as if the guitar had been made just for him. Then Annabel captured the moment in a photograph.

They left the antique store a little while later, items wrapped up in their bags, Emile's guitar sheltered inside a bag on his shoulder. Joan was wearing her new coat, the colours of purple and navy blue gliding with her movements. The road took them further into the town, and soon they reached a road where marigold lights glowed on the trees which lay in formation along the pavement. They walked on, and then, right beside the inn in which they were going to stay the night, in a little front garden behind a wooden gate, Annabel noticed a framed photograph standing on an easel, displayed towards the road. She stopped as soon as she saw it. In the photograph, coastal oceans glistened thousands of sparkling lights like tiny white crystals floating on the surface; on the side, someone was standing by, their blue dress blowing in the wind, their arms up towards the sky and the sunset beaming out on the horizon. The photograph was astonishing, but there was no name attached to it, only a tiny note on the bottom that read *June, 1988*. In the front garden, there was a walkway that appeared to lead be a bakery of some sort. Noticing Annabel's spark of interest, the others huddled around her to see what she was seeing, and after a moment, Emile opened the fence gate and, with an investigative smirk, gestured with his head for the others to follow.

Walking in, warmth came over them immediately and a ravishing smile from a kind-faced old woman behind the counter greeted them.

"Welcome!" she said brightly. "What can I get for you?"

There were loaves of bread and cakes and all kinds of baked goods on display, from sweet to savoury and a plethora of shapes and sizes.

"I'll take one of these," said Emile, pointing to a pile of cinnamon buns. "Anything for you guys?"

"One for me too, please," said Annabel.

Joan, Nolan and Giselle ordered some of the savoury pastries, and then the woman, with a congenial smile, gave them their treats on miniature woven bamboo baskets.

"That photograph outside, did you take it?" asked Annabel as she sniffed the aroma of her bun.

"Oh no, you wouldn't be able to tell but that's me in the photograph," she replied. "It was taken by my husband, a long time ago now."

"It's beautiful," said Annabel. "Does he still take photographs?"

"No, not anymore. It was something he did a few decades ago. He never really shared his work with many people. It was only quite recently that I started revisiting all of his old work, and I was taken aback. I never fully appreciated them in the past, and I thought what a shame it was that all these wonderful photographs have been sitting here unseen for all these years.

So I've slowly been in the process of getting them printed. Each week I put a new one on display outside."

"What a lovely idea!" said Annabel, grinning.

Just then, an old man in paint-stained jeans came in from a door on the side. He was holding a dustpan and a brush, and there was a careful attentiveness to his step. The woman caught his attention through a wave and gestured her hands in sign language. Her facial expression emanated a cheerful glisten. He responded with a similar expression on his face and then turned to see Annabel and the others, lifted his glasses up the line of his nose a little and took a moment to acknowledge them before signing back to the lady.

"He says he appreciates it. He says it makes him glad to know that people are now connecting with something he did such a long time ago," the woman said. "Mick's a little shy about his work. He didn't want me to put them outside at first, but I told him there would be people who would be touched by them, just like yourselves, and that made him reconsider."

"I'd love to see more of his work," said Annabel, "if it's possible."

The lady excitedly signed again to Mick, and he responded to her with a timid smirk and a little nod of the head.

"We have a laptop somewhere upstairs with all of his work. Take a seat and I'll go and grab it," she said. "I'm Beverly, by the way."

Annabel introduced herself and the others and then they went and sat at a table. Mick walked around the room sweeping the floor and smiling to himself.

They were munching into their pastries when Beverly came back, a clunky laptop in her arms. She placed it on the table and took a step back. "Here they are."

The others gathered around to see as Annabel flicked through the photographs slowly and with effortless concentration. Every single photograph was a beautiful surprise, each telling a story so unlike the rest of them but with a stroke of brilliance that was evident in them all. There were places, things, colours, humans, and creatures, all captured in a series of spectacular scenes. Annabel was set alight by a flame of admiration that took away her voice, speechless at how in awe she was at such moving pieces of art. Somehow these photographs captured the essence of each setting so greatly; somehow they captured the happenings of the world and everything in it so brilliantly, so boldly and masterfully. The magic of the collection was endless and completely unpredictable. And there was so much to see: a bird captured mid-flight as it hovered over the horns of a deer; the hand of a child reaching to touch flowers under the shadow of a willow tree; a hunched-over elderly woman on a train knitting a scarf, her glasses ricocheting the light from the moon through the window; an abandoned treehouse in the middle of a sunset-lit forest. The magnificence of each shot was persistent, never ceasing to amaze, and at the final photograph, the astonishment within Annabel was one that scarcely came, that rare feeling where one is touched by a thing of so much beauty that it that grabs them and screams life into their soul.

"They are just magnificent!" she cried with a real spark of enlightenment in her words.

And the others were enthralled too, nodding their heads in agreement.

"I'm so glad you think so," said Beverly before signing to Mick who was standing behind the counter, his eyes squinting with affection.

Then Beverly took the laptop and held it to her chest. "It just makes me so happy to see people appreciate Mick's work. He never took them for the adoration of others; it was always a personal enjoyment for him. But I've seen recently how his work can touch others, and to me, that's such a lovely thing to witness."

And touched was precisely what Annabel was feeling as they walked out, waving goodbye as they exited through the fence gate, the photograph on display shining brightly.

The sun was preparing to set, and their tired bodies were calling them to rest, so they headed into the inn. They walked through the front door and checked in at the reception. Inside, it was small and filled with an incredible warmth which quickly impelled them to remove their gloves and scarves. In the back, there was a little garden with a porcelain floor, and sheltered inside of a pent shed were a handful of bikes for the guests to use.

Up a creaking wooden staircase that twirled upwards to the floors above, they made their way to their room, laid down on their springy beds and fell into a much-needed afternoon doze. But, once again, Annabel did not sleep, and whilst the others drifted into their unconscious worlds, she lay awake, and though she had fallen into the calmness of the afternoon, she was alert in her mind, occupied by her flourishing thoughts. Streams of memories of Mick's photographs, bright and stark, flowed into her mind, guiding her steadily into waves of inspiration, until it became a time of magic, a moment where wonderful ideas sprung to mind and creativity approached on the fluttering wings of luminous, floating clouds of good ideas. She thought about the landscape she had seen earlier that day, and how she wished she had captured it before the bus turned down a bend in the road. And, with a swift surprise, she was met with an idea, an idea so excellent, so true to her instinct, that it only landed on her mind for a second before she sprung to her feet, wrapped up warmly and, as quietly as possible, dashed out the door. She flew down the stairs, out to the garden, took out one of the bikes from the pent shed, walked it out onto the road and then jumped on and pushed her feet on the peddles. She paced up the hill at a steady speed. The early shadows of darkness were beginning to spread over the town, but the street lamps and winter lights and the dim residue of illumination in the sky kept the town lit up. She peddled and peddled, and as she reached the steeper part of the hill her legs began to slow down the pace, but she continued, persisting in her task, until she reached it. And there it was, the perfect sight, the scene she so fervently wished to capture, there in the sunset, embezzled with the blazing colours of the setting sun, this time even more beautiful than before. And then she took the photograph, capturing it right in the midst of its pure, pristine perfection. Now she had caught it, and how great it was to hold it in her hands, knowing that she'd now get to keep the scene for as long as she wished. She breathed a grand breath and released it back into the air, seeing the wintry fog disperse over the hill like the seeds of a dandelion spreading out with the wind. She turned the direction of the bike so it faced down the hill, and then sat on the seat and lifted her legs off the ground, allowing the hill to guide her down its body, along with whatever speed it was that gravity would impart. Within only seconds, her feet were flying, piercing through the gale like a needle through a cloth, and her ears heard nothing but the mighty winds that travelled north to south, surrounding her and hugging her with unseen arms. And the speed at which she moved caused her heart to beat to the rhythm of exhilaration. And then the feeling of the moment rose and became breathtaking. As she moved rapidly, she remembered the musing of experiencing things as if for the first time, and, all at once, it was as though the realisation of it had actualised within her, for she understood it in a way that the words alone failed to make her understand. Now the wind was communicating through its cold sound, whispering and crashing all around her, and it submerged her in its benevolent grasp, breezing between every strand of hair like dry waves of moving water. She had felt the gushing wind a million times before, but now it was melting all over her in a way that she had never felt. And where the wind touched, a thrilling joy did too. She felt alive, and she smiled at how she cherished the freedom, how wonderful the sensation of the speed was, the soft way in which the bike carried her, the pathway before that revealed itself anew with every second that passed, the atmosphere around and its ubiquitous beauty, and the air — she marvelled at how beautiful and fresh the air was, how it never ran out or ceased to be, and how it was there for everyone; it was just as much for the strangers that whizzed by as it was for her, or the birds in the sky flying overhead. And how beautiful the sky was, too, forever picturesque and unendingly putting on a spectacle to look up towards.

When the evening came around, the candle that flickered on the windowsill cast a bobbing shadow on the wall, and amongst that light, and the glow of a colourful stained-glass table lamp, all five of them ate dinner together. This time Nolan and Giselle had cooked a stew, and it soothed them and warmed them from the inside out. The nighttime was growing in, and they all shared a mellow feeling, a tiredness that came from a long day. The trip had been truly satisfying for them all, and now it was coming to a restful close.

After dinner, in the aftermath of venturing out into the hallway, Joan made a discovery: up the wooden stairs that curled upwards, and then through a narrow corridor with slightly crooked flooring, there was a roof terrace, prettily decorated, open to guests, and with a rather spectacular view of the town. Together, they sat up there, looking out at the dazzling scenery. From afar, headlights of cars moved through the thick layers of the bushy trees, like tiny, luminescent creatures searching for treasure through thickets of leaves; and tiny lights from hundreds of windows on homes shone in tidy rows along the dim horizon. Nolan and Giselle imitated the screeches of the foxes lurking on the dark roads, warbling and wailing a cacophony of sounds. Joan stood nearer to the edge, a blanket wrapped around her, swaying side to side, silently looking out to the view. Emile sat on the floor, crossed-legged, his guitar resting on him and his hands carefully strumming along the strings. And then the wind came around and bounced onto the guitar and then carried along with it the melody that played, sustaining the sound of the notes, launching it out to the atmosphere. Startled and astounded, everyone gathered around to see and hear what was taking place. And Emile, laughing in a daze of surprise and amusement, strummed each chord. And the wind that came continued to carry the chords along, drawing out the sound for a while longer until it vanished into the air.

Soon, the bright stars glinted heartily in the painted night sky. They looked up to notice, and up there, they saw an aeroplane skim the edge of the crescent moon. And then, after what had been an evening to be remembered, the atmosphere had become quietly calm and the nighttime enclosed everything.

Dust and Dinner

The week that followed came and moved along gently into the past. It began with a thick fog that arrived suddenly, lurching over and sprawling throughout the city, submerging everything in its large, milky haze that floated along, moving imperceptibly, unfurling and then quickly silencing the streets. And then it passed by and left the air to return to purity, and then splashes of heavy rain fell and soon after the rain turned to sleet and the sleet to snow, and the snow settled on the ground for a single day, before melting as the temperature rose just a little and the sun shone glimmers of winter light.

For Annabel, each day moved slowly and gradually, and within that gradualness, there was a serenity that somehow she could often find when she focused her mind on the present, in the very moments as they arrived, whether she was at home, or work, or out and about in the corners and cracks of the city. Fortunately, she didn't find herself lost in any worries or stuck in any spirals of bothersome thoughts during the week. It turned out that the trip to Cornwall was one of a great catharsis after all, for since she had returned, a smoothness with which she moved through the days had come and ceased to leave. She laughed more than she was used to, and suddenly it felt more natural than ever to smile at the little things around her; and whether it was in small glimpses, or musings that required great reflections, she often stopped to recognise the world she had built around her and intended to cherish everything within it. She spent quite some time with Emile, tucked up cosily at home or wandering through the city, admiring the winter festivities all around, and occasionally Nolan and Giselle would join and together they would venture and enjoy each other's company. At times she had heartwarming conversations with Dusty on the kitchen table over a cup of tea and a slice of cake; this too was something she cherished, often looking forward to it after an exhausting day when all she wished to do was unwind with good company. And she enjoyed her alone time too, taking time out of her day when she could be with just herself and her mind; at times she read books underneath a blanket; other times she would listen to music or watch films by a flickering candle; on some days she would take small naps in the afternoon or relax by the view of the window, and whenever she found the time, she'd go on walks alone with hopes to discover something new in her path. At work, days were getting busier; customers came in at every minute, and although most shifts were tiring and consumed much of her energy, she enjoyed them, especially as either Muna or Adia were there to accompany her with their homely presence. It was clear, through their sweet words and unvarying attentiveness to her needs, that they were grateful for her help and regarded her as a significant part of the pottery shop; and they cared for her too, and she for them.

Occasionally, Annabel spoke to Edith over the phone, letting her in on the happenings of her life, big and small. She had promised her that she'd spend a weekend with her and Judy back in Edinburgh, so one mid-December morning, she boarded the train and set off on the journey. It was the first time she had visited since leaving, and although with the return came a strange feeling — a mixture of nostalgia and melancholy simmering beneath her in a thin undercurrent — she was eager to see her family, Edinburgh, and reminisce on the earlier chapters of her life, this time surrounded by the very walls of her past.

The train exited the harsh blackness of a long tunnel, the light of day abruptly piercing through the windows. The station was approaching, and Annabel, with squinty eyes adjusting to the light, looked out the window to see outside. The skies were overpoweringly white, covered entirely with clouds that appeared thick and solid, and the sunlight, with an immensely wide presence, came melting through the background, lighting up the sky and everything below.

Stepping onto the platform, she looked at what lay around her. This quiet town, along with everything inside of it, was the place she called home for the longest time, and what a fascinating thing it was to be there without that sense of ambivalent belonging she once felt. The chimneys, with their unvarying structures and pointy tops, stood in tightly organised rows behind the station gates, and as she walked over a bridge that arched over the tracks, she could see clumps of trees and village homes and the weak colours of all the distant buildings amongst the pointy street lamps. It was a beautiful place, and being here after a while only made her realise this even more. As she walked, there was a sense of restfulness in the way she moved, from the swing of her arms, all the way down to the steps of her feet, and she smiled with a sense of pleasantness that came from the sweet familiarity of merely being there; but all the while, there was a noticeable sense of disconnect: some close affinity she had once felt with the place was now removed, leaving her with the impression that this was a place she would no longer instinctually call home, but one she would gladly pass through and re-visit when in need of a certain familiar tranquillity.

When she walked out the exit, Edith was there, standing tall in a feathery coat that fell all the way to her ankles, with a smile on her face that she rarely revealed. And then, as if pushed by the wind, Annabel's arms opened and so did Edith's and the two of them embraced each other with a hug, and though it was brief, Annabel couldn't help but take joy in the shortly-lasting embrace of her mother, for she couldn't remember the last time she had held her so dearly.

"Oh, look at you!" said Edith, gripping her arms. "Are you happy to be back?

Annabel smiled and nodded. "Of course. I've missed you."

'I've missed you too," said Edith, before letting out a small sigh of pleasure and then opening the car door. "Now, come inside dear."

The journey was a winding one, the car roaming nimbly down the curves and twists of the small town roads that Annabel knew so well. An air freshener dangled from the rearview mirror; it was the shape of a tree in a dark, pastel crimson colour and filled the space with a musky and, to Annabel, almost sickening scent of an artificially sweet forest. It was a scent she had known for the longest time, a scent with which she associated the sickly journeys to and from school as a young girl. Then, coming swiftly into the spotlight was the smell of Edith's perfume, another scent that was permanently ingrained in her memory, almost as if she could sense it from miles away; it was a fruity, flowery aroma with a harsh bite and somewhat of a hint of strong liquor right at the tip of it. Faint music from the radio played in the background, and Edith hummed quietly along to the tunes, her head often turning from the road to Annabel so as to acknowledge that she was actually there with her. Annabel gazed outside at everything passing by. She saw places she had known her whole life, places she used to visit often: convenience stores, post offices, little gated parks, bookstores, old rustic coffee shops tucked away in the corners. Then Edith huffed a little as they passed a market stall where together they used to visit to pick up fresh fruits.

"What a shame they're closed! I'm sure Mary would have loved to see you. She always asks about you whenever I visit. She tells me she misses seeing you with your basket full of pomegranates," she said brightly, turning the wheel.

"Oh, Mary! I always looked forward to seeing her on the weekend mornings."

"And you haven't forgotten Angus and Bryce from the tavern?"

"Of course not," said Annabel, laughing.

"Well, they always ask about you and how you're getting on in such a big city. Everyone asks me about you. They all miss seeing you around here. I tell them all you're getting on just fine."

Annabel listened as her mother told her about all her old fellow neighbours, people she was so accustomed to seeing often, and then suddenly not at all; it was quite a peculiar thing, to hear about all these people she saw routinely for years and years before she moved away, these peripheral characters that, for so long, would pop up in her day-to-day life, with their features and their mannerisms that she could still picture so distinctly, with voices still marked in her imagination.

They swivelled around a roundabout and slowed down on a road with a small bump every few seconds.

"You must be hungry," said Edith. "I've got a pie in the oven. I'll fix you a warm slice as soon as we get home."

"That sounds amazing!" said Annabel, her eyes widening at the thought of eating.

The windshields wiped away specks of rain that landed gently on the windscreen, pattering quietly on the glass, along with the sound of Edith's fingernails tapping on the steering wheel, a continual rhythm, so constant and persistent in timing it was almost unsettling. Delicately, Annabel leaned her drowsy head on her mother's shoulder, sinking slowly into the plush texture of her coat. The coat was so soft that naturally she moved her head around tenderly to feel it touch her ear. She could hear the wreathing of the fabric brushing past her ear as she moved her head around in minuscule movements. Somehow the sound reminded her of the ocean, and though muffled and muted, the swishing and swaying permeated through her just like the waves of living waters, soothing her into a tranquil state. And it reminded her of the wind too, like forceful gusts pouring through a forest of trees, smoothly carrying her into a space of calm meditation. She was glad to be there, to have a moment alongside her mother, glad to be visiting the town she used to call home.

Amidst a recognisable whimper of a creaking door, they stepped into the pleasantly warm home. Annabel looked around as she slipped out of her shoes, then she hung her coat up on the rack and slowly entered the living room. Everything was perfectly placed and neatly organised, from the alignment of the ornaments on the windowsill to the positioning of the candlesticks by the fireplace to the books sitting on the shelf. She quickly noticed that something was different, something prominent had changed, but she wasn't quite sure what it was exactly; it wasn't the brand new gleaming string lights set up along the windows, nor was it the Christmas tree with its shiny red baubles, or the humungous bouquet of purple perennials sitting in the crystal glass vase on the dining table; there was a distinct air to the home, a slight but evident newness about it she wasn't quite familiar with. Edith, whilst pacing to check the pie in the oven, was on the phone with Judy discussing the evening plans. Her voice bounced with a certain spark, one that scarcely ever made itself known. Annabel walked through the hallway and then up the stairs, hearing her mother's conversation falling away into the distance, running her two fingers up the bannister the way she used to as a child. At the top, she made her way towards her old bedroom, placed her hand on the doorknob, turned it slowly and then swung open the door to let the room reveal itself. The curtains were closed and only a fraction of light entered, so she walked over to them and flung them open, a cloud of dust scattering out in the new light. Then she turned around to see the room, and stood there, motionless, her eyes scanning from corner to corner. This was once her magical territory, her space of vastness, where she could spend time alone in eternal possibility. It appeared that everything was exactly the same as she had left it; not a single item had been moved, not a single thing had been changed. She walked across the room, purposefully stepping on a particular point in the floor that let out a whining creak — one she could recall as if it were recorded in her memory — and then sat on the bed. With her weight on the mattress, she noticed that the feeling of the fabric was a lot stiffer than her bed back home, more solid and with less bounce. She looked at the wall on her left above the bed frame, and all of the cutouts, photographs and paintings scattered across, each item with their own memory attached to them. Then she lay down, flat on her back, her feet dangling off the edge and pressing firmly into the carpet, placing one hand on top of the other over her chest. With a swift pull of air, she breathed deeply in and out, and then let her mind wander as she gazed at the ceiling and all of the minuscule chips and marks scattered across in an erratic disarray like bird droppings. Under the bed, she felt something touch the back of her feet, an object with a soft touch, but she wasn't quite sure what it was, so she heaved herself off the bed and bent over to see. A cardboard box, dusty from plenty of time in solitude, was just at arms reach. She had forgotten about that box and it had been a long time since she last opened it; she had pushed it under the bed many years ago, into deep darkness. She pulled it out and turned over the top flaps. Inside was a surplus of things: used pens, withered key rings, ripped paper receipts, worn-out scraps from magazines, little toys and collectables from her childhood, old letters she had received as a child and adolescent. She looked through some of the things, inspecting them between her fingers. Then she picked up a handful of the letters, browsing briefly through their contents, and then took out one letter that caught her attention, pinching the edges delicately so as not to risk tearing it. It was written on a pale-pink, almost tissue-like piece of paper, with a blue marker in a shade so light that the words had almost faded, but were just about discernible to a focused eye. It was a letter from a much younger Joan, thanking her for a birthday gift, and at the bottom was an illustration of the two of them holding hands — an endearing little piece, their heads as large as their bodies. Giggling, she decided she'd take that one home with her as a keepsake, so she folded the letter and placed it neatly in her pocket. This wasn't a box she often perused, and she looked a little longer, twiddling with all of the memorabilia, before closing the box and pushing it back under the bed, patting off any dust from her trousers as she stood up. Then she walked towards the window, noticing the thin sheet of frost on the edges of the glass, creating a hazy border on the outline of the outside scene, and the sweetest little robin sitting on the oak tree outside. On the windowsill, some old photographs inside brass frames sat charmingly. She picked one of them up; it was a photograph of her younger self, caught in the middle of an excitable movement, her cheeks rosy as a red sun. She had Nina's blue scarf wrapped around her neck, and she was grinning brightly. It was a photograph of natural delight, a glimpse of a real, precious moment. Holding it between her two hands, she blew away the thin layer of dust on the surface, and, floating in her mind inside the memory in the frame, traced the outline of herself with the tip of her finger. Suddenly, she heard the sound of movement and the tapping of fingernails on the door behind her and turned around to see Edith standing in the doorway, peering through with one finger on her lip suggesting both her urgency and reluctance to intrude.

"Annabel, dear. I've left your pie on the table downstairs. Don't let it get cold, okay?"

"Oh, thank you! I'll come and eat now," replied Annabel. "I'm just looking at some of my old things. Do you remember this photograph?"

Edith walked over to see. "Oh that one, yes it's lovely."

Annabel looked up at her quizzical eyes and her laid-back smile.

"Do you remember this scarf?" she asked. "I wore it all the time."

Edith crossed her arms and furrowed her eyebrows as she leaned in a little closer.

"Let's see... Yes, I do remember it," she said before leaning back. "Listen, I need to make some calls now so I'll be downstairs. Would you help me with the dinner in a little while? We have quite a few guests arriving soon."

"Yes, I'd be happy to help."

"Great," said Edith, nodding. "Please don't forget your pie."

Then she lightly patted Annabel's shoulder — one of her odd gestures, this time suggesting she was glad to have her around — then ambled out of the room. Annabel stared at the photograph for a little while longer, trying to picture the moment with as much clarity as possible, and then smiled to herself as her thoughts branched out to other connected memories. Then she remembered the pie that was waiting for her, carefully placed the picture back on the windowsill and made her way downstairs.

By the time the evening came along, they had cooked a wonderful dinner together, an assortment of different plates of delicious foods. The guests were on their way, coming down to celebrate the holiday season, and so they both rushed upstairs to get dressed. Annabel scurried through her wardrobe for a nice garment to wear for the evening. She speculated for some time as she browsed through her hanging assemblage of clothes she had left behind, before deciding on a dungaree dress and throwing on a colourful patterned cardigan over it. Then she put on a pair of emerald earrings and sprayed herself with a perfume she found sitting on her desk — an oaky, sweet clementine scent. Suddenly, from afar she could hear the sound of Edith calling her, and with a tiny nudge of concern, she stepped out into the hallway and followed her voice into her bedroom.

"Ann, would you help me zip this up?" asked Edith. She was sitting on the bed, pointing to the zip at the back of her blouse.

"Of course," replied Annabel, smiling and rolling her eyes endearingly as she walked over to her.

She zipped up the blouse and Edith thanked her, her words morphing into a breathy sigh as she reached to grab a hair-comb on the bedside table. She was hunched forward and her movements were slower than usual, lacking her usual swiftness and a certain vivacity that usually came over her on a celebratory evening such as this one. It was clear that something was wrong with her; it was as if a gloomy grey cloud hung over her, just above her head, keeping her in a dismal shade.

"Here, let me," said Annabel, holding her hand out and bending down to sit beside her.

Helplessly, Edith handed her the comb and then she began combing through her hair, the tangled clots breaking with every stroke. There was some pleasantness in this that Annabel found, something satisfying about tending to her mother's needs, this simple deed of care that would only happen with a certain vulnerability, something Edith only ever showed in times when she could no longer hold up her tough walls with which she guarded herself.

"When I was little you used to comb my hair just like this," said Annabel.

"Every day," whispered Edith.

Annabel noticed that her eyes were avoiding any contact with her own, and there was a quietness and hoarseness to her voice, an indication that she was on the verge of tears.

"Is everything okay?"

Edith said nothing, staring straight at the wall for a little while. She breathed in as if to speak but then bit her lips and let the words fall out in a breath. The seconds of silence that followed felt thick and unnerving, and then Edith looked at her and then looked down at her own hands, her fingers twiddling on her rings.

"What is it? You can tell—"

"I've decided to move homes," she said, still looking down.

Annabel's eyes opened wide. "What? Why?"

Edith looked up to her. Her eyes seemed sharp and wet. "This house, it's... I don't feel right being here anymore, alone, without you to share it with. It's too large just for myself."

Annabel was surprised to hear her mother say this. "But you love this house, don't you?"

"Well, recently I've found myself uncomfortable in such quiet solitude. It's lifeless here, Annabel. I don't hear your voice anymore echoing down the hallway, or, you know, your songs playing on the turntable, or your footsteps on the floors. You being here with me made this place a home for me, and now, it just doesn't feel right for me to be here alone. Sometimes when I walk through the corridor I remember you as a child, running up and down, giggling. Some days, I'll be cooking in the kitchen and I'll remember how you used to sit on the counter and watch me. And then reality slaps me in the face and I'm reminded that none of that exists anymore. And, there are memories attached to every room. I can't even go into your bedroom anymore without feeling like I want to cry."

"But I'm here now," said Annabel, with reassurance in her voice. "But a visit is not the same. After this you'll go back to your life — and please don't misunderstand me; I'm glad you found a city and a home and a life you adore so much — but I'll be here alone again. And this place, it's just far too large and desolate for just me. I've talked to Judy about it. She thinks I should re-decorate the space, and I've tried, I really have, but still, this dreariness doesn't go away. I even tried gardening. And I hate gardening. The garden was your place, you loved it, but without you here there's no need for me to have it." She stopped twiddling her fingers, took a sharp breath and looked up. "So I've decided to move, and I don't know if I'm making the right decision but I don't want to carry on living here like this. And it's a difficult decision for me to make and I'm incredibly attached to this place, but I think I've made up my mind."

She sighed once more and then placed the back of her hands to her eyes to catch her tears. Instinctually, Annabel leaned a little closer to her and pulled her in. She took her hands in her own, feeling the wetness of tears on her fingers. She had never seen her mother cry like that, nor had she ever comforted her in this way.

"Hey, listen, it's okay. We'll get you a new place. Somewhere you feel right at home. We can decorate it together if you like, and hang up all the old pictures. We'll just have to make sure that there's a spare room, or that the sofa turns into a bed, so I have a place to sleep when I visit you."

Edith stared ahead as if transfixed on her daughter's consolation. Then Annabel held her hand a little tighter and noticed her mother's eyes begin to change shape, changed by a tone of hope; and then a smile, though small, peeked out of her lips and her cheeks and then her eyes and she chuckled a little before coming back to herself and sighing. Then she puckered her lips to the side, took a sturdy breath in and then, all of a sudden, sat up and wiped the residue of tears from her eyes. Her face had turned neutral.

"Right, enough of that. I've got to finish the food," she said in a serious tone, and then walked over to the door. "I'm glad we spoke about it."

Annabel watched her leave, then looked at her own two hands and the glisten of tears smeared across them. A chime of a clock in the corridor sang a melody across the home, and as the tune played, she questioned if this were the first time she had seen her mother cry. She recalled old memories of catching her upset, but within each of these memories was Edith's determination to hide her tears. But in this very moment — even though the emotion was one of sadness — to witness her unguarded vulnerability was like catching a glimpse into a purity deep inside, a real, untainted character, almost like witnessing a swan reveal its true form.

The guests were soon to arrive. Annabel was in the dining room, aligning the glasses with one another, rubbing away any noticeable smudges with a handkerchief. She could hear Edith talking to herself in the kitchen, in that low, breathy voice she did when speaking her thoughts aloud, usually as a response to nervousness. The doorbell rang suddenly, shattering the quiet, and Annabel skipped to the door and opened it to a happy surprise. It was Judy, standing there looking dazzling with a bottle of wine in her hand and a delightful wide-eyed, beaming smile across her lipstick-painted lips. They hugged tightly, Judy screeching like a playful mouse.

"It's so great to see you, Ann! Honestly, I feel like it's been years!" she exclaimed whilst she took off her jacket. "Now, is it too early to pour this wine? I'm itching for a glass."

Annabel showed her to the dining room and Judy screeched again in delight at the wonderful set-up of the dining table, clapping her hands in tiny bursts at the beautifully detailed display of plates, silverware and candles. She popped the lid off the bottle, poured herself a glass of wine and got to drinking.

"There's so much you have to tell me, Ann! I want to know everything about your life in London!" she said excitedly.

They spoke for a little while. Edith was in the kitchen touching up on the last-minute details of the food. Annabel told Judy about London and the main parts of her day-to-day life there, and her trip to St Ives and how much she loved it. Judy had always been a good listener, and as much as she loved the chirpy sound of her own voice, she responded to the words of others with steady attention and a sweet gleefulness, sometimes gasping at every minor turn of a story. So she listened, before sharing some of her own stories, which were mainly just work-related endeavours — although she always made them exciting — and then followed by some neighbourhood gossip she couldn't resist throwing in. Her mood was wild and vivacious, and Annabel enjoyed this and found herself giggling at her wine-enhanced spiritedness. Then in the midst of the conversation, the doorbell rang just as Edith was alighting the final candle on the table. The first guest had arrived.

"Here we go," said Edith sturdily, straightening her posture before marching off to the door.

The dinner commenced smoothly amidst the honey-coloured glare of the candle lights and a smooth selection of music from the radio, sprinkling the ambience with a pleasant quaintness that remained through the night. Guest after guest arrived at the door; at first, it was an uncle, an aunt and their small child.

Annabel had not seen them in a very long time; she realised this through the enthusiastic cheers of greeting at the door, cheers suggesting that much time had passed since their previous meeting, and when she knelt to greet the child she remembered a past holiday dinner where he was crawling around on the carpet like an excited puppy, attempting to hoist himself onto his feet and failing at every attempt; now he was standing there in his little polished shoes and the smallest red bowtie, smiling shyly and hiding behind his mother's legs whilst peeking out to say hello. Then shortly after, their cordial neighbours came to join, and then a few of Judy's friends, and lastly, another aunt and some of Annabel's older cousins, who walked in, shoulders back, with confident countenances and hunger for dinner in their eyes. They both nodded as they greeted everyone formally and then gave Annabel a strange hug that avoided as much physical contact as possible and felt oddly identical. There was always some sort of unpleasant air that came with seeing these cousins; she found that as children their connection was open and natural and usually involved them playing games and chasing each other around the home, but it was a playfulness that withered as they grew older no matter how much she had tried to relight a connection with them on occasions like this.

Once everyone was seated, Edith laid out the food on the table, positioning the platters in a way that gave every dish, plate and glass a perfect amount of space between them. She was smiling and attentive, and as Annabel looked into her eyes, she noticed just how polished and put-together she seemed; no one would have known that, just moments before, she was sobbing away her sadness. She was also quick to add more food to the plates and refill the glasses, moving around hastily and watching the guests' plates like a hawk, and after the savoury foods had been eaten down to the scrapes, she brought out the dessert and popped open some more bottles.

Judy was the real spirit of the room, the loudest one to cackle at every joke made, the fastest to speak out of a small moment of empty silence, the first to laugh at a spillage of red wine on the white linen tablecloth. She was bringing in new topics of conversation and speaking in expressive bursts and chuckles and gasps and responsive sounds between every bite and sip. The conversation seemed to be moving naturally around the table which made the night move through time quickly. Everyone was getting along, and there was a merriness in the air, and though it was nice to be there and be with her mother and Judy and amongst all of the smiles and the friendly chatter, Annabel couldn't help but wonder about the oddity of such a night. Here she was, sitting at a table, celebrating a holiday with good people, friendly guests, and she looked at all of their faces around the table, their smiles and their roving gazes, yet she didn't truly know them, nor they her, and despite their interest in her endeavours and keenness to display some absorption in finding out about her life, at the end of the evening, all of the guests would go back to their own lives and forget about the bulk of these fleeting interactions, perhaps never even speak again until the next seasonal celebration. But regardless, the night was pleasant, and it moved like a film, scene-to-scene, consisting of listening to the chitter chatter, sipping on red wine and nibbling on the packets of chocolates that Edith was dishing out perpetually, attempting to talk with her little cousin in small, broken words, playing a game of chess with her uncle who had an unfaltering solemn expression on his face throughout, and then watching each and every guest leave with full-stomachs and sinking eyes as they waved goodbye and headed out the door.

Now that all the guests had left and the environment had simmered into steady quietude, Annabel sat on a cushion on the floor by the fireplace, the heat at a perfect level on her face. She stared into the dancing fire, at the tiny sparks of light shooting out of the core, at the glowing embers, hearing the crackling sounds that reminded her of her childhood. And behind her was the faint chattering of Edith and Judy in the kitchen, discussing the evening and their observations of the guests. As she stared into the burning heat, everything around fell into a quiet hum where everything but the fire was dimmed and she could hear her internal discourse. She was reminded — through a whimsical excitement that flew through her — of her home and the life that awaited her. This would perhaps be the last time she would sit by a burning fire in front of this fireplace, she thought, and that saddened her, but when she thought of home and her future, the sadness began to evaporate. She stayed there for a while, huddled up beside the warmth as if it were a companion, and she could feel the unseen force of the fire touching her face, nourishing her with an incentive to think kind and pleasant thoughts. And the fire blazed on until it reached the end of its dance.

A New Truth

The chirping of birds and the gentle pitter-patter of the rain came falling onto the window. And the gentle winds, quietly howling like a sad ghost, came through the cracks. Faint footsteps echoed from downstairs, and the shrill whistle of the kettle came rising through the floors. Annabel woke from her sleep and opened her eyes to a booming morning in Dean Village. That peculiar confusion, the one that occurs when waking to an unexpected surrounding, came over her, and then a little air of motion sickness crept up on her as if something was being stirred behind her eyes, moving in slow sways. With a little push of effort, she flung herself onto her feet and stretched her arms out wide. The blinds were drawn, and opening them gave refreshing light to the room. The trees were wobbling and swaying outside, and she watched them move, the same way they always did, the same motions and gesticulations on the same road she had looked out to for years. And she saw the homes on the other side of the road, the red bricks and the brown chimneys and the curtains and the stained-glass doors. The image of it was engraved in her memory.

It was early, earlier than her usual time of waking up on a free day, but she had planned to head back home in a couple of days and she wished to relish every bit of her time there, perhaps pay a visit to Joan or some friends she hadn't seen in a while. So, with a bit of a wobble to her step, she made her bed, washed, dressed and then fluttered down the stairs to join her mother for breakfast. Edith was sat at the table, engrossed in the weekly newspaper, her expression hard and stern as she sipped on black coffee. Her work required her to be out of bed bright and early and she refused to work if she hadn't yet had her morning coffee and got her fix of the local news. She had never been a natural morning riser, and her demeanour would often come off as cold or bitter in the early hours, but on this day, she smiled as Annabel entered the room, evidently pleased to see her.

"How was your sleep, dear?"

"Great actually! I slept like a tired bear. And you, are you feeling better?" replied Annabel, before chugging down a pint of water. As she drank she could feel the coldness moving down inside of her, giving her a new glint of life, feeling a tiny bit better with every gulp.

"All great. Listen, I was thinking we could do something nice tonight. Maybe we can go out for dinner, or see if any shows are playing at the theatre. Just the two of us."

"I'd like that very much," said Annabel, leaning over a pile of fruit and biting into a shiny red apple. "I'll probably head out very soon, but I'll be back in the afternoon!"

"Perfect. I finish work at five," said Edith, looking back to the paper, then quickly up to her again. "Oh, I forgot to tell you yesterday, there's a little pile of letters for you in the hallway cabinet. They've been piling since you've been away."

Annabel's face lit up with a bright spark. Somehow it hadn't even occurred to her to check for letters. Speedily, she made her way to the hallway cabinet and opened it to a small pile of envelopes, each with her name on the front. She put on her jacket and shoes and placed the letters in a small bag she dangled from her shoulder.

"I'm going out to read them!" she called out as she dashed out the door, munching on the apple.

Briskly, she moved down the steps and out through the gate, and then waved to a neighbour as she strode down the pavement and round the corner to a wooden bench at the edge of a small patch of greenery she knew so well. Shiny foliage, mahonia and beautiful berries with tiny speckles of frost on the surface came through a bush from behind and trailed along the bench. Sounds of life in the distance buzzed through the open spaces, and children's laughter, playful and bouncy, ricochetted through a brick tunnel ahead. And the cold was alive, shimmering in the air all around, potent but gentle and refreshing like a water fountain.

She held the letters between her hands, placed a few to the side and then opened the first one, tearing the envelope delicately so as not to rip it, and then pulled out a piece of paper. It was a letter from a friend of hers who was living abroad, a response to a letter she had sent many months ago. She sat there and read, carefully and with every grain of focus in her, smiling easily at the handwritten words, and when she finished reading she folded it back up, carefully placed it back into the envelope and then beside her underneath the pile. The next was a card from her aunt and uncle, wishing her a happy holiday, with a black outline drawing of a snowman under falling snow. Another was a postcard from a family in Portugal she lived with as an au pair a few years back. She read the writings adoringly in a half-whispered voice and then took a little break and pondered and placed her hands together and breathed warmth into them. There were a few more letters to go through, and she held the next one in her hand. The envelope was a biscuit-beige colour, the touch of it textured as if it were handmade. On the front, her name was written in handwriting that swooped and fell and glided through each letter with poise — a style of writing she could not recognise — and it was sealed with a crimson wax stamp with a beautiful botanical garland design. Stunned by its appearance, she placed her eyes fixedly onto it, studying every corner of detail, then, attentively, opened it and pulled out a folded piece of ivory paper. She opened it and began to read.

Dearest Annabel,
I've been staring at this blank piece of paper for a while, thinking of what to say to you, wondering how to put the noise in my mind into words.

I've tried to search for you, but so far my attempts have been unsuccessful. It seems that getting a hold of you is tricky. So, my search has now led me to write to this address. Somehow I still remember it after so many years. Do you still live here? I doubt you do. But maybe this letter will fall into the hands of someone who will know how to reach you.
The night I saw you, I was so swept up in shock, and for a while, I didn't believe it was you standing there before me, and though even now I cannot be certain, something deep inside me tells me it was you.
There's so much I want to know, so many questions running through my mind. But I'll refrain from putting them all on here, although I hope that we'll be able to get there eventually.
First, I'd just like to know that you are okay.
I hope to hear back from you,
Nina

Life stood still, stiller than a painting on a wall, less capable of movement than the coldest ice. If she could have seen herself objectively she would have wondered how words could have smote her with so much ferocity, how the contents of a letter could plunge into her with an impact so great that it caused everything around to become sucked into non-existence. Her fingers grasped onto the corners of the paper and her eyes did not move from the name written at the bottom of the page. It seemed there was no doorway out of the reverie she found herself in — it was a hollow, magnificently humungous depth with a force that dragged her in, powerfully and unrelentingly, to the lowest point, a ground of utter incredulity, where she remained for what could have a been a single second or hundreds of them, and a force that then threw her out vehemently, back into the world. Her ears registered not a single sound, and then only a toneless ringing, or perhaps it was more like a hiss, far beyond the limits of what she could see, and then, after a timeless instant, the hiss became sucked into the wind, and then the ambience came back to life, driving into her from all around. Then she was up, suddenly standing on her feet, the letter firmly held in her hands. A spit of gentle rain began to fall, and just as a droplet landed on the surface of the paper, smearing a speck of ink just slightly, she folded the letter and placed it into her jacket pocket, then she packed the other things away and started moving back towards home. She needed so much to be back home, to think where there were no distractions, so, with firm, heavy footsteps she walked, whilst the ground below felt as if it were extending in length, stretching out further through the distance. She made it along the pavement, past the gate, through the front garden, up the steps and straight back inside, where the air was warm and hushed. She took everything off — her shoes, her bag, her jacket, and emptied her pockets, sat at the bottom of the steps and took out the letter once more. And she read it again, but this time, from someplace in her mind, she could hear that mellifluous voice reading it to her, layered with echoes, beautifully delicate, with urgency and a silken sweetness. At the bottom of the page was the address of a place in Madrid, most likely where Nina currently resided, she thought. She read the letter a few more times over, scrutinising the words and whispering them aloud to herself. Disbelief flooded her, and then, pushing through the currents came something new, a feeling that made her eyes water. It was a joy she felt, a torrential rain of delight, of excitement, and then, in a matter of seconds, confusion came kicking in, a whirl of bewilderment. She was feeling everything, altogether in an absurd amalgamation. From the other side of the wall, she could hear the turning of pages and the clicking of a stapler and the tapping of fingers on a keyboard; the sounds brought her mind back to her environment, and once again, she folded the letter and placed it into her pocket. And then she stood up, her running thoughts at a halt, then walked through the corridor and into the kitchen. A touch of frosty air came in through the slightly-open window, and bright, distant echoes of a neighbour playing the saxophone simmered through gently, as well as the laughter of children playing in a garden next door; but somehow every sound fused into one as she found herself wrapped in the contents of the letter. She sat at the table and opened the letter again. She could see the words as if they were being written before her eyes, the bold, black ink swirling through each word in tiny connected journeys, weaving through the page. And she could hear Nina's voice blooming inside of her mind. As each minute passed, she fell greater and farther into the words of the letter, and when she finally remembered to breathe deeply, she breathed as deep and as extended as she could manage. Now that the initial shock had passed, she began to wonder how this was all possible, how Nina could have possibly known her, and how in the world she was without a single memory of it. These feelings of longing she had felt for all these years, all of them, had been for a reason, it now seemed. But what could all of this mean? Something huge was missing. Now she dwelled in rumination so deeply it felt that not a single thing could pull her out. But then Edith walked into the room. She walked in hastily, so focused she didn't even notice Annabel sitting at the table. Swiftly, she turned on the kettle and then reached into the cupboard, grabbed a box of coffee and placed it firmly on the counter, and as she turned around to get to the fridge, she squealed with fright as she saw Annabel, who looked up to her, her eyes emitting sheer perplexity, like a spotless window revealing a glimpse into her inner conundrum.

"What's the matter?" asked Edith, her voice feeble with concern.

But Annabel had no words to respond with, and instead, she looked up to her, her eyes soaked in vulnerability, seeking an answer. Then she put out her hand, almost mechanically, and passed the letter to Edith who, with no hesitation, grabbed it and lifted it to her glasses. With every fibre of her attention, Annabel watched her read it, the intricate movements of her head and the way her eyebrows caved in and the movement in which her lips parted after a few seconds. She studied her vigorously, so caught up in the intensity of the moment, the moment that felt as if it were not real at all, but instead, a surreal dream from which she was seconds from waking. And then she noticed her own heartbeat pounding vehemently, like a deep rumble in the earth, a great shake that would cause rivers to tremble and birds to flee from trees. Then Edith looked down at her, without making a sound. Her eyes were cold, as though coated with a thick outer layer of ice. Annabel could feel a vibration forming in her throat, almost like a persistent humming growing from within her, travelling through heavy waters, upwards to her mouth to form words that she hadn't yet realised she was preparing to say. And then she spoke.

"Do you know who she is?"

Thick, unnerving seconds passed. Edith did not respond, but stood there, hard and cold as though a spell had been cast on her, rendering her mute and motionless.

Then Annabel spoke again, words conjured by a force within the depths of her chest. "Do you?"

Edith, still unmoving, slammed her eyelids into a forceful blink, appearing to knock herself out of whatever was keeping her from speaking. She opened her mouth to speak, but she did not answer the question, and her voice was deep and firm. "Where did you see her?"

"I found her," Annabel responded quickly. "I was searching for her, and I found her."

"Why? Why were you searching for her?"

"I briefly met her once. It was during the time Judy took me to London, nine years ago. I caught sight of her from afar, and I don't know why but I was drawn to her. I wanted to connect with her in some way. So I approached her. She's the one who gave me the blue scarf. The one in the photograph. But it was a brief encounter. And recently, I... I searched for her and I found her again."

"But, why?" asked Edith, sharply. "Why did you go looking for her?"

"I don't know." Annabel looked down, then to her mother's face and then at the letter, firmly grasped in her hands. "There was something about her that enticed me, and I wanted... I just wanted to see her again."

"And what did she say to you?" Edith's voice was beginning to sound urgent.

"Nothing. We didn't get to speak. I went too far and found myself in a bad situation, so I left before any words were spoken. That was the last time I saw her."

Edith crossed her arms tightly, the letter between her hand and her chest, her mouth tightly shut, sealed by a tightly sewn thread. Her face was solid, unfaltering and completely emotionless, and she let out a sharp breath, but it was wordless, cut off at the very beginning of an utterance, as though her mouth forbade her to express her thoughts. She was unshakeable, impossible to see through. Not once had Annabel witnessed her with such a broken expression, such a sunken countenance. She could tell that Edith was holding something from her, restraining her words and inhibiting herself from letting it out, and she watched her and waited for her to say something until the urgency for her to speak became so immense that she just could not refrain from shattering the silence.

"You know who she is, don't you?" she asked in a broken voice.

Still, Edith did not say a word, let alone move a muscle. The solidity of her face was startling, and her breath was utterly silent. Then she opened her mouth to speak and then faltered before pulling out the words, and then she sighed and looked once more at the letter. One shaky hand moved up to touch her lips, and the other held the letter tightly as she skimmed the sentences once more, and then quickly folded it up and handed it back to Annabel. Now her face displayed emotion, a distraught and somewhat melancholy air, but it wasn't quite a sadness, nor did it appear to be anger she was emanating. It seemed she was struggling to hold back her words, words that pushed eagerly behind her lips until she couldn't keep them in anymore.

"Nina was your carer," she said, her face still as a solid object, "from when you were a baby, up until you were about three and a half years old."

Silence. Total numbness. That was all. That was everything that lived in the moment, all that could be. Everything else had collapsed, crumbled into thin air and vanished. Gone was any shred of perceptivity, gone in an instant. Annabel could feel nothing but the beating of her heart, and she sat there with not a single thought behind her steady gaze. And then, like a sudden crash of an ocean wave, thoughts came from all over the place, frazzling, shooting all around. A new truth had been unveiled, shattering everything before it. It was the flesh of a new conception, the shotgun impact of a devastating, brilliant, utterly bewildering revelation. She breathed in sharply, realising her breathing had come to a halt as she gasped for a taste of air, and staring, unblinking, straight into her mother's eyes, she felt a sudden shift, a positioning of compounds, an alignment of understanding come into place, and with it, a continuum of sensations came flooding in, like a rainbow spectrum of emotion all at once.

"Why haven't you told me about her?" she asked in a voice that shook with a broken tenacity. "How could you keep that from me?"

She could feel her eyes welling up, but she couldn't quite tell if tears were brewing. Edith walked over, pulled out a chair and sat down. Then she placed her hands on the table, interlocked her fingers tightly and exhaled a breath of discomfort, looking up and then around as if searching for a place from which to somehow pull words out of the air. Annabel did not move her eyes from her mother, observing the way she tightly squeezed her hands together and nervously bit her lips. And then Edith shuffled in her seat and sighed a heavy sigh. "It's more complicated than that, Annabel. There's so much... There's so much I—"

"Then tell me. I want to know everything." Annabel crossed her arms and sat back in her seat, her eyes wide and sodden, her heart pounding, and although the hunger for an answer was beating robustly from within her, elevating a little more with every second of silence, she somehow found a calm place in her steady breath. Edith stood up, walked to the counter and poured herself a cup of steaming black coffee, took a gulp and then came and sat back down; the entire time, Annabel's eyes were on her, following her like the prying eyes of an alert animal.

Edith placed her hands together again and then breathed in a long inhale, exhaled sharply and then cleared her throat, preparing to speak. "Nina responded to an advertisement I put out when you were a baby, just months old. I was in need of a carer to help me take care of you. Judy wasn't around at the time and my mother had recently passed, so I was looking for an extra pair of hands to watch over you at times when I had to be away for work. I remember we spoke over the phone and she seemed polite and well-mannered and I invited her over. So she came, and she met me, and she met you, and shortly after I hired her."

She paused and took another sip of coffee, the sound of the gulp loud and sharp. Annabel could say nothing, but watched her in silence, waiting anxiously for her to continue. Then Edith cleared her throat once more and proceeded to talk.

"She was only eighteen at the time. She was so young, and smart, and she carried herself with this sense of composure that I felt was way beyond her years." Edith's voice was sonorous and sad, and she was staring ahead so deeply. It seemed she was perhaps reflecting on memories she had been hiding away for the longest time. "She lived not too far away at the time, in Glasgow, and she started helping me with you once or twice a week. And it was great. She was excellent with you. She would stay with you for many hours, sometimes all day whilst I worked if I needed her to. I felt very lucky to have her. As the months went on I started to trust her more and more.

Eventually, it got to a point where she would take you out, bathe you, tuck you into bed at night. And she was so conscientious, she knew it was a job and she worked well, but the way she cared for you was so... she was tender with you. You two, you had a bond, and I knew that you were precious to her."

She paused and took another sip of coffee, then breathed in to speak. "Time went on and she would come and go, and I noticed how much she cared for you and how much you loved having her around. She started coming more frequently too. She was there when you started crawling, she was there for your first words, and so, a little after your first birthday, I asked her if she'd like to work more often, to which she told me she'd love to. It was... Tuesdays, Fridays and Sundays. Yes, that was what we arranged. And she was always here, on time. Never once did she have an excuse not to turn up. Not once. And that's how it went for a long time. You grew very fond of her, and every day I noticed just how much she cared for you."

Edith stared ahead for a handful of seconds without speaking, then looked at Annabel with a hollow expression, took a sip once more, and then straightened her posture. She was vulnerable, more vulnerable than Annabel could remember ever witnessing her.

"So, much later on," she continued, "when you were two years old, almost three, I offered her a full-time job, and she took it. On weekdays she worked and lived here in the spare room, and on the weekends she would leave and go to Glasgow, sometimes to London to stay with her brother. I started working longer hours and I was in the office a lot of the time, but we both took care of you at different times of the day. She was here so much but she never really built a life here. I remember her working on her art a lot when she wasn't with you, and she was always quite protective of her work and her space. She was always making things, privately. Her room here became a sort of creative haven for her, I guess. When she wasn't with you she was painting and when she wasn't painting she was with you.

But, soon after there came a time when you two became inseparable, and it was getting more and more difficult to take you away from her. I started noticing how much you longed to be around her when she was absent, how you smiled and the way your eyes lit up when she walked into the room. Oh, the way you smiled with her. You never smiled at me like that, and, I suppose a big part of me became envious, and bitter." Her voice had become colourless. "I treated her wrongly and I'm ashamed of myself for it. I often raised my voice at her over the smallest things, and I... I ridiculed her when I was in a bad mood. I remember your third birthday came along, and she couldn't make it. You waited at the door for her, hoping she would walk through, and I distinctly remember how you cried for her when you discovered she couldn't be there. Something broke in me that day. I don't know what it was, but I saw that she gave you something I couldn't, and it broke me... I was so bitter..." She paused once more, sat in a moment of desolate silence, and then began again. "Anyway, more time passed. I sometimes used to wonder why she was still around considering the inexcusable way I treated her, but I guess the adoration she had for you conquered the tribulations I caused. So time went on. You two were so entwined. And then, one day, I noticed the drawer in my room was left slightly ajar, and the things inside were not as I had left them, but I had so many things in there that it was hard to decipher what was missing. I couldn't put my finger on it. But I didn't think about it for too long, and soon after I let it go, but then as time went on I started noticing things were going missing, belongings of mine around the house. At that time, my stress levels were high and I thought I was losing my mind because I was looking for things and then finding that they weren't where I had left them, and then I thought perhaps I was making it up, or misplacing things. It happened variably for months and months, until one day — it was a winter morning, I remember this day so well — I couldn't find a particular necklace. It was a necklace my mother gave to me and I scarcely wore it, but it was my mother's birthday and I specifically wanted to wear it in memory of her. I knew precisely where I had left it — inside a little box hidden in the back of one of the cabinets in my room. But when I checked, I saw that the box was gone. So I searched everywhere else it could possibly have been, but it was nowhere in sight. I was furious and I blamed Nina. She was out at that moment and when she came home I had packed her suitcases. She denied ever taking anything but I was enraged and indignant and I fired her and kicked her out of the house and told her never to return. And I threw away every trace of her, every photograph of the two of you. I kept telling myself that I wasn't going to let someone steal from me, no matter who it was, and I don't know why I didn't consider the possibility of it being someone else — I guess my envy of her and my anger blinded me — but at the time I believed that removing her immediately was the only solution. I remember she... she tried to say goodbye to you but you were asleep in your room and I refused to let her go in to see you. So she left, in tears... She would call, every day, asking to see you, to say goodbye to you, and each time I told her never to call again. She even turned up here one day unexpectedly. She wanted to give you a gift of some sort, and I screamed at her and sent her away." Edith's voice began to tremble and a tear trickled down her cheek. Her eyes emanated an air of disgust, almost like a layer of self-hatred. A moment of silence filled the room before she began again. "You had a piano teacher, Marcia. She would come to our home once a week to teach you. One day, many months after I had fired Nina, I caught Marcia snooping in my room, going through my belongings." Edith let out a whimper. "It was her all along. She was the one stealing from me all that time. Of course, I was furious and had her leave immediately, and, as for Nina, I—" she put her hands on her cheeks, rubbing her fingers on her temples, and then placed them on her knees and bit her lips, swaying slowly back and forth, "I did nothing. I was too embarrassed and I had too much pride to apologise to her. And I didn't want her back. I had too much hatred of her. It pained me too much to have her around. She resorted to writing letters to you from time to time — I guess this was her last attempt to reach you — and I returned every one of them, for many months, until we stopped receiving them. And it hurt you to be without her, I know it did. You often cried for her and I used to tell you she had gone far away, and I distracted you from her every day until you mentioned her less and less. It wasn't until much later, perhaps two or three years later, that I tried to write to her. I was thinking of her at the time and I felt guilty. I wanted to somehow apologise to her for all I'd done, but still, my pride wouldn't let me. So I left it. I decided to move on. Eventually, you forgot about her, and I tried my best to forget about her too, and that's what I did and what I've been doing all this time. Occasionally something reminds me of her and I'll think of her and wonder how she is, but for the most part, I left her far away in the past."

Edith huffed and sighed, and then nothing was heard other than the distant winds bouncing onto the chimney. Her story had rendered Annabel voiceless, without concrete thoughts that she could form into words with which to respond. She was stunned, wedged right in the middle of a spiderweb of stupefaction. The air in the room had changed; something about it had become sticky and humid, making it barely possible to digest the vastness of what had now been spoken. This story — uttered through words that hammered down and then sliced with the sharpness of daggers — had struck something at her very core. She sat there, still, watching Edith's hovering eyes, unable to unpack her thoughts and make sense of how she was feeling. And then she saw herself objectively in that very moment, sitting at the table with her mother, and how from the outside it would have seemed to be an ordinary scene, but now everything had changed, drastically, in ways beyond anything she could have anticipated.

A Great Novelty

Patterns, textures, edges, hard and soft, light and dark, colourful and colourless, big, bright, green, blue, red, yellow, white, buildings and bridges, forms and thorns and round bushes, big fields and small flowers, fruit and leaves, smooth and harsh; her eyes watched everything pass by in rapid blazes amongst tranquil scenes, staring right into the centre of the hypnotic setting of whizzing land, the moving substances wreathing into each other like ink in running water. And the magic of the movements fleetingly lifted her mind afloat from the waters in which her thoughts swam. Things were different now, far different than she would have ever predicted.

What happened in Dean Village changed everything. She had never seen her mother in the way she appeared as she told her of Nina; she was like a statue, drenched in some sort of potent affliction, holding her emotions in and then releasing fragments in small whimpers when it all became too much to keep inside. The conversation she had with her mother over the kitchen table had, at first, pushed her into turbulence. The only way in which she felt capable of reacting was to be silent, to let the story sink into her mind; and when it finally did, she could do nothing but wrap herself in a scarf and sit outside on the steps in the garden, where she could allow herself to be and think in the flow of natural air and digest what she now knew. It was a long time, perhaps hours, that she sat outside, staring into the treetops and the spaces between the branches where the light poured through, and then eventually she found herself laying on the grass and looking up to the sky. Discovering the letter alone had bestowed on her a huge surprise; just the knowledge that Nina knew of her existence was enough to render her speechless, to send her into a whirl of rumination, but with what followed it was like having her entire world inverted. There was so much to fathom, so many things to come to terms with, and so she let herself do just that until her mind wandered away and her eyes drooped and by the time they opened again, she was sprawled on the grass, waking up from the cusp of a dream, and she looked up to see the approaching dusk and then down to see a large coat thrown over her before turning her head to see her mother sat at her side, her cold hand resting on her own. But Edith spoke no more — perhaps she felt there was nothing more for her to say — and instead, she sat there, quietly settled on the grass, looking out to the darkening sky and now and then down to Annabel, who waited a few minutes before moving any part of her other than her blinking eyes. And when she felt the urge to move, she sat up, and with soft words she began to speak, driven by a keen urge to say all the things that were now churning within her. She felt it was her turn now to speak into the flame that palpitated between them. Now she wanted to be listened to. She began by telling her mother about the first time she saw Nina, sitting alone, wearing the blue scarf; she told her about the way she felt in the aftermath, of the allure and the fascination that pulsed from inside of her and how she could not fathom such indefinable feelings; she told her about their transient interaction, her awkwardness and the oozing curiosity she saw written in Nina's eyes, about the scarf, and about how she held onto the memory of that evening for the longest time; she told her about how she had recently come close to making contact with her again, about how her impulses led her into a harrowing situation, and about how she ran away immediately after those unforgettable seconds in the doorway; and she told her about Nina's painting in which she saw herself, and how she wondered long and hard about why she had painted her. And lastly, she told her of how, in recent days, she had somehow managed to let go of the bulk of all the strain she had been holding inside for all those years, that impossible longing that, at times, had control of her, and how she had finally accepted that perhaps there was no answer to her questions, no shining light at the end of the elusive quest, and how, in letting this go, she had finally allowed herself peace. And when she arrived at the final thread of words, she looked around and realised they were sitting in almost pitch-black darkness; she had wandered so deep inside the light of her memories that she hadn't even noticed the absence of light around herself. Edith was still and soundless, unspeaking, her spectral silhouette unmoving and her facial features submerged in rigid shadows, but Annabel could just about see that her hand was up somewhere on her face and she was looking down as if she too were somewhere other than there in the unlit garden. She wondered if it were herself or her mother that the evening had brought more shock upon.

Out there in the bare night of the garden, only the wind spoke, and after a short moment it grew colder and sharper and began permeating through the layers of fabric, and so they went back inside, walking closely beside each other. An emotionally-drained Annabel gravitated to the warmly lit living room and threw herself onto the sofa, and Edith followed her in and sat next to her. Now Annabel could see her face through the glare of the lamp; the aching, stinging edge that earlier lay within her eyes was no longer there, and now she seemed to be passing through an influx of feelings in motion, heavy and light, dark and bright, sweeping through passages only she herself knew behind the glint in her eyes. She was sitting there, her hands on her lap, her guard down, looking ahead into empty space. Her mouth fell heavy and sorrowful, and it seemed she was incessantly on the verge of speaking but failing to find adequate words. But Annabel did not rely on any more words from her, and whilst looking at her in the glowing light, she was seeing her in a new way, as though she was looking *through* her and not *at* her, and somehow she felt no bitterness towards her. And then, without an ounce of forethought, she leaned in and wrapped her arms around her; it was the only way at that moment she could think of to show that she felt no contempt, to express her desire for tranquillity between the two of them, and it was with her arms that she found it, and through the interlocking of her hands, and in that calm place of being held back by her mother's arms, those two suspended limbs, sturdy and firm with eagerness; through all of these things, they had reached an equilibrium. She heard Edith whisper a mumble, some sort of apology and a small cry of remorse in heavy, gluey words, and then she felt the fall of tears on the nape of her neck, and when they pulled away she saw, up close, beyond the outlines and the wetness and the chestnut browns, a beam of some sort, a small glow, like a ray of essence pouring out from the crux of her; it was a tenderness, a softheartedness, gently exuding out from the shape of her eyes, a part of her mother she'd never known. There was nothing more to be said, nothing to convince each other of; everything that needed to be expressed had been expressed. Then Edith wiped her tears, and as she did so, Annabel could read a perplexity in her demeanour, an incredulity, and she thought perhaps Edith was wondering why she was not projecting any resentment towards her, why she wasn't throwing a rage of anger in her direction, but somehow, whatever fragments of resentment that had been there had suddenly became washed away in the bonding of their arms and their eyes. And shortly after, in the nurture of the wordless connection they had found, Edith relaxed into repose, and after some time of being there, she leaned into a quiet rest. Annabel laid her down gently and covered her in the warmth of a blanket. She looked at her, her blank eyelids, her eyes beneath them lost in the trance of sleep. The pace of her breathing was calm and steady. She was rested, no longer wrapped in the hard shell she so often kept around her. Then Annabel switched off the lamp, leaving her in nothing but the washed-out glare of the moonlight coming through the curtains, and made her way to her bedroom. Standing in the doorway, looking into the darkened room, the faint outlines of things appearing like blocks of shadows, she thought about how this would most likely be one of the last sleeps she would sleep in this room. And somehow, the very moment she placed her weight on the bed and her head fell onto the pillow, she dozed off effortlessly.

"Can you tell me more about her?" she asked her mother the following morning.

On the kitchen table, they were seated together, eating breakfast, accompanied by the sweetest sound of an old, rusted wind-chime dangling on the tree outside. There was a lightness now in the space between them, a calm air of trust, of understanding. Edith was wrapped in a dressing gown, her hair down, and her face was brighter; the stale tiredness that appeared under her eyes was no longer there.

"Well," she began, "Nina was kind. She was thoughtful. Oftentimes she had a smile on her face. And she was bright, and talented. I remember, when you cried, she sometimes would sing to placate you, and her voice, it was just lovely, and it soothed you in ways I never understood."

Drawn deeply in, Annabel could somehow picture the words clearly and effortlessly, as if the scene had been painted precisely from an infinite pallet of colours in her mind. Edith stared at some point downwards, appearing to be in a zone between the edge of a smile, an empty stare, and a trance-like serenity.

"She was gentle too. And I remember her hands; she used them in ways I had never seen before; she would speak with them; she sort of moved them around in patterns along with her words. Sometimes it was as if she were tapping on some kind of piano in the air. And her appearance, it was colourful, it was creative, bold; she wore beautiful, deep colours, these flowing garments, and, I remember, she always wore earrings, magnificent earrings, and they were large and they dangled from her ears. I remember vividly the sway of them when she'd turn her head." Edith spoke with a steady concentration and then lightly chuckled, her face transfixed in memory. "I remember, sometimes, on warm days, I would stand here by the window, and I'd look out to see her laying with you in the garden. She'd put down a picnic blanket and the two of you would lay together, right out there in the middle of the grass, often for hours. I remember she would read children's books to you, and she'd show you paintings, photographs, and music... In the evening, when you were asleep, she'd go for walks alone, and she'd come back here and paint in her bedroom, for hours at a time. And she often sat by the windowsill in the living room; I'd see the shape of her from behind the curtains. I guess it was her place to ponder. She always seemed to be absorbed in something, whether it was you, or a piece of art, or people, or anything. She was fascinated by the world."

There was something profoundly heartening about hearing her mother speak of Nina in such a way; it almost didn't feel real, as if it were a mirage, a vivid hallucination that could be wiped away instantaneously, as if perhaps to press firmly against the eyes and to pinch the skin at the back of the hand was an appropriate response to this convincing illusion. But, nevertheless, it was beautiful, and perhaps that's what made it nearly unbelievable, the mere fact that it was too beautiful to believe.

"Will you write to her?" asked Edith after a moment of quietude.

"I will," replied Annabel. "I think I just need a bit of time to come to terms with everything first. All of this has been so sudden. I'm feeling a whole lot right now."

The sun beckoned through the windows, and then its hands of light struck the thin, frosty surface of the glass and then came through to touch their hands that were rested upon the table, and they noticed it, and smiled together along with the smile of the glisten and the glow that now filled the room.

And that was how the unravelling of the story of Nina came to be. Annabel spent her final day in Dean Village with her mother, just the two of them at home, talking, eating, and just being in each other's company. There was still so much Annabel felt she needed to digest, and she knew it was the same for Edith; everything had happened so abruptly, without any warning or preparation, and perhaps this quiet time to be together in reflection and let it all wash over was exactly the thing they both needed before she departed.

And so, the views from the window passed along smoothly through the vistas and the spectacles of land and rural civilisation. Trees flew by in a vast parade falling sideways incessantly, moving on and on, briskly and unendingly, each tree coming and then vanishing in a flash as transient as a blink; and the overflow of fast motion — the feeling of steadily moving into what was approaching, again and again — engendered a new energy upon her. The stream of things being left behind meant only that new things were approaching. Something bright kindled within her, and she found herself tapping her hands on her knees to the rhythm of alacrity. She was approaching something remarkable. A lot of things were about to change, she felt. A great novelty was calling her.

And when the train arrived in London, she took a deep breath before stepping out onto the platform. Walking through the train station and out to the city street, passing the signs and stalls and cafés, amongst the endless rows of moving crowds, she started to smile to herself, effortlessly, as if the edges of her lips were lifted by two invisible strings. Now, in everything she looked at, she saw what she now knew, unable to think a single thought separate from the excitement that was beginning to pulsate within the core of herself; now the whole world, through the vast coalescence of things around, was reminding her, and through the layers of sounds around, was whispering to her, what she now knew, bringing it to her mind again and again. And within each footstep she took, she bounced on the ground with exuberance, and her feet stepped triumphantly along the pavements as though magically attached to springs. And then, sitting on the bus that carried her home, through the traffic lights and the buzzing streets, this city around her, a place she was beginning to know so well, now revealed itself to her eyes with a remarkable freshness. Joy was in the air, real joy, and she could laugh, and she could cry, and as a tear trickled onto her open smile she noticed she was doing both. She looked around at everything beyond the windows. Not a single shade of blue bloomed as freely as the shade of blue in the depths of the sky; not a single child had ever seemed happier than the child outside with an ice cream in one hand and a balloon in the other; nothing had glistened more profoundly than the ricochets of the white lights on the satin dress of the person through the window of a bar. And to look around, here and now, to just be and breathe and look and feel was a great world of contentedness, a feeling of equanimity. Everything made sense; the puzzle pieces had found their place in the grand picture; the fog and haze had made way for a clear day; the painting had been made whole with the final flick of colour; what on the surface seemed to be a day of the ordinary was now one of wild adventure; now the roads were growing and unravelling to remarkable surprises. Passing by a lake of ducks, coots and swans on a lake flaunting effulgent streaks on its surface, sinuous and bright and shimmering like broken pieces of moonlight, she held her two fingers up as if to hold a swan between them, and her fingers, now pierced by the sharp edges of its beauty, held the splendour of a magnificent creature between them before brushing past the pretty surfaces of trees as the bus rolled on. And then, stepping off the bus in her neighbourhood, the ease with which she breathed now was as liberating as the wind. She walked along her road and approached her home, her dear home she cherished. And whilst walking up the stairs, she thought about just how much she adored the great height of her comforting abode. Then, up on the fifth floor, she turned the key in the lock, noticing the clicking sound of the door opening, that sweet sound of home that belonged to her. Dusty was sweeping the hallway floors, humming along to the songs of Ella Fitzgerald, and Annabel greeted her and then ran upstairs to her bedroom, placed down her bags and flung herself onto her bed, curling her body into the duvet and then happily unfurling her arms and legs, spreading her body out wide like a starfish on its favourite rock. The walls around cradled her in tender arms, and the ceiling, tall and mighty, gently watched over her. Now, laying there in nothing but stillness, she saw her thoughts on the ceiling. The stories her mother had told her, of Nina, were designing themselves vividly in her mind until it was almost like recalling a riveting dream one could never forget, or reliving a memory one revises now and then with hopes that it will linger forever. This pondering sent a tickling shiver through the depths of her, and now she suddenly felt the weight of the impossibility of such a thing, the tremendousness of it all, and perhaps this was the belief of it beginning to sink in now, and to be so incredulous about it was just the next step in the process. Nothing in her life had been so out-of-this-world bewildering before; this had superseded the threshold tenfold. She placed her hands on her chest, instinctively. Her heart thudded in a way she didn't know; it was brisker, but not racing, and it wasn't quite beating at an anxious pace, nor was it pulsing with restlessness, but the speed and the intensity that it carried was much greater than usual. A moment later, she noticed the rising and falling of her chest, the expansion and contraction of her lungs beneath the layers, the accepting and releasing of oxygen, the to and the fro; and she observed without the distraction of intervening thoughts, and with this undisturbed observation, the rate of her breathing slowed down, naturally, until the bobbing of her chest was similar to that of the rock of a boat on a quiet lake; and as her movements became stiller, her heartbeat calmed too, and all the while, her limbs, heavy and loose, sunk into the soft surface the way the falling sun sinks into the ocean in the coastal horizon. Gently, she closed her eyes, and in an instant, she was floating, hovering, swimming in musings of diverse colours, somewhere that was partly there, in the fixed location of the weight of her body, and somewhere else, somewhere separate from her vessel. And through a hazy veil, like looking at some dusky scene in the reflection on the surface of her mother's vulnerable tear, within the currents of an invention of her mother's memory, she saw herself, much younger, and Nina beside her, outside in the garden, laying down on a blanket thrown over the grass, their heads almost touching, strands of their hair perhaps gently interlocking. And though their voices were indistinct, arriving to her with the faintness of sound through a thick wall, they were laughing together, and speaking amongst one another breezily and with relish, but what they were saying was unintelligible from the position from which she peered, as if their words remained solely between Nina and her past self. As she followed the movements of Nina's fingers, tracing the blue sky as she spoke, she wondered how distinctly Nina remembered moments such as this one, if she could remember the sound of their blending laughter, the affection of the silence between them, the power of their mingling presences. She wondered, deeply: did Nina remember the shape of her face? Her scent? Could she recall the look in her eyes when she was happy, or sad? Could she perhaps still quote particular conversations between the two of them? Was their time apart, that nefarious separation, so prolonged as to cause her to forget memories she once perhaps believed were permanent objects? Or did she hold onto these memories with enough tenacity for them to remain as a part of her now, in the substratum of her mind? And she could have lingered there, brooding and dreaming in realities far from herself, if it were not for the sudden thought of Emile that sprung to her mind and the feeling of how she wished to see him, to talk to him and hear his gentle voice. She had been spinning in such a whirlwind that it was only now as the crux of everything was beginning to sink in that she thought to reach out to him. And now, as she wondered what he was doing on this Sunday afternoon, all she wanted to do was to see him. So she lifted herself from the bed, picked up her phone and dialled his number. After a few seconds, he picked up. His voice was filled with a light jolliness and a spark of excitement to talk to her and find that she had arrived. And he told her that he had just been thinking of her, and she told him that she needed to see him and had so much to tell him, and, perhaps sensing her alacrity, he suggested that they meet right away. So, without much time at all, she wrapped up once more, skipped down the stairs, called goodbye to Dusty, who called back to her with a giggle in her voice — seemingly startled by her whimsicality — and raced out.

They met at a corner of the canal, just outside of the music studio in which Emile had been playing. There, he was sitting on a bench, in a faded blue denim jacket, a cloth tied around his neck, his head in a book perched upon his lap. His deep, brown eyes gleamed below his raised eyebrows as he caught sight of her approaching, and then they hugged and sat on the bench together, beside the rippling surfaces of the river. Within seconds, he leaned in and turned his head with a puzzling mysteriousness in his eyes; it was evident that he had suspected that there was a huge heap of things to say hidden behind her lips, things that urged her to be spoken of, despite her trying to keep herself collected. So, without holding anything back, and with a steady control of her words, she told him everything, in detail, from the very moment she found the letter, up until her mother's final words of the story in the kitchen; not a single speck of information was withheld, and she spoke fluently as though everything was there, predestined and in order. Throughout her words, Emile jolted and moved around sporadically in surprise, and the incredulity on his face from her point of view was almost laughable. And when she finished talking, he sat there in silence, his eyebrows firmly raised, his eyes wide as a nightbird caught in a flash of light, and, through the curling of his expression, he seemed as if he had forgotten the ability to utter words. In the midst of his shock, her unexpected calmness, and their mutual wordlessness, Annabel turned her head to see the river, and she began to laugh as she thought about how unbelievable it must have been to hear it all delivered in one short story, wrapped in a ribbon of calm composure. Mysteriously, telling him everything had somehow caused it all to sink in even more for herself; now she was starting to finally come to terms with everything, and really believe it, the palpability of it, to know it as a fact and not some abstract conception or dream-like story wafting around her mind like a restless ballerina spinning behind the haze of a misty window. The currents of the river rippled on, endlessly pushed by the gentle winds that skimmed over the shiny blanket of glaze on the surface, forcing the ripples to fold over like flaps of wings returning to their place of safety, and moving them constantly into motion. Some lights from homes across the river were turned on as the light of day began to say its goodbyes. She turned back to Emile, who now had the briefest hint of a smile on his face; now, it didn't seem as though he was so shocked, but rather that he was delighted with an energy simmering beneath his sparkly eyes. With bouncy words, he told her that what she had just shared was perhaps the most incredible thing he had ever heard, and he leapt up onto his feet with joy, so much joy that his cries echoed out into the skies; and through his joy, her spirit enlivened too. And they talked about it all, the amazement after everything she had been through, the journey of her longing reaching such an unexpectant climax, the beautiful fortuity of such a thing. And then, some moments into their intertwining rejoicing, she told him how much she wished to write to her, and how up until now she couldn't express this wish because of the sudden impact of finding out everything all at once. Emile sat there, pinching his chin, and asked her what she was waiting for whilst he reached into his satchel and pulled out a pen, a playfulness written on his face; and perhaps he was right, she thought, nothing more was to be discovered in this ever-unfolding story other than through contact with Nina herself. Maybe now that she had taken time to assimilate everything, and with all of these feelings itching to be expressed, it was the perfect time to write to her, during such a momentous peak of irresistible curiosity. And indeed it felt just right.

Down the river bank they walked, past boaters and red-berry bushes and exploratory cats on fences in the growing evening, until they stumbled into an old bookstore with rows of letter sheets and envelopes on display. Annabel went to take a look, her finger wandering steadily over the lot, and then she pulled out a pack wrapped in twine and held it in her hands. This was it, she thought, the ideal moment to write, and so they purchased it and then walked a little more down the river, discussing the multitude of things she could write. It seemed there were a million ways she could write to her, a myriad of ways in which she could fill the pages, and whilst contemplating the endless avenues of such a significant letter, she decided that she'd let her mind stay fresh and write what came naturally to her at the moment. Then, just as they stepped over a small bridge that overlooked a flat, motionless portion of water with a raft of ducks paddling through, from afar, they could see, through distant windows, the warmth of lights from lamps hitting the rustic stone walls of a building, and walking up in keen footsteps of curiosity, they began to make out just how remarkable it was. It was a Parisian café, a hidden treasure, and somehow there was an unspoken agreement that it would be the place to write to Nina. So, naturally, they walked to it, and when they stepped inside, immediately they were submerged in the homely spell of the place, by the chime of the dangling bell on the door and the hum of friendly chatter and the elegant strings of a harp from a gramophone radio. The entire place was speckled with charm; there were paintings in every side and corner of the room, intricately painted works of oil depicting landscapes and lavish scenes; a distinct pecan tone of colour shone from the dark wooden floorboards, creaking with antiquity; books were piled on shelves, forming structures like little hardback towers; the yellow stone walls were big beautiful things, poised and wide, holding up the tall ceilings where the elegant lights shone like tiny suns; and above everything, the gold light swung through the arch columns and bounced around the entire room. At the front, a smiling woman in striking red glasses took their order of tea, and then they sat at the back, at a round marble table. They remained there for some time, in the present moment with each other, drinking their tea, talking with steady anticipation and excitement, and when Annabel decided it was time to write the letter, she took out the paper and the pen and placed them in front of her on the table. Emile, with his usual altruistic self, stuck his head into a book so as to give her time and space to get into the calm mentality from which to write such a monumental letter. She looked down at the piece of paper, wordless and blank but beaming with infinite possibility, and whether she would write a lot or a little, she did not know, but she knew that whatever she would write would come from a place deep inside of her so long as she wrote with the right purity and vulnerability that, if she focused enough, she knew she could summon. She looked around the room, thinking just how wonderful it was to be there, and then to Emile sitting opposite her, and she thought about how much of a treasure of a friend he was, and how he was just the perfect person to accompany such a significant endeavour. And then she looked back down and, unthinkingly, flicked the lid from the pen, and somehow, even though she was without any sense of clear direction, the words flew out of her the moment she touched the very tip of the pen onto the surface of the paper; somehow it all came so effortlessly, every word branching onto the next like trailing vines, as though each word held the hand of the subsequent word, gracefully flowing and forming a union of writing. And she wrote and wrote in one swoop of motion until the page was filled with what felt to be unequivocally the truest expression of what she wished to say. And when she marked the end with the final dot of ink, her eyes flew back to the top of the page to read what had somehow, instinctively, flown out of her.

Dear Nina,
I'm not sure exactly how I intend to phrase what I'm about to write.
I'm not even sure exactly what it is I wish to write, and perhaps that's because there is so much to say that I don't know where to begin.
But, the first thing I want to tell you is that it's me, Annabel.
I want you to know that I've had an inexplainable, inconceivable desire to find you ever since you gave me the scarf, the scarf that, through my recent rediscovery of it, revealed to me your name through the hidden thread that I had somehow overlooked for years.
All this time, as unbelievable as it may sound, I've been unaware that you ever even knew me, and I you. It wasn't until yesterday when I read your letter and was confronted with the truth about us, that my mother told me everything.
Before yesterday, I never understood my desire to seek you whilst I've been without the knowledge of our past, and to try to understand the longing I've felt has been unendingly perplexing and at times has felt as if it were an impossible puzzle that I would never have the satisfaction of figuring out. But now that I know what I know, it seems that all of the little pieces have come together in a way that is just so beautiful.
The moment I caught eyes with you, nine years ago, as you sat in your blue scarf, there was something there I could just not ignore, and now I recognise that it was a powerful familiarity that lived within me even though my memory had failed to keep up with it. And now, as I remember that look you had in your eyes as you sat there and stared into mine, the look that seemed as though you were trying to figure me out, it all makes so much sense to me, finally. You were trying to decipher if I was the child whose side you stood by, if I was that little girl you made smile for those three precious years.
Since that day, I was left with a lingering sense of longing for you, and a deep curiosity, and it persisted, even until recently when I moved to London. And here, after I discovered your name, I found out who you were, that you were an artist. I even saw a photograph of you; I'll never forget that moment I saw your face for the first time in such a long while. And I know I could have made contact with you, but the insurmountable task of finding words to explain how I felt, along with the fear that you'd never understand, left me with no choice but to find

you and discover you myself, and with that discovery of you, to hopefully make sense of the way I felt.

And now, my mother has told me about you, how you took care of me, how much you tended to me and how close the two of us were. I'm sorry about the way she treated you and shut you out of my life, and I'm sorry that she kept you from saying goodbye to me. I wish I could have taken away the pain it must have caused you. She's told me of the guilt she's lived with for years, how she could never bring herself to apologise to you, and how as I grew to forget you, keeping the memory of you away from me was all she could think to do. I cannot understand why she did what she did, and maybe I never will, but as I write to you now, I feel it's best to focus on what I do understand, what I know now, and how much clarity knowing all of this gives me. It seems that things have aligned in such a way that I would never have anticipated. I feel that even the most daring night's dream could never have predicted this.

As of right now, I find myself feeling so much. I want to cry and laugh and dance and sing and cry again. There's so much that I want to tell you, and even more that I wish to know from you.

I cannot remember anything from the years of being in your care, but I would so love to hear about the memories you keep, even if there aren't many; maybe getting a glimpse into yours will be the closest thing to igniting my own. How much do you remember about us?

I wish I could see all that is going on in your mind as you read this. There's so much to be shared, but I know we will get there with time. I will wait patiently for your reply.

With love, Annabel

And through the stream of those words, her face emitted the light of a smile that refused to let go, a smile with a luminous heart lodged into the spark of her eyes and the bending of her lips, and one that remained throughout the evening as she sat there in the golden glow of the café, as she walked out into the freshly new night with Emile by her side, and throughout the moment she slipped the letter into the postbox under the embrace of the sky.

Is That You?

In the morning after, Annabel awakened to a sense of lightness, a feeling that she was, fleetingly, akin to a feather in the breezy air, carried by the gentle edges of the wind; it was a remarkable feeling, and it felt as though even gravity could not stop her from floating upwards and touching the ceiling if she wished to do so. And when she rose to her feet and looked outside towards the increasing lightness of dawn, the day felt bright and new like no other. She ate bread and fruit and drank earl grey tea downstairs at the table, along with pleasant melodies on the radio. She saw things this morning with a stark admiration for beauty, with an eye that noticed the wonder of things around. The leaves of the weeping fig by the window shone their green edges spectacularly; the freckled strawberries in the wicker basket beside her looked sweet and ripe and ready to be bitten into; the bouquet in the clay pot on the shelf beautified the ambience with a garnish of harmonious colour; the sweet and cinnamon aroma of the candle alight on the table bestowed her with the comfort of home. All was safe and well, and she sighed with sincere appreciation, with a light glow of pleasure wedged into every breath that came through her. And that glow remained throughout the day, and the days that followed, even in times when she became caught up in nervous anticipation as she thought about the letter, the letter that was now on its way to the hands of Nina.

Each day seemed to pass slowly, and she was often reminded of the letter in the most random hours, and though she tried not to think of it too much, to dwell in the avenues of what could happen, at times she could not help but dip her mind into imaginary possibilities, to garnish the painted scene in her swirling thoughts with specks of finer detail. She sometimes thought about Nina's reaction, the surprise bursting through her at the ripping of the envelope, and she speculated all the ways she would possibly act in response to the words, and whatever form of expression her surprise would take. Sometimes she pictured her reading it in the daylight of morning, just after waking and rubbing her eyes to rouse herself fully, half-whispering the words in quiet stupefaction; other times she pictured her through the light of lamps in the bliss of the evening, reading the letter on an upholstered armchair, almost spilling wine from a glass in her other hand at the sudden shock of realising the contents. And to imagine what she would possibly be feeling as her eyes would travel along the words was an elusive quest, one that sent waves of powerful suspense. How startling it was to imagine the power of those swirling streams of ink.

The evening she sent the letter, she and Emile walked along the river and the roads of residential blocks, and as they walked they talked about the plethora of recent discoveries, about the unbelievability of it; and it was a mountain of which they were only just treading along the foot; there was still so much to fathom, so many pieces that perhaps with more time they could put together to enrich the picture of a thousand colours. It was enlivening to ponder it all, to discuss the multitude of past chapters now that the answer, previously unknown and perceived as impalpable, was in fact real and right in the palms of their hands. And it felt so nice to dwell on such a great discovery with him, to share the weight of something so paramount. Emile had a wonderful trait of focusing on the good in every situation, squeezing out as much enthusiasm as possible, and sharing the weight of the bad, the troublesome parts that could lead to one feeling frightened or overwhelmed. So to have him beside her was all she could ask for at a time like this.

Eventually, at some point in their sauntering, the evening came, dusk began to slice through the trees and the call for rest came upon them. And so, they went their separate ways, and when Annabel arrived home, she joined Dusty on the sofa who was watching a documentary of wild birds on the television. The home was filled with its usual tranquil evening ambience. Dusty had her elbow on the arm of the sofa, and her chin rested in her hands, and when she looked over to Annabel to greet her, there was a dash of concern in her eyes — perhaps she was suspecting the absorption of her inner thoughts on her face — and she enquired, naturally, in a comforting tone, "Is there something on your mind?"

Her voice, so gentle and nurturing, reached Annabel with a warmth that made it feel as if speaking her mind was the most natural thing at that moment. So that's what she did. She hadn't yet made Dusty aware of the existence of Nina, partially because their interactions were usually fleeting, and partially because their dynamic had evolved into a happy coexistence where she felt no pressure to share the details of her life. But now, on this fine evening, she told her about Nina and about all that had occurred. The more she spoke the more Dusty leaned into a position of deeper concentration, variably turning down the volume on the television until the birds on the screen appeared as silent spectators too. And it was cathartic to tell her, to share the details of such an unbelievable story, to confide in her and to witness the natural shock in her eyes at the unfolding of the story, as though in some way she was sharing a piece of her own bewilderment.

"Now, that may just be the most magnificent thing anyone's ever told me," she said at the end. "I knew you were a valiant one."

She spoke in a voice of sheer astonishment, garnished with pure affection, and she interlocked her fingers beneath her chin and shook her head with sincere admiration. She then shuffled along the sofa, put out her arms, asking with a kind expression if she could offer a hug. Annabel smiled and nodded and then accepted her warm embrace, her chin resting on the soft embroidery of her blouse, and she couldn't help but feel touched by the kindness of her care. Then seconds later, Dusty stood up onto her feet, animatedly, before leaving the room and then returning with two small dishes which she delicately placed on the table in front of them. On the plates were two slices of homemade peach crumble, and as they ate, they spoke more about it all — the longing for Nina she had felt over the years, the shock of discovering a forgotten past, the anticipation that was stirring through her. Annabel could see, with a newfound observation, the entire story and all of its components becoming more and more apprehensible; it seemed to be forming into something that she now knew to be very real. All of the uncertainty of the past, all of the confusion and the ambiguity was now slowly being washed away in a tide of certainty and clarity. Now, when she thought of it all, everything simply made sense. Dusty told her how courageous she thought she was, how only a resilient spirit would have gone to the lengths she did to find the truth, and how glad it made her to know that the truth, after all, was the most beautiful conclusion to such a vast and wild story. Annabel smiled at her words, and she looked at Dusty, her wide, gracious eyes, the way she stared into her thoughts with such finality, the proud grin at the edge of her lips, the creases by her eyelids, like innocent little smiles, fragile as a rose petal. And then, moments later, when the pleasant conversation had turned into tuneful sighs of satisfied somnolence, Annabel could feel her eyelids beginning to droop. She lay back on the couch, and a short moment later, as the quiet creaks of the room and the imperceptible flickering of the candle mingled together into a blur, she felt the warm touch of a blanket placed over her and the touch of gentle hands tucking in the edges all around her. And this gesture, though little, brought her back to her days of being a child and the heartwarming sensation of being taken care of with a gentle love; and she was touched by this, so much so that her lips formed a subtle smile naturally. She remained there, her eyes closed, floating into a cloud of equanimity, soaked into the feeling of home, and in this state of lightness, a small tear brewed under her eyelid, and perhaps it fell and trickled down her cheek, she wasn't sure, but it didn't matter, as she was just on the very brink of a blissful sleep.

It was over the next handful of days that she would stumble into a state of sheer restfulness within herself, where disquieting thoughts could not exist, and instead, there was a calm welcome of the moment and an unhurried joy in the expectancy of what was to come. She spent these days working in the pottery shop, and she soon came to realise that this environment was just the thing she needed to get her mind off the letter for a little while, and as she did, naturally, this peaceful state of being found her. These busy days entailed her focusing on the task at hand and giving all of her attention to the customers that came and went. She was usually with either Muna or Adia, and sometimes both, and sometimes, during the quiet hours of the days, she was alone; in these rare moments she would read a book, or flick through a photography magazine, nibbling on fruit — usually sweet oranges — from the fruit basket, and during busy hours, when people shot in and out of the store incessantly to sculpt and paint and purchase goods, she found that the time would pass along swiftly, the morning shifting quickly into the afternoon.

On the last day of consecutive work days, whilst she dusted the shelves and prepared for closing time and the approaching weekend, Muna and Adia ushered her into the creative room in the back. It was dark in there other than a flick of street lights streaming through the curtains, and as Adia drew them to light up the room, Muna whipped off a cloth that covered something on the shelf, and then the two of them presented it to her with spirited smiles of excitement on their faces. It was a small ceramic ornament, about half the size of a palm, and Muna held it in her hands, lifting it for her to see. Annabel looked at it, leaning in a little to see it up close, and as she did, she saw that it was a sculpture of her younger self, prancing with a dancing ribbon on the top of a hill — a specific treasured memory of her childhood that she had briefly mentioned to them one day during a heartfelt discussion. It was so remarkably detailed, and somehow captured the very essence of the exact moment; the posture, the heart of the smile, the bending and the flow of the ribbon — all of these elements culminated into one beautiful form; even the invisible force of the wind was captured in the flick of the little swaying carvings of the grass. She became stunned and almost speechless, and she thanked them and told them how much she adored it. From within, an abundance of sweet, reminiscent thoughts were running through her and it showed in the frantic breaths between her words of appreciation. Muna and Adia told her that they wanted to make her a small gift together, something that represented how thankful they were for her continual help. They told her that prior to her generous contribution, they had been having trouble finding the right person to be an addition to their treasured store, and choosing her, they told her, was the most wonderful decision they could have made, and they'd continue to cherish her company for however long she would stay with them. With glee and appreciation, Annabel held the sculpture up closer within her gaze, following the trail of the edges with her eyes, tracing the breadth, noticing the shades and colours of the paint and the lustre of the glazing, and the details, from the thinnest lines that imitated the character of hair, to the individual fingers grasping to the ribbon, to the infinitesimal curving of the mouth. This little recreation of a special moment, much like the memory of it, though now in a solid, tangible form, somehow brought back to life that familiar warmth, that sentimental glimmer held securely in her mind; this small thing, moulded with the pressure of hands, but a careful pressure that came from the depths of care, of a desire to reciprocate a certain love, had become, instantaneously, a thing she knew she would hold dear to her heart for a very long time. And she wanted to show them her thankfulness in whatever way she could, so she hugged them tightly and dearly, and when she waved goodbye to them as she left, the gift wrapped and tucked neatly into a bag, she thought about how much it meant to her to be thought of in a way that inspired an act so kind. And what a remarkable thing the act of giving was, she pondered, how great it was to realise that, if obtained or assembled in a thoughtful way, a gift, in whatever form it holds, can hold the substance of one's truest affection.

And afterwards, she was inspired to extend that feeling, and when she met Emile, she gave him a bouquet of colourful flowers wrapped finely in cotton twine. He was waiting for her outside a train station, his guitar on his back, and his face lit up with a wonderful surprise as he took the flowers in his hands and dug his nose into them to smell them.

He took her down to a block of residential homes, and then, cutting through the middle of two buildings, she followed him straight into a mysterious passageway of white brick on narrow walls that trailed down the sides. The passageway was dark, and their steps filled the tight silence with tiny echoes, but through the light at the end, they arrived at a concrete square with an array of beautifully intricate mosaic walls all around. The thousands upon thousands of colourful stone tiles displayed patterns, plants, animals and naturalistic scenes, and even on the ground below their shoes, intricate geometric patterns beamed. They walked by, Annabel tracing her fingers along the amber leaves of a mosaic autumn tree, Emile admiring the arrangement of patterns, detailed and labyrinthian, surrounding his espadrilles. Then they sat on a bench against a wall and ate pieces of sliced mangoes and strawberries, the grand exposition before them.

"When I was a kid," said Emile as he ate, "back in France, my family and I used to live in an apartment just above a little park with mosaics just like these. We'd get ice cream and sit and look at the walls. You see that hare over there? There was one just like that on the wall in France. Sylvie and I used to play a game where we'd stand in the middle of the square, close our eyes and take turns throwing marbles on the ground, and try to see how close we could get them to the hare."

Annabel chuckled, imagining the scene. "The hare reminds me of an Albrecht painting," she said, before pointing, "and that shepherdess over there, above the sheep, there's something about the way she stands. It's powerful and commanding, but at the same time so gentle."

A breeze blew over them, ruffling through their hair and sending the trees swaying in a wave-like motion, and for a moment, the whistling wind and the rustling of the trees with their thousands of twigs encompassed the atmosphere, until the wind passed and the trees found stillness again.

Annabel looked ahead and then turned to Emile. "Can you put your hand out and point your finger just a little? I want to see something." She placed the camera up to her face, her eyes squinting in concentration, then put it back down. "No, that doesn't feel right."

Emile chuckled. "I wish I could see whatever it is you see when taking a photograph."

"What do you mean by that?" asked Annabel, her camera to her eyes as she looked around for a shot.

"I guess to feel what you feel when you get the impulse. It's fascinating to see... What is it you love about taking photographs so much?"

"Well, that's a good question. What is it I love so much? It's just something I feel compelled to do. For me, taking a photograph is more than just capturing a little souvenir for a memory. If I find something beautiful I feel some kind of need to seize it in its beauty. Look up there, do you see that robin sitting on a twig over there? And the yellow flowers through the window just behind it? And over there, there's a silhouette through the window below. Someone's washing the dishes. Can you see some kind of collaboration in all of these things together? You'll never see this exact thing before you again, with all these specific, fleeting elements. Taking photographs, in my mind, is making a beautiful sight that will soon pass, live on."

"Immortalising a flicker of life," Emile chimed in, playfully.

"Yes, exactly!"

She took a photograph right before the robin flew away, and then seconds later, the person through the window finished washing the dishes and closed the curtains. Now the picture had changed, and she smiled as she noticed. Then Emile smelled the flowers, and so did she.

"Kind of like Camomile!" he called.

"And something sweet, like maple syrup," she responded.

"Yes, I'm getting a hint of that too. But there's something more, something—" He paused, then placed the flowers down. "Oh, I meant to tell you. I finally wrote a song."

Annabel gleamed. "Is that so?"

"Well, it's only half-finished. I'm still working on the lyrics. I heard a chord progression in my mind this morning as I was just waking up, and I rushed out of bed to find it, and I slowly built it piece by piece. Would you like to hear it?"

"I'd like nothing more."

He took out his guitar, held it in his arms and started tuning it, quietly humming along the notes as he twisted the pegs. Then he closed his eyes, took a breath and relaxed his shoulders, before plucking and then strumming the strings. As Annabel listened, her head turned upwards as though her gaze clung onto the wings of the unfurling notes, and her eyes trailed up to the sky, like a bamboo plant seeking light. The song was soft and euphonious, and Emile began humming and gently singing in delicate, broken words to the melody of the guitar. His emotions bled through the notes, and the melody, sweet and mellifluous, spread outwards into the air, reaching her ears like trickling honey. And after he strummed the final chord and the music grew faint until it faded into the wind, Annabel gasped in delight, and stood on her feet, her hands together and her head shaking with alacrity.

"You like?" asked Emile.

"Emile, I think it's absolutely wonderful!"

As sunset passed by, they strolled along the quiet stream of a river walk, taking small steps together with no particular destination, enjoying the freshness of the outside and the colours of the sky above them, lost in conversation. Somehow their enthusiasm led them to the topic of future plans, and they talked about places they wished to go, things they wished to do and see, new experiences they wanted to share, how they saw their lives branching out, and the eagerness of all of the unwritten possibilities, big and small, awaiting them and yet to be known. The winding road led them over little bridges, under little tunnels, and round the bends where drifting boats with luminous windows and softly-playing music came into view, and carefree dogs with sticks in their mouths ambled by, and clusters of ducks floated along, sticking their heads in and out of the water that reflected the vibrant colours of lampposts and glittering garden lights and the moon that surfed on the tiny ripples. And when it was time to go they said their goodbyes at a crossroads and went their separate ways. As Annabel walked away, she stopped and looked back. Emile was trodding away in lighthearted footsteps, one hand in his pockets, the other holding the stems of the flowers, his head looking up to the treetops from below, and then he too stopped and turned around, locking eyes with her from afar. The two of them laughed, and he waved, and she waved back, before going their separate ways into the developing night.

The air was growing colder as the light became subdued by the night. Annabel walked into the underground train station, down the steps and to the platform. There she sat, and as soon as she was given this moment alone with herself, she began to wonder if her letter had reached Nina, and if so, if Nina had written back to her yet. Perhaps her response was on the way now, one among thousands of other letters on the journey to their recipients, or maybe it had arrived that very day and was waiting for her at home. And as she pondered this possibility, suddenly, a surge of energy, a rich fervour bolted through her. And then on the train, with every second that shortened the distance between her and home, the energy elevated. She couldn't help but anticipate, to dwell in the excitement of awaiting a response.

Shortly after, she arrived at her destination, and as she walked along the street, she listened to Ravel's *Daphnis et Chloe, Lever du jour*, her gaze drifting along the chimneys, her feet moving with a little more speed than usual at the small chance a letter was waiting for her at home. And when she arrived, she dashed to check the sideboard at the end of the hallway; it was the place Dusty would put aside her letters and packages when she wasn't home. But not a single letter was there. She sighed, staring at the emptiness, and then smiled. She would wait patiently, she thought, no matter how long. And as she took off her jacket and her shoes, she sat at the bottom of the stairs and breathed slowly into calmness. Then she got up, inspired by the thought of hot tea, ambled into the kitchen and switched on the light. The kitchen, now flared with an enlivening, honey-golden light, revealed, perched on the middle of the oak table, wrapped in an indigo ribbon that was tied thoughtfully in an intricate little bow, a letter. She moved a few steps closer to it, spellbound by the sight of it. On the letter, her name was written in the blackest ink that danced in curves and bends. She halted, falling into stillness for a small moment, before reaching out her hand and holding it up to her eyes that squinted through a fresh layer of wetness. A stark inhale, a breath of wonder, gallantly travelled through her astounded expression, and like a ray of light shooting through prismatic glass and dispersing a spectrum of colours, the air she drew in breathed a vast coliseum of colours into her. This anticipated moment was here, at last, and she wished to savour it and be in it with every ounce of herself. She lit a few candles and brewed some tea, then she drew the curtains to allow the night sky to be witness to the magic of the moment. And when she felt she was as ready as she could be, she sat down by the table, unravelled the ribbon, tore open the envelope, opened the letter and read the words.

Dearest Annabel,

If only I could express to you how thrilled I am to receive your letter. I read it this morning and I was truly filled with mountains of joy. Throughout the day I've been thinking about how to respond, waiting for the right moment to sit and find the words to convey my feelings.

Right now, as write to you, I am sitting by the window. It is night time here in Madrid and the moon is brightly shining. A gentle wind is blowing over me, and as I sit here, I am being reminded of memories I hold of you, moments I still remember. And to answer your question, I remember it all. I remember the day I met you, holding your tiny hand in mine. I remember the way you'd laugh when I'd tickle your chin. I remember when you first started to walk, the day when you snuck out into the garden and ran across the wet grass into the rain before toppling down, and I remember you smiling as I washed away the mud. I remember taking you to the parks, watching the sky with you on hills, and when you began to speak, talking with you, singing with you, reading poetry to you, even though you didn't understand. I remember your penchant for observation, the way your eyes widened at the sight of what you deemed to be beautiful, your blooming affinity with colours, with birds, the sky, with photographs, music, the way you'd trace your fingers along the streaks of my paintings, interpreting them in your own innocent way. I remember your curious eyes, your eyebrows that shrugged with a special kind of sensitivity, the little mole under your nose, the way you squeezed my hand when you wanted me to hum lullabies for you, the way you cried when you were upset, and danced and swayed when you felt like it.

To read about your story, to learn that an obscure feeling has been with you for so long and that all this time you've been longing to connect with me has filled my eyes with tears.

When you were a small child and I was suddenly forbidden from seeing you, I became lost. I felt as though I had lost a little sister, a dear friend. I felt I was a bird that had lost its wings, forlorn, without any real purpose. But as time moved on I found solace in the hope that you'd keep memories of me, as withered and fragmentary as they may be, and that perhaps when you grew old enough to make your own choices, you'd find a way to reach out to me. And although time had resorted to taking your memories from you, it seems that from your story, Annabel, something remained, something more than a lasted memory, an indelible engraving, an unbreakable invisible thread between the two of us. I guess nature has its own mysterious ways of leading us to our elusive desires.

I am overjoyed that you found me. And I'd like to know more about you, Annabel, about the person you are today, and if it's possible, I'd love to tell you about myself, the person I am today.

Tomorrow I will be leaving for San Fransisco, far away from here. I've been offered the opportunity to showcase my work in other parts of the world, so I will be travelling across America, and soon after I will be going to Asia. So unfortunately it seems that there is no way for us to meet in the near future, and I'm afraid, with my varying destinations, it will take a long while for any future letters to reach each other. So, on the back of this letter, I will leave a telephone number that you can call when you wish to speak to me, whenever that may be. I'd love to be given a chance to hear your voice and discuss everything in greater detail.

So I will wait for your call.

With love, Nina.

The written words were like an incantation, and as she read them, she could have sworn dust-like particles of evanescent colours were exuding from the paper and over her gaze. And she remained where she was, still and immovable but engulfed with a moving force of wonder, her tears and the drips of wax on the candle beside her falling together in synchronicity. The letter, held with tenacity between her fingers, was all there was in this very moment; nothing else was real enough to be perceived. Her focus was fixed on the words, words drawn by the hand that not only wrote thoughts, but painted them, fondly and carefully. She read it a few times over, reading with a little more whispered vivacity each time. She wanted to shout with joy, to howl like a wolf and the entire world to hear and be revitalised in that joy, as though her cries would inspire the sun to rise and light up the sky and begin a beautiful morning prematurely, and the birds on the treetops would sing to the music of her rejoice, and the sounds of the birds would pierce the sky and send away the clouds and make way for every colour. Yet it was a quiet night, and she was alone with the ambience of a closing day, and everything around was still. And yes, she thought, this engraving, the invisible thread, as Nina had wonderfully described it, was truly there and real as anything tangible in the world. And though unseen and incapable of being understood, it was incredibly large and significant, like the beating heart of a passing stranger, or the bones of a whale. She turned over the letter and looked at the telephone number written at the back, and as she did, something within her urged her to call it — impatience, perhaps; but the thought of calling her in that very moment, as the moon shone and the quietude of the night gave her not a single distraction, seemed riveting, as if it were a timely opportunity. And there was no longer a reason to be patient, there was nothing to wait for. Right there in her hands was the opportunity to speak with her, with nothing but generous time and a desire to know more between them. She looked at the clock. It wasn't that late yet, and she knew Nina was a lover of the night, and she thought perhaps right at that very moment, Nina was up, standing by the window, maybe looking at the trees and the shadowy buildings of Spain, or reading a book, wondering when she'd hear the ring of her call. And now seemed like the time to try. So, with a conscious calmness in her steps, her heart beating firmly, she moved into the living room, sat down by the rotary dial phone which lay on a small side table surrounded by plump cushions, and with a hand that was overtaken by a steady tremor, moving her fingers firmly, she dialled the number. It was only seconds before she heard a voice on the other end.

"Hello?" the voice called softly.

Annabel quietly gasped instantly at the sound of it, now flooded by silence and nothing but her fluctuating rhythm of breath. A few seconds of wordless silence took place between them, and then the voice spoke once again: "Annabel, is that you?"

The Ease of Being

Salty tears curving around the edge of cheekbones, one by one; words, thousands of them, coming after one another incessantly like the steps of galloping horses on an open meadow; feelings, multifaceted and in waves, moving in large, vehement motions, surging through every layer of understanding right to the core. These were the components of the night, the night that swept by in such a surge that it felt nothing at all like a night but instead a single hour of dusky skies that hurtled into the early hours of the morning. In fact, it was the first note of a bird's morning lullaby that nudged them out of the spell in which they had found themselves wrapped so tightly and made them realise that they had been talking for many hours. It was the rarest kind of conversation, a conversation remembered with the ease with which nature blossoms a seed to a flower; and to Annabel, this seed became the most remarkable flower the earth had ever seen, a flower of every colour imaginable, with shimmering petals of a lovely affection, and one of mere simplicity. They spoke with care and listened to one another with equal focus and keenness. There was so much to say, so much to be brought to the light that shone between them, and so they allowed themselves the time to say it all.

The conversation had begun with Annabel suddenly losing her ability to speak to an unseen force that had instantaneously taken her breath away, a surprise at the very moment Nina's voice came out through the telephone speaker and tickled her ear with its lovely rasp and tender curiosity. And as she pushed herself to respond, to greet her back with whatever words she could muster, her voice came out soft and frail and lacking the lively rigour only moments before swam throughout her being. But then, as Nina spoke, clearly sensing her mute astonishment, and told her how delighted she was that she had called, and on such a beautiful night too, the speechlessness that kept Annabel's lips tightly shut began to lose its hold on her, and she told her just how thrilled she too was to be finally speaking with her, on a night she too deemed beautiful. But this very instant, this long-awaited interaction was the real beauty of the night to them both; and from that moment on, after the initial greeting and receiving of each other's voices, the conversation flowed fluidly and effortlessly as though a sweet syrup trickled along the line of their blending thoughts and interlacing sentences. And they spoke about everything, about all they were inspired to say, about all of the events that occurred between them leading up to the moment Nina sent the first letter, and their words were natural, unadulterated, bouncing back and forth and weaving like yarn through a loom. At first, they spoke about the day they crossed paths those nine years ago; Nina told her about a strong uncertainty, a potent ambivalence she remembered feeling the moment she looked into the face of Annabel standing before her, her features still of a child yet significantly matured over the years; she said that although there were striking differences compared to the face of her three-year-old self, there was a glint of a familiar core, an essence — although almost imperceptible — that she was familiar with in the outline of her features and the pupils of her eyes. She told her how she could have sworn she knew the person behind those eyes, and the moment she heard her voice being called, her mind raced with so much intensity that it caused her heartbeat to feel as if its beat were frozen in time. And because it was clear that Annabel didn't remember her, she knew that she could say nothing about the past; but as she watched her turn away as her name was called through the crowd, the chance to say or do something began to slide away in a blink, and she knew that to let her leave just like that would have been throwing away the incredible, surreal moment that unbelievably came to meet her; she just couldn't let her leave without doing something, anything, and a voice inside of her implored her to give her the scarf, because in doing that, she felt she would somehow establish a link between the two of them, something that connected them once more. And it was a quick impulse, she said, a spur-of-the-moment decision, but one she was so grateful to have made. She told her how thankful she was that she listened to that voice from within, and how wildly beautiful it was that the scarf connected them once more after so many years. Then Annabel told her about it all from her own point of view, how despite the fact that she was living without a single memory of their shared past, somehow, in some fragmentary portion of herself, buried deep beneath the outer layers of her mind, she did remember her, and in fact, knew her deeply. She told her about all the times she tried to find her, about her visit to the café, and the showcase, about the night she followed her and ended up trapped in the house by the river. In a way, it was hard to say these things aloud to her, embarrassing almost, but hearing Nina's voice come through so endearingly on the other side of the telephone, as she expressed her heartfelt concern for all of the hardship Annabel had pushed herself through, somehow washed away all of the resistance that held her words back. And she told her exactly what had happened that night, the night she followed her and hid behind the curtains. Nina listened and responded with understanding, and although there was astonishment in her tone, her words were gilded with an appreciation for the truth and wholesome, thoughtful empathy. She told Annabel about her own experience that night, how when she turned on the light and saw her standing there, and after the initial seconds of shock had passed, she had not even the slightest idea that it was her, and all she could apprehend was the appearance of the figure, obscured by shadows and blots of mud on the face and across her neck. But, in some peculiar way, as they looked into each other's eyes, Nina knew that she posed no threat, that despite how startling the initial sight of her was, somehow she sensed that her intentions were innocent and pure. She told her how days after, whilst digesting the shock of it and pondering on such a bizarre instant, a small thought in the back of her head nudged her towards the idea that maybe it was Annabel, and though as absurd as it seemed at the time, the part of her that believed it grew a little more each time she thought about it. Somehow to imagine that it was her made sense in a way her thoughts could not comprehend. And they spoke about the painting Annabel had seen at the exhibition, the one of her dark silhouette in the glare of the lamp. Nina said that she had been ruminating about the image of her for a while after she saw her, and the only way to release it from her mind was to paint it, and in fact, it was in the painting of it, in the unimaginable reviving of such a vague picture of someone within such a striking memory, that she began to truly believe that the girl standing there was Annabel. Somehow, as she painted and brought back to life the memory, she just felt it, and knew it. And she began to believe it so much so that she couldn't settle the persuasive impulse to write to her, and so she did.

As the swirling hours of the night kept on moving, they spoke about themselves, their lives, the things they cared for, how they spent their days. There were moments during the conversation where Annabel fell into utter bemusement, a starstruck wordlessness, and she could sense the steadiness of her breath was slipping away as her mind struggled to process what exactly was happening, that she was *really* talking to Nina, hearing these things now, here, on this very night. But Nina spoke with such a gracious, compassionate voice that soon washed away all of this overwhelm until at some point they bothered her no more. And they continued the conversation with a sprout of enchantment beneath their words. They spoke about their love for creativity; Annabel told her about her adoration for taking photographs, something Nina was so delighted to hear. And at some point amidst the passing hours, a small silence lay suddenly between the two of them, and that's when Annabel's eyes began to brew full-hearted tears, as her disbelief was slowly transforming into a beautiful wonder, and somehow she knew Nina felt the same.

And what was more, the two of them listened to the other with a keen enthusiasm that lasted through every single minute, each piece of communication blooming and emerging invariably through both ends of the telephone. And then they spoke about the very distant past, about specific memories Nina remembered of the two of them, like the time they tended to an injured hedgehog that a two-year-old Annabel had found in the back garden, and how she wanted to leave with it when it fled the moment they set it free; or the time, shortly after Annabel began walking, she took her up to a hill on a winter's day where the ground was submerged in thick white snow, and that it was the first time Annabel had walked with settled snow beneath her feet, and how she smiled and yelled with glee at the touch of it, and how they built a snowman together that soon turned into a deer with antlers made of long, twiddly sticks; or the time, during a rainstorm, they spent a whole day at home surrounded by cushions and blankets and watched cartoon films, laughing and melting into the warmth, and were so comfortable that they fell asleep beside each other and didn't wake till the next morning. It was slightly surreal for Annabel to be told of memories she didn't remember, but strangely, she felt as if she didn't need to remember them, for these stories elicited thoughts that were as intricate and ornamented as any memory could be. And to hear them now, through the words of Nina herself, was everything she could have wanted.

And finally, when the bird chirped to praise the morning, along with the first hints of light that graced the sky, they realised they were talking now with heavy eyelids and episodic yawns. Nina suggested that it was best they both got some sleep, and Annabel agreed, the two of them laughing drowsily. They had been so swept up in the conversation that time had not even the lightest hold on their perceptions. They told each other how incredibly happy they were that they had found each other, and, at last, spoken and gotten to know one another; and the two of them promised that they would speak again, soon. There was a sweetness to the tones that graced their farewells, a warm reverence that had formed between them during this beautiful time between night and morning. Then they said goodbye. Annabel hung up the telephone, and then sat there for a quiet moment, perched on the one cushion she had been sitting on for hours, her head planted into the palms of her hands as she smiled with all of her heart, another tear falling on the ground and laying there, luminous and whole, beneath her smile. And then she got up and stepped outside onto the balcony with a sudden caprice to feel the morning air. She looked up at the sky, and all around at the trees and homes on the street glowing a little brighter with the growing light. The morning was arising along with her booming heart, and the single bird that sang out to the world woke up the neighbouring birds who began joining the song with their little chirps and whistles. She quietly began to hum and sing along too, imitating their songs, and then her melody turned into a small, fragile chuckle and then into dulcet, teary laughter that poured down like pattering droplets of rain. She stayed there until the rush of weeping tears passed by, and by the time it did, the sun was being welcomed to hold sway over the world and the skies were brighter. She stood up, made her way back inside, and drifted up the stairs. As she brushed her teeth and washed her face with fresh water, the bathroom light falling onto her eyes, she looked at herself in the mirror — her dishevelled hair, her tired, wet, gleaming eyes — and she nodded to herself and smiled with the compassion and sensitivity of nature, the growth and bloom of spring's most welcoming flowers bursting forth with colours so sharp and poignant. And here and now, she felt home, free, boundless. Her prosaic reality had become an ethereal dream. And moments after sliding into bed and engulfing herself in the embracement of soft quilts and pillows, she curled up in the softness and then leaned against the windowsill and looked up to the sky. There she was, meditatively reflecting on the past but absorbed by the moment as if she stood at the opening gateway of a winding road with a wondrous journey ahead. She let her body find repose and her mind wander, without a worry or a single plan for tomorrow, and she allowed herself to glide effortlessly into rest, carelessly, and her mind to focus on nothing but the simplicity of the presence and the ease of being. She closed her eyes to a realm of dreaminess until she was weightless, truly contented. A light breeze came over her as she breathed out a whispering sigh, feeling as if she were floating in a stratosphere of boundlessness. But above all, she felt, at last, that she was exactly where she wished to be.

Two Keen Hearts

In many ways, an ending is also a beginning. When a tree dies and returns to the ground, from it, new life bursts forth, and its nutrients return to the soil, beginning the journey of new life; the final words of a conversation always lead to a web of new ideas, realisations and connections, and without the ending of a conversation, a new one could not begin; the final thread of a note in a song only leads to the next, seamlessly flowing on and on and on into continual melodies that end and begin and end and begin, and when the song closes, the final seconds only make way for a new song.

This story ends with the final inch of this thread of words, but the beginning of a great connection, an illuminated passage. And so we end and begin here, the day Annabel and Nina met one another again, at last.

It happened in a large, distinct room, a room in an arts hall by the bank of the river, a room with an exhibition, where a grand display of photographs was scattered across the walls, telling stories particularly unique to each one. Here, Annabel stood, with Emile by her side, in a world of awe and wonder. She looked all around to see her beloved photographs framed and hung in a thoughtful arrangement on the large walls before her, surrounding her with memories she once captured with relish. Photograph after photograph, beside one another, some above, and some below, swooped along the walls, set in a particular placement that formed a trail to be followed in a precise order. The beam that shone from Annabel's face couldn't have been any brighter. Tears hung at the edge of her eyelashes like morning residue abiding on the tip of the grass. This was, for her, a magnificent day, a monumental moment. And here she was, unaware that this day would only unfold into one of the most unforgettable clusters of minutes in her life so far.

All around, she saw her treasured memories displayed before her eyes, her creative world in frames, a world that once lived only in the depths of herself; and now it was being released, out into the open to touch and inspire others. Across the dimmed room, ravishing lights lit up the photographs, garnishing them with the sheen of a soothing glow, and softly blossoming lights of fluorescent amber lit up the corners, poignant and majestic, embellishing the air with the ripples of a potent hue and moving the space to a place through which insight flew spiritedly. And melting sounds of soft piano fell from the ceiling above, prancing through the atmosphere, the melodies covering the room in the resplendence of enlivening symphonies, a life-enhancing orchestra. Throughout the day there was a wide, heartfelt sharing of felicity and adoration all around, from loved ones, and even from many she didn't know. The door was open to whoever wished to enter, and indeed, streams of people came in to see what lay beyond the door, many leaving with a fruitful spirit. And towards the end of the day, as Annabel lingered in the final hour, one of those people was Nina.

Now the lights were dimmed, the music was raised, and the visitors had dwindled. This instant, the very second she walked in, completely and utterly unexpected, with the spirit of the stars in her face and swaying by her ankles the flowing hem of a red dress, would endow Annabel with a surprise so breathtaking that it would lift the beat of her heart somewhere that seemed to be above her own being. This moment landed on a day many months after their first telephone conversation, which afterwards led to many more, which eventually led to them talking only from time to time when they could both find a synchronistic moment out of their teeming lives to converse. Over the months, they had formed a strong connection in their distance, one that remained regardless of how often they spoke, and the roads and avenues of their lives were taking them in very different directions, so eventually they didn't feel the need to talk often, although when they did it was wonderful; and as the two of them lived their own lives on other sides of the world, they knew someday they would meet, but it didn't matter when, or how, for they knew it would happen eventually, that with time their roads would cross, and it would be beautiful. The last time they had spoken, Nina was still far away, travelling across Asia, with no idea when she would return. And perhaps, this startling surprise garnished such a long-awaited meeting with just the perfect touch of magic to be the unforgettable memory it would become.

She walked into the room with footsteps of a feather, her wide eyes looking around at everything before her, mesmerised by the beauty in the air all around. Annabel looked towards her, noticing first the amber light that came above her head, casting a lustre, like a halo, painting the stark outline of a beautiful human. And like the salty sea percolating the sand, changing its form, its texture and its structure, Annabel felt changed at the mere sight of her. It felt as though the unreachable had come into reach, arriving like the summit after a thousand upward steps, as though she was witnessing the physical forming of a dream of her own, half-imaginary concepts moulding into being. And much like the gasp at a rare culmination of a song that pours through what it touches, or the twinkle in the eye that revisits a cherished painting, or the awe that enfolds one at the sight of a remarkable vista, the breath she inhaled was not just a breath of function, it carried along with it traces of fondness, affection, of a tender enchantment that could only exist in a genuineness such as this one. She watched Nina's head turn to face her own, and then, her eyes — those round and prismatic little worlds — look towards her with the sincerity of a heartfelt sonata, interlocking with her own gaze. And then she watched her place her hand on her chest as her smile deepened into the shape of kindness. She was there, real and magnificent in this unlimited instant, this time that was without a beginning or an end, and for only the two of them, within the spaces through them and between them. And there, in the bursting and the blossoming of something so pure and so true, in the merging of these two keen hearts, a care had formed. And this care washed over all the turmoils of the past, and now it cast a wonderful light upon the moment, and it would continue, certainly, to cast that light upon every moment that came to be.

Printed in Great Britain
by Amazon